# Chapter 1
# Five Years Ago

Matthew ignored the snakes crawling around his feet under the pews as he read quietly from his bible. The snakes were all dangerously poisonous, everything from rattlesnakes to vipers, and their scaly bodies made slithering noises as they moved across the rough wooden planks that made up the floor of this remote West Virginia snake-handling church. The soft organ music didn't block out the sounds made by the snakes as they moved beneath the pews. Almost one hundred parishioners sat quietly in the hand-hewn log cabin that many of them had helped build thirty years ago.

For fifteen years Matthew had attended this church with his parents. He had learned over the years to keep his feet down, his breathing regular and his fear at bay. Now it all seemed rather commonplace to him.

Glancing at his mother, he noticed beads of sweat had formed on her forehead but she calmly turned a page in her bible. When she tipped her head down to read, her long blond hair half covered her face. Matthew felt a surge of love for his mother. She was kind and patient and loving. She was in fact beautiful except for the ugly scar that went from her temple down to her chin across her left cheek.

Her scar had been there since before he was born. He wondered if she had been in an accident. Years ago he had asked her how she got scarred, but when she started to cry he felt so badly that he had never asked again.

Matthew looked over at his older brother, Mark, who was starting to nod off and had not turned a page in several minutes. Matthew nudged him in the ribs with his elbow. Mark snapped awake and quickly started reading his scriptures again.

After several minutes Reverend Forester looked up and smiled at his congregation. No one had been bitten this Sunday and he nodded his approval. Several men seated in the front stood up and began carefully gathering up the squirming snakes and putting them into the decorated boxes where they lived.

Reverend Forester never let his congregation know ahead of time when he would release the snakes. Some Sundays the snakes stayed in their boxes during the entire service. Other times, members went up and picked up the snakes on their own. It was their way of showing that they were willing to follow all the teachings in the Bible.

According to the Reverend Forester anyone who was bitten had sinned and it was God's punishment meted out for his or her transgressions. If the poison did not kill them, it was God's way of saying they had repented and were forgiven of their sins. If they died then their fate might well be hell and everlasting burning.

In his younger days the reverend was bitten by a rattlesnake, and he still had the scar to prove it. But God had forgiven him and he had "given away his sins" and trained to become a preacher. His ideas were a little different than most Pentecostal preachers and he had started his own church, *The Pentecostal Holiness Today* church.

When Matthew was six years old he had asked to see the reverend's scar. His mother had turned white and grabbed Matthew with shaking hands, offering apologies to the reverend. But Reverend Forester had smiled and pulled up the sleeve of his shirt to show Matthew. His left arm had a huge scarred indention that showed where the poison had killed skin and muscle almost down to the bone. Reverend said the injured area had decayed and sloughed away, but no poison had gone to the rest of his body. God had kept his heart beating and forgiven his sin.

Matthew's mother had quickly pulled him away before he could ask what sin the reverend had committed. Afterwards she had told him that was not polite and that he was never to ask those kinds of questions again. She was so upset that tears were running down her cheeks, and she had hastily brushed them away. He had promised to do whatever he needed to do to keep her happy. She had hugged him then and he knew everything would be all right.

Matthew's father, John, was a solemn and fair man who worked hard to make a living from their small farm. He had built their house and the barn himself with help from close neighbors. They always had food to eat, but things they could not make were sometimes in short supply.

His mother, Anna, supplemented their income by sewing beautiful quilts. She spent months drawing the designs then sewing the intricate pieces together. Matthew knew she was happiest when she was creating these works of art. Sometimes he felt guilty when she had to take time to make new clothes for her sons because it took time away from her quilts.

Her quilts were not only beautiful, but practical in their extreme warmth. They were filled with the wool batting she made from the sheep her husband raised. She patiently cleaned and carded the wool into soft fluffy batting that was in high demand from wealthy buyers. When John took the quilts down to Richmond they sold in a shop for upwards to one thousand dollars each. Anna normally turned out at least five quilts a year and that money was essential to the survival of her family.

Once a magazine had offered to write an article about Anna and wanted to display photos of her and the quilts. She had adamantly refused. His father had backed her on this decision and Matthew saw fear in both their eyes when they discussed it.

Reverend Forester had come to their house as soon as he learned of the offer. Anna had assured him that she would never consider any such thing, even though they needed the money to pay for repairs to the roof. The reverend had left smiling and the next week new shingles had mysteriously arrived fully paid for.

Matthew had wondered about it at the time but didn't dare to ask any questions, he just helped his father make the repairs to the roof.

# Chapter 2
# Present Day

Elizabeth brushed her light blond hair then pulled it back into a ponytail. There were the beginnings of dark circles under her blue eyes, evidence that she had stayed up too late last night studying for her algebra test. She quickly slipped on her shoes and rushed downstairs.

Her mother was feeding the three year old twins their breakfast and they were happily munching away at it. Maggie smiled up at her and looked so cute with milk dripping down her chin that Elizabeth had to laugh. Maggie's twin brother, Martin, had cereal on his face and Elizabeth wiped it off before she kissed his cheek. They were both cute as could be with curls the same color as their mother's dark hair.

"Be good for Mom you two," she coaxed. "And I'll read you a story before bed tonight." She patted Maggie's head and picked up her book bag.

"Do you need the car today?" asked Elaine.

"No, I'm riding with Maria. And don't forget, I'll have to stay a little late to go over some chemistry problems with my teacher this afternoon."

"Just so you have time to practice the piano this evening," reminded Elaine.

"I will. I'm still struggling with that one piece for the concert on Saturday," complained Elizabeth as she finished a piece of toast.

"You'll get it, you always worry but then play brilliantly."

Elizabeth smiled. "Mother, you're my best fan. Thanks."

"True. But your father's coming around, too. Classical music just isn't his favorite. He loves it when you play jazz music for him."

Elaine waved as Elizabeth went out the door. There was a loud crash and she turned around to see Martin looking up guiltily.

"Sorry, Mommy," he said his chin quivering. "I spilled."

His broken cereal bowl lay upside down on the floor, a puddle of milk and cheerios spreading out from it.

"That's all right, honey. I'll take care of it. Don't touch the broken glass," warned Elaine as she grabbed a broom and dustpan.

The bright spring sunshine felt wonderful to Elizabeth as she and Maria arrived at the high school. Flowers were blooming all over San Diego and white Shasta daisies filled the flowerbeds in front of the school.

Neither girl was aware they were being watched as they walked from the school parking lot. They were discussing the upcoming algebra test, hurrying to get to their lockers.

Matthew and Mark Hensley had been stalking Elizabeth for two weeks now. They had even gone to one of the high school's swim team matches and seen her win a second place medal. They admired that she was tall and slim and very athletic. That match was where they had first seen Maria. Elizabeth and Maria both swam on their school's team in the relay competition and their team had taken first place.

When the girls had gone shopping together one evening, Matthew and Mark had followed them to the mall. They were impressed by the fact that the girls did not flirt with all the boys like some of the other high school girls did. They seemed to be more serious minded and didn't fall for the obvious enticements the boys flaunted at them.

During the days following the swim meet, the Hensley men had occasionally followed Maria home and watched as she helped her single mother care for her three younger brothers. They were impressed by her loving attitude and homemaking skills. Parked outside her house one evening they had seen her prepare a lavish dinner for several visiting family members. Mark had commented that he couldn't wait to taste some of her homemade enchiladas.

"I hope Ma lets Maria do some of the cooking," he told Matthew.

"Sure she will," grinned Matthew. "Isn't she always complaining about how you're a bottomless pit and she's tired of trying to fill you up?"

Mark punched him in the shoulder. "You eat as much as I do, little brother," he had harshly commented.

Now they watched both girls as they left the school parking lot for class. Mark turned to Matthew and smiled slyly. "You're sure it's the blond girl that you like?"

Matthew nodded. "She has hair like mother's and I like her smile. She plays the piano really well and the reverend's been complaining that we need someone new to play for church meetings. You like her friend, don't you?" he asked.

Mark shrugged. "Yeah, she's real pretty and she has big ones."

Matthew blushed. "Don't talk like that."

"Well it's true," he grinned. "Besides didn't we decided it would be better if we took two girls who were already friends? That way they won't be so afraid."

Matthew nodded and turned to follow his brother back to their van. Now that they had found two perfect girls, they would have to make plans on how to kidnap them.

*\*\*\**

Elizabeth woke with a start and jumped out of bed. Today was Sunday and it was her birthday. She was eighteen years old and graduation was only a month away. It seemed that this day would never come, but finally it had. She could hardly wait to see what her parents had gotten her for a present.

Her mother had been smiling and teasing her all week about becoming an adult. Elaine had told her that her stepfather had a surprise for her and promised that Elizabeth would love his gift, but she wouldn't even give her a hint as to what the gift actually was. Hurrying as fast as she could to brush her teeth and get dressed, she rushed downstairs to the kitchen.

Brandon looked up from his cup of coffee and smiled. "Hi, Birthday Girl," he said grinning. He looked at Elaine and winked.

Elizabeth grinned at him, her eyes wide. "Do I have to wait until my party tonight to see what you got me?" she asked, her eyes pleading. "You are the best step dad in the whole world. You won't make me wait, will you?"

Brandon looked over at Elaine. "Should we make her wait?" he asked as he pulled on his cowboy boots. He'd worn them when he lived in Texas and still thought they were more comfortable than shoes.

Elaine wiped her hands on a dishtowel as she turned away from the sink. "It's up to you. I know you have to head to the station in a few minutes …"

Elizabeth groaned. Brandon was a police detective. There were times when one of his cases kept him away from home until all hours. If he didn't give her the present now, it could be late tonight or tomorrow before she saw it.

Brandon laughed when he saw the disappointment on Elizabeth's face. "I wouldn't be that cruel. Come on." He stood up and reached into his pocket.

She watched wide-eyed as he pulled out a key.

"Is it locked up somewhere?" she asked laughing.

"No," he said. "This key is used to drive it."

He dangled the key in front of her face teasingly.

She reached up and he dropped the key into her outstretched palm. There was a small imprint of a galloping horse on the end of the key ring. Taking her by the arm, he led her out the kitchen door to the yard.

There parked in the driveway was a dark green Ford Mustang convertible.

Elizabeth screamed for joy and grabbed him in a big hug.

"Oh my gosh, oh my gosh! I don't believe it! You got me a car!" She ran up to the car and caressed the hood. She ran back and hugged him. "I absolutely love it!"

Elaine stood there laughing at her from the open kitchen doorway, with the twins peeking out beside her legs.

Maggie squealed and ran outside with Martin close behind. "Lizzy got a car! Lizzy got a car!" she exclaimed excitedly.

Brandon opened the driver's side door. "Get in," he told Elizabeth.

She climbed in and put both hands on the steering wheel.

"I thought you were getting me a string of pearls or something. I never dreamed it would be a car. And not just any car, a Mustang!" she gushed. "Thank you, Brandon."

"Well, it's not brand new, but it's been overhauled and cleaned up. It's low mileage and in great shape. We had it painted your favorite color."

"I love it! Wow, a Mustang convertible. Wait until I show Maria!"

Elaine snapped Elizabeth's picture as she sat behind the wheel of her new car.

The twins were jumping up and down as they raced around the car.

"Hey you two," called Elizabeth. "Get in the car before you get hurt."

She laughed at them as Brandon helped them both climb in the back seat. Elaine brought out their booster seats and strapped the children in.

Brandon showed her how the stereo worked and how to raise and lower the convertible top while Elaine snapped more photos. Brandon's cell phone rang just as Elaine was climbing in the front passenger seat. He listened for a few minutes.

"Well, you all go enjoy a drive, I've got to head to work." He leaned in the window and gave Elaine a kiss. "I'll do my best to get back for the party. Hopefully the local criminals will all take the day off."

After driving to the corner store and buying ice cream cones, Elizabeth dropped everyone off back at home. She helped Elaine take the twins' seats out of the car.

"I can't wait until tonight to show Maria the car, I'm going to drive over to her house now if that's all right with you," she said.

Elaine smiled. "Sure, have fun and be back to help me set up for the party."

Elizabeth gave her a hug. "Thanks again. This is the best birthday present ever."

Elaine watched Elizabeth back out of the driveway, then she hurried into the house with the twins. "Let's go wash the ice cream off your faces," she told them.

Within a few minutes Elizabeth was parking the car in front of a white stucco house. She honked the horn and waved at Maria's brother, Luis, who was looking out the window. His eyes popped wide when he saw Elizabeth at the wheel.

"Maria, Maria, come quick!" he shouted. "It's Elizabeth!"

He rushed out the front door and ran down the sidewalk towards the Mustang.

"Oh wow, Elizabeth! Is this your birthday present?" He reached out to touch the car, then quickly pulled back his hand.

"It's OK, you can touch it Luis," laughed Elizabeth.

Maria broke into a grin as she came rushing down the sidewalk towards them.

"Hi. Happy Birthday. Your mom told me about the car last week and I've been biting my tongue ever since to keep from saying anything," informed Maria.

"You knew I was getting a car?" asked Elizabeth in surprise.

Maria nodded. "But I hadn't seen it. It's beautiful."

"I can't believe you could keep a secret for a whole week. You can never keep a secret."

"It was really hard," admitted Maria. "If I had known it was a Mustang convertible I probably would have cracked under the pressure."

"Hurry and get in and we'll go somewhere," laughed Elizabeth.

"Where?" asked Maria as she climbed into the car.

"I don't know. I just want to drive it."

"Can I go too?" begged Luis.

"Sure, get in the back."

Luis' face lit up and he quickly opened the back door and climbed in. "I hope I get a great car like this some day," he said as he buckled his seat belt.

"Maybe in seven years when you're eighteen you can get one, too," said Elizabeth.

Maria laughed. "Luis, you better get a job tomorrow and start saving for the next ten years if you want to be able to buy a car."

Luis grinned. "Yeah right."

They waved at everyone they passed in the neighborhood as they circled the block three times. When she finally stopped in front of Maria's house again, Luis spotted his two younger brothers in the yard. "Can they ... " he started.

"Yes, help me get them in," interrupted Elizabeth with a grin.

When she had them all settled in the back seat she drove around the block again. Jose and Servando were as excited by the car ride as they would have been by a ride at the carnival.

Maria's mother, Adelita, waved at them from the doorway when they pulled the car up to the curb. "It's time to come back inside, boys," she called. "You have bothered the girls enough for one day. And it's almost time for lunch."

"You didn't bother me," Elizabeth told them as they climbed out of the car.

"I love this car," sighed Maria. "You are so lucky."

"Oh Maria, I hope this doesn't make you feel bad."

"No, don't worry," Maria interrupted. "I'm thrilled for you. After everything you have been through, it's good to see you so happy. Besides I'd be afraid to drive a car this nice. My old Dodge Dart is just my speed and it's very sturdy if I hit something."

"That's true. It didn't even get dented when you bumped that light pole in the school parking lot," reminded Elizabeth with a laugh. "I'm so glad you're not jealous."

"Are you kidding? We've known each other for a long time. I know how hard you've had it, what with your real mom dying, then your illness. I felt so bad when you had to be in that wheelchair. It's such a miracle that the brain surgery worked ... and look at you now. No one would ever know that you almost died," Maria paused to take a breath. "And then for your father to be murdered ... " Maria stopped, afraid she had said too much. "I'm sorry, I shouldn't bring that up."

"No, it's all right," assured Elizabeth. "It feels like both my parents are with me today. And I'm so lucky to have Elaine and Brandon. I don't know what I would have done without Elaine after my father died. I do feel lucky even after everything that has happened."

"I shouldn't have brought it up on your birthday. I just wanted to make sure you knew I could never be jealous of anything good that happens to you."

"Thanks Maria. You're the best friend ever."

"Well, I better go help my mom with the boys," said Maria as she got out of the car. "See you tonight at the party. Do you need me to come early to help get things ready?"

"No. I think Elaine and I have it under control, but thanks."

\*\*\*

Anna Hensley looked up from her sewing machine, one hand still holding the fabric in place. "When will Matthew and Mark be back?" she asked. "I don't remember them ever being gone this long camping before. Where did you say they went?"

Her husband kept his back to her as he continued to sharpen the saw. "I don't think I mentioned where they have gone. I'm not quite sure myself."

"Did they take enough food and supplies with them to stay this long?"

He hesitated. "I gave them some money, too."

She inhaled sharply. "You did? You've never had to give them money before to go camping," she said accusingly. "What are you not telling me, John?"

He placed the saw on the cabinet and turned around slowly.

"Reverend Forester sent them hunting," he reluctantly told her.

Anna gasped. "No!" Her hand flew to the scar on her cheek.

John walked over to her side. "You know the boys would never do anything to hurt anyone. We've raised them better than that."

"How can you say that! Taking someone away from their family and everything they know hurts them!" she exclaimed.

John hung his head. "I know. I'm so sorry. But the reverend says it's the only way for the young men to get wives."

"How many? How many men has he sent hunting this time?" she asked, her voice shaking with emotion.

"Seven," he reluctantly admitted.

"Oh my God. Where are Mark and Matthew now?" she demanded.

"They went to California. All of the men were told to go far away so as not to be too close to home. Reverend doesn't want the women to come from nearby ... "

Anna started crying and John put his arms around her.

"Have you never been happy here with me, ever?" he asked sadly.

She sobbed harder. "Of course I have. I love you, John. And the boys ... but it's so wrong to do this to innocent women. I've learned to accept this life, but it was never the way I had planned my life to be."

"It's been twenty-five years since they brought you here. There have been no new women since then. There aren't enough girls here for our boys to marry. Reverend says the gene pool is still too small. The babies could be born deformed or simple minded," he sadly repeated the reverend's warning words.

"Don't tell me what the reverend said!" she shouted pushing him away. "There are other ways for our boys to find wives. Why can't they go to college and get a better education and fall in love like other young men? Why does he insist that they steal wives? I hate this. I don't want our boys to think like the reverend!"

"Hush! Don't talk like that! Someone might hear you," he gently put his hand over her mouth. "It will be different with our boys. They are gentle men and I've taught them to respect women, you know that."

She pushed his hand away and stood up to face him.

"You have always been kind to me. But I still have this scar to prove that not everyone here is as good and kind as you are."

He reached up and gently ran his finger down the scar on her face. "I'm so sorry about that, I wish it had never happened."

She slapped his hand away and ran to their bedroom.

Anna lay on their bed for hours, remembering. Remembering the horrible things that had happened to her all those years ago, and now it was happening to other innocent young women. After a while she fell into an exhausted sleep. But the dreams that had not plagued her in years returned.

Dreams about the terrifying experience of being dragged from her dorm room and being drugged, and of waking in the back seat of a strange car with another frightened girl. She remembered the terrified look in the other girl's eyes and knew it mirrored that of her own eyes.

Anna woke with a scream as she again saw the knife coming towards her face.

# Chapter 3

The Hensley men sat in the back of the van eating sandwiches for dinner. Mark had been talking for hours about his plans to kidnap Maria. Matthew's head hurt from listening. Mark wanted to break into her house at night and steal her from her bed.

"I don't think that's the best way to do this," insisted Matthew for the second time. "She has all those little brothers. What if someone woke up and got hurt?"

"All right. Then what do you think we should do?" asked Mark sarcastically.

"There's another swim meet tomorrow. Let's go there and see if we can try to make friends with the girls and talk them into going out on a date or something."

"Right!" snapped Mark. "Then everyone there will know what we look like."

"Not if we wait until after the meet and talk to them in the parking lot. You know, tell them we watched them swim and were impressed. They usually park in the student lot and that clears out pretty fast after a meet. We don't have to tell them our full names or anything."

Mark reluctantly nodded. "Maybe they would agree to go out for hamburgers or ice cream. The main thing would be to get them into the van. That might work."

"We'll wait near Elizabeth's new car. They change out of their swim suits after the meets and most of the parents and visitors are gone by the time the girls get dressed."

Mark laughed. "You're right. It sure takes them a long time to get dressed. The guys are out in ten minutes and the girls take an hour fixing their hair and make up. They'll have to get over that when we take them home with us. Reverend won't let them wear make up or dress like whores."

"Elizabeth and Maria don't dress like whores," corrected Matthew angrily.

"You know what I mean. Most of the girls we've seen in California barely wear enough clothes to cover themselves. Anyway, I think your idea of waiting for them is worth a try." Mark crumpled up his sandwich wrapper and threw it in the back. "If that doesn't work we can always do it my way."

Matthew nodded but in his heart he prayed that it would work. Elizabeth's father was a policeman and he didn't want to think about what might happen if they had to break into her house to get her.

Matthew didn't like the reverend's method of obtaining a wife, but he didn't know any other way to find one. This was the first time they had even been allowed to leave the mountains of West Virginia and the world out here was alien and sometimes frightening to him. He was a country boy and the big cities in California were almost too much for him to comprehend. How could all these people stand to be jammed together this way? He just wanted to get back home where he felt safe, well safer anyway. Even the snakes at church didn't seem so bad compared to some of the things they had already seen on this trip.

***

Elizabeth was pleased that the swim meet had gone well for her school. She had taken second place in the free style swim and Maria had won first place in the butterfly stroke. The school's team had also won the relay race in which they both had participated.

They were excited and happy as they said goodbye to their families and went to the girl's locker room to dry off and change out of their wet swimsuits.

"Is your family going to take you out to lunch?" asked Maria as she got her clothes out of her beach bag.

"Not this time. The twins have a birthday party to go to in an hour so Elaine gave me money for lunch. Do you want to go to Pizza Hut for the buffet or get a burger?" asked Elizabeth as she rubbed her wet hair with a towel. "Darn, I forgot my blow dryer and I'll never get my hair dry with a towel. I guess I'll just pull it back into a ponytail."

Maria laughed as she brushed her thick black hair. "It takes hours for my hair to dry." She brushed a little rouge on her cheeks. Her dark brown eyes had thick dark lashes and she didn't need mascara.

"That's because you have that beautiful Mexican hair," sighed Elizabeth.

"Everyone from Mexico has this hair. I wish I had blond hair like yours."

"You could always bleach it," said Elizabeth as she slipped on her t-shirt and shorts. She applied some chapstick to her lips. The chlorinated pool water always dried them out.

"My mother would kill me if I bleached my hair! No way would I do that." Maria shrugged and finished dressing. "Besides, I complain about it, but I really like my hair."

They didn't hurry as they folded their wet towels and put them with their suits in plastic bags. Elizabeth put her medal in a side pocket of her bag and zipped it shut. "There, I'm ready."

The student parking lot was empty when they finally left the locker room.

They were both discussing where they should go for lunch when they reached Elizabeth's car and threw their swim bags into the back seat. She had the top down today and she felt a thrill just looking at her own car.

"Hey," said a masculine voice behind them.

Elizabeth looked back and saw two young men standing behind them. They were both clean cut, tall and muscular. She could tell they weren't from around here because they both wore jeans and long-sleeved shirts. California boys were all wearing shorts, t-shirts and sandals this time of year.

"Hi," said Maria flirtatiously as she looked at the men. The taller man smiled and two dimples appeared. He was really cute. He had sandy blond hair and blue eyes.

"We saw you swim. Congrats on winning first place," he said to Maria.

Maria blushed. "Thanks."

"You were pretty impressive," he said in a soft Southern drawl.

The other man looked at Elizabeth and smiled. He was nice looking too, but not as obviously cute as the taller man. He seemed somewhat shy and held back a little. His eyes were dark green and his hair brown and curly.

"My name's Matthew and this is my brother, Mark," he said.

"My name's Elizabeth and this is Maria. What brought you to our swim meet?"

"We have a cousin from the other school," lied Mark. "Your team beat the heck out of them today. He wasn't too happy about that."

Maria laughed. "That's true. We had a good day."

"Well, it was nice meeting you, but we have to go," said Elizabeth as she walked around the car and opened the driver's side door.

"We were wondering if you would like to go to lunch," said Matthew hastily. "With us, I mean." He was nervous and hoped he didn't sound that way.

"We're not from around here," admitted Mark. "Maybe you could come and show us a good place to eat. I'm buying ... "

Maria turned and looked at Elizabeth and mouthed "Please", her eyes wide.

"Well, I guess that would be all right. We were kind of thinking about pizza," said Elizabeth. "Do you like pizza?"

Mark smiled. "I love pizza." His eyes sparkled when he looked over at Maria. "So is that a yes?"

Maria blushed at his obvious flirtations and nodded. "Yeah, sure."

"We're parked over there, it's that white van," said Mark. "We can bring you back later for your car. By the way, I love the Mustang. Is it yours?" he asked Maria stepping closer.

"No. It's Elizabeth's," she admitted. "It was her birthday present last week."

"Wow, that's nice," he leaned in towards Maria. "Come on, Beautiful, show me where to drive for the pizza." He reached out and took her gently by the arm.

Maria blushed and started giggling as she walked with him towards the van.

Elizabeth looked at Matthew. "Seems that Maria is pretty taken with your brother," she said smiling. "Shall we follow them?"

"He can be rather charming. Hope you don't mind being stuck with me."

"I don't consider it being stuck. I'm not that impressed with charming men," she stopped short. "Sorry that didn't come out right." She blushed and shyly looked up at him. "I didn't mean that you're not charming, too."

Matthew laughed. "That's OK. As the younger brother I've learned it's best to be myself. He can be kind of obvious at times."

They followed Maria and Mark over to the van. Matthew politely opened the side door for the girls to get in.

"Wow, looks like you've been living in here!" exclaimed Maria when she saw blankets and pillows folded up in the back. There were coolers on one side and suitcases on the other.

"Where did you say you were from?" she asked Mark as she sat down.

"We've been traveling and the hotels are so expensive, I admit we have been sleeping in the van for a few nights," said Matthew hurriedly. "Sorry it's such a mess."

He climbed in the front passenger seat and turned around towards them. "We came down from Oregon to see our cousin swim."

"Really? Wow, that's a long way to come for one swim meet," said Maria buckling her seat belt. "It's too bad his school didn't do better.

"Well, we wanted to see southern California anyway," said Mark as he started the van. "He was always bragging about how much nicer it was than Oregon. So where do I go to find this pizza place?"

Elizabeth gave him directions and he drove out of the parking lot. As they turned the corner Maria saw her friend, Angelina, standing on the sidewalk and she waved to her. She pointed at Mark and made a thumbs-up sign. Angelina laughed and waved back.

"If you guys are from Oregon, why do you both have southern accents?" questioned Elizabeth. "Obviously you weren't born there."

Matthew frowned and quickly lied, "Well, we lived in Alabama when we were younger. I guess the accent has stuck with us." Wow, she was smart. He hadn't thought about that when they decided to tell them they were from Oregon.

"It sure has stuck," she laughed.

"So, I guess graduation is getting close," said Matthew. "Are you excited?"

Elizabeth nodded. "Of course we are. I can't believe we'll finally be finished with high school."

"What are your plans after that?"

"I've applied to several different colleges and universities. I'm hoping to get a music scholarship to one of them," she said shyly.

Maria interrupted her friend. "You should hear her play the piano," she told Matthew enthusiastically. "She's fantastic! I'm sure she'll get a scholarship."

"What are your plans?" asked Mark glancing back at Maria.

"I'm going to the community college in town. I want to be an LPN, a nurse. My mother can't afford a four-year college. I have three little brothers," she explained. "But I can be an LPN in twelve months if I work really hard."

"That's an admirable goal," said Matthew.

"Well, I like to help people and nurses do that."

As they came up to a cross street, Mark looked over at Matthew and nodded.

"I'm really thirsty," Matthew told the girls. "Mark can stop at that 7-11 for a minute and I'll buy drinks. What do you girls want?"

Mark slowed down and pulled into the 7-11 parking lot.

"Thanks. I'll have a Sprite," said Elizabeth.

"I want a diet Dr. Pepper," said Maria.

"OK, I'll be right back," said Matthew opening his door. "This will only take a minute."

He quickly reached into the glove box subtly pulling out a twenty-dollar bill and a small bottle. The girls were too busy talking to Mark to notice anything strange.

In the store he went to the back and pulled cups from the fountain drink display. After pouring half the little bottle in Maria's drink, he poured the rest in Elizabeth's. He put ice in the cups and then soda. He got himself a bottle of water and a Gatorade for Mark. It was easier to carry the bottles under his arm and the cups in his hands and there would be no way he might have a chance of mixing up the drinks this way.

Back at the van, he handed the girls their sodas and buckled his seat belt. "OK, let's go get pizza, I'm starved."

Neither girl noticed anything strange about the taste of the drinks and they sipped thirstily. "Swimming really makes you thirsty," said Maria. "Thanks for the soda."

By the time they made it through all the lunchtime traffic to the Pizza Hut, both girls were asleep in the back seat.

Matthew turned around and said, "Hey you two, don't you want to eat?"

There was no answer from either girl.

Mark grinned. "Reverend said it only took about twenty minutes to work. They should sleep for about twelve hours now."

Matthew got out and climbed in the back beside them. He leaned both girls' seats back and covered them each with a light blanket. This way anyone looking in the window would only notice two girls taking a nap and their faces would be harder to see.

"Thank God that worked so well," said Mark. "Now we can head home. Bring me one of those sandwiches from the cooler."

Matthew got out two of the sandwiches they had purchased that morning from the Wal-mart deli. There were twelve more in the cooler as well as chips and apples in a bag. They didn't plan to stop except for gas and bathroom breaks until they got back to West Virginia.

***

Melinda Lakes whimpered in her sleep and woke herself up. She sat up in bed and looked around her room. She felt scared but there was no one in the room and all she saw were her toys and the Disney decals on the walls.

Her Little Mermaid nightlight illuminated the stuffed animals and games on the shelf by her bed. She shivered and climbed out of bed. Her 'Hello Kitty' nightgown was damp with sweat and she still felt afraid as she hurried down the hall to her parent's bedroom.

Janice woke up when Melinda crawled in bed beside her. She rolled over and asked, "What's the matter, honey?"

"Mommy, I had a bad dream," Melinda whispered.

Janice hugged her close. "It's OK, sweetie. Go back to sleep."

"Mommy, a bad man took Elizabeth away," said the child.

"What are you talking about? You mean in your dream?"

Melinda nodded. "He made her fall asleep and he took her away."

"It was just a dream, sweetie. We'll call Elizabeth in the morning, OK? You can talk to her yourself. Go back to sleep."

Five-year-old Melinda snuggled up against her mother and fell back asleep.

***

Mark was outside pumping gas when Matthew noticed that Maria was starting to wake up. She rubbed her face and looked over at him. Her eyes flew open and they were suddenly full of questions.

"Where am I? Did I fall asleep?" She looked over at Elizabeth sleeping beside her. "She fell asleep, too?"

"Sort of," admitted Matthew.

"I'm so sorry. Oh my gosh, it's dark outside. How long did I sleep?" she asked, completely confused.

Maria looked out the side window but there were no familiar city lights or tall buildings outside. In fact it looked like they were in the middle of the desert. All she saw was a small gas station surrounded by sand and rocks and cactus. Suddenly she felt terrified. Something was definitely wrong.

"Where are we?" she cried trying to sit up in her seat.

"Somewhere in New Mexico."

"New Mexico! What are you saying? Why are we in New Mexico?"

She tried to unbuckle her seat belt but suddenly a wave of dizziness overtook her and she leaned her head back. She looked at Elizabeth still sleeping soundly beside her. "I don't understand."

"You've been asleep for fourteen hours, Maria. It is two o'clock in the morning, Sunday morning," informed Matthew.

Maria shook her head. "What are you saying? How could it be Sunday? What is going on? In doesn't make any sense." Her head hurt and she couldn't think straight.

By this time Mark was finished pumping gas and he climbed back into the van. He looked over at Maria.

"Hi, Beautiful. I'm glad to see you're finally awake." He started the van and pulled out of the gas station parking lot.

Maria was terrified and started shaking. Even in her confused brain the truth had finally penetrated. She and Elizabeth were being kidnapped.

"Why are you doing this? What do you want from us?" she asked in a frightened whisper. "I don't understand why you would do this."

Matthew was watching her. He could tell that she had figured it out.

"Try not to be too afraid. We aren't going to hurt you, I promise, Maria," he said soothingly. "I know you're frightened, but it will be all right."

"Then why are you kidnapping us? Our families are not rich. In fact my mother is poor." She was so confused, none of this made sense. How could she have slept for fourteen hours? Then it hit her. There must have been something in the soda.

"Please, don't do this," she whimpered. "Take us back home. I promise we won't tell anyone."

Mark glanced around and laughed. "Sorry, Beautiful. You're going home with us. You are going to be my blushing bride. We've been out wife hunting."

"Don't tell her like that!" said Matthew disgustedly. "Gee, you're so tactful."

"Well, she might as well get used to the truth now as later," retorted Mark.

Maria was shocked. She shivered and hugged her arms to her chest. This couldn't be really happening. Men didn't just go out and kidnap women to marry them. That was ridiculous. Not in this day and age. What was he talking about? She rubbed her eyes trying to wake up and make sense of this.

"Where are you taking us?" she asked weakly, trying to hide the quiver in her voice. "This isn't the way to Oregon."

"We're not from Oregon," said Matthew. "We live in West Virginia, way back up in the mountains. It's really pretty up there ... Lots of trees and flowers and animals."

Maria stared at him in amazement. What was he trying to do, convince her that she would like living in West Virginia in the mountains? She couldn't believe this was happening. She felt dizzy and nauseated and she couldn't think straight. And worst of all, why wasn't Elizabeth waking up by now?

***

Luis answered the phone with a "Yeah?" and his mother scolded him.

"Don't answer the phone like that, please." She took the receiver from him and said, "Hello, this is the Gonzales residence."

"Hi, Adelita, this is Elaine. May I speak to Elizabeth, please?"

"Elizabeth is not here, Elaine," said Adelita confused.

"Oh, is she already on her way home?"

"No, I thought the girls were spending the night at your house."

"No. They never came back here after the swim meet. They talked about spending the night together and when they didn't come back I assumed they were over there with you."

All of a sudden Adelita felt chilled with a cold fear. "They didn't come here. Where could they have gone? Now I'm worried."

"I'm sure they're fine. I'll call their other friends, maybe I misunderstood where they were having the sleep over. I'll call you back when I find them," promised Elaine.

She hung up and turned to Brandon. "That's strange. They aren't at Maria's either. Where could they be?"

"I'm sure they'll turn up soon. I didn't always tell my parents everything when I was eighteen either," assured Brandon casually.

"But that's not like Elizabeth, you know that."

"True. She is more responsible than I ever was," admitted Brandon sheepishly.

"I'll call a few of her girl friends, someone is sure to know where the sleep over was," said Elaine trying not to let the niggling fear she felt grow stronger.

Brandon stood up from the breakfast table, picked up his keys and gave her a hug. "I'm sure they're fine. Let me know what you find out. I'll be at the station all morning." He gave her a quick kiss.

After Elaine got the twins settled at the table with their morning cereal she started calling Elizabeth's friends. No one had seen them since the swim meet yesterday at noon and a panicky feeling overwhelmed her. She immediately called Brandon.

"I'm really starting to worry," she admitted. "The girls all said there was no big sleep over planned for last night. Maria and Elizabeth were planning to stay here. Where could they possibly be, Brandon?"

"I'll swing by the school and see if anyone there knows anything. Try to stay calm. I'm sure everything is fine," soothed Brandon. "But one thing's for sure, I don't care how old she is, I'm giving her a big lecture about worrying you."

"Call me just as soon as you find out anything," said Elaine.

Brandon put down his desk phone and looked over at Belle. She was busy working on her computer finishing up some forms.

Belle Aspas was the only black woman in this precinct who had made it to detective status. She was a petite woman who looked half her age and completely helpless. That was far from the truth. Her marksmanship was better than most of the men on the force and she held a black belt in karate.

"Hey, Belle, have you got time to take a ride with me?" asked Brandon.

"If it gets me away from this computer I'm game for anything," she said shutting down the program she had just finished.

They drove over to the high school in their unmarked police car. On a Sunday morning there were no students to be seen. The only person around was sweeping the courtyard in front of the building.

Brandon flashed his detective's badge and asked, "Have you seen any students around here this morning?"

The man leaned on his broom and shook his head. "Nobody's here. I always come in to clean up on Sundays and I never see anyone." He paused then pointed around the side of the building. "I did notice there was a car parked in the student lot out back."

"Thanks," called Brandon as he and Belle hurried down the walk. He stopped short at the edge of the parking lot and muttered a curse under his breath.

"What's the matter?" asked Belle.

"That's Elizabeth's new car. She would never just go off and leave it parked here with the top down. Something is definitely wrong."

They walked over to the Mustang. Both girls' swim bags where still in the back seat. "This is officially a crime scene," he reminded Belle. "Don't touch anything."

Belle looked at him in disgust. "I figured that out for myself."

"Sorry," apologized Brandon. "I'm not used to having a family member involved in something like this. Elaine's not the only one worried now."

\*\*\*

Janice phoned Elaine around nine o'clock.

"Hi, would it be OK for Melinda to talk to Elizabeth?" she asked. "She had a nightmare last night about her."

"She's not here," said Elaine. "In fact Brandon just called me and said her car was left overnight in the school parking lot. I'm scared to death something awful has happened to her."

Janice gasped. "I don't believe it. Melinda said that in her dream some man drugged Elizabeth and took her away."

"What? How in the world would she know that?" asked Elaine.

"I don't know. But you remember how they almost seem connected sometimes. I don't understand why or how, but Melinda woke me up in the middle of the night scared to death. She said a man made Elizabeth go to sleep and took her away."

"I have to go," said Elaine shakily. "I'll call you later."

When Elaine put down the phone, she was shivering and wrapped her arms around her chest. It was uncanny how sometimes Melinda and Elizabeth seemed connected. She prayed that this time Melinda's dream was not true.

She tried to reach Brandon, but his line was busy. As she was washing up the breakfast dishes Brandon stopped by the house.

"Any news?" she asked him.

"Not yet. I was kind of hoping she might have contacted you," he said.

"No. But Janice called and said Melinda had a nightmare about a man taking Elizabeth away. I know you don't believe in that type of thing, but the two of them seem somehow connected and ... "

"Now, don't go off the deep end here," he interrupted. "I'll find Elizabeth."

"Brandon, there are some things I never told you about Melinda," confessed Elaine. "Maybe it explains how they seem to know things about each other."

"What do you mean? I already know all about how Dr. Franklin saved Melinda's life and kept her alive in that artificial womb thing of his. I know that he died protecting her and that she and Elizabeth have always been close. What have you not told me?"

She took a deep breath and told the secret she had kept to herself for five years. "When Melinda was in his lab all those months, he played audio tapes of Elizabeth reading stories and playing the piano. He was trying to give the fetus Elizabeth's memories because he was planning to kill her and use her brain tissue to save Elizabeth. He came to his senses and never did that, of course, but I think all those tapes somehow created a psychic bond between the two of them."

"You know I don't believe in that stuff," scoffed Brandon.

"Well, how do you explain that Elizabeth knew before Janice called that Melinda fell and broke her arm last year? Or that I can never tell Melinda what presents we buy to give Elizabeth because somehow if she knows, then Elizabeth knows, too?" she asked. "You know that's not normal, don't you?"

He shrugged. "I don't know. I don't understand that either. I'll go and talk to Melinda, but how is a five-year-old little girl going to help us find Elizabeth?"

"I don't know," said Elaine as she reached over and gripped his arm. "But we have to check into everything."

\*\*\*

Adelita sat at her kitchen table feeling sick and frightened. Elaine had just called and told her that Elizabeth's car had been found in the school parking lot. There was just no explanation of where the girls had gone.

She picked up her address book and started calling every one of Maria's friends to see if anyone had seen them yesterday after the swim meet. She was near the bottom of her list when she finally found the one person who knew something.

"I saw them leaving the school parking lot in a white van with two really cute guys," Angelina Sanchez told her.

"When was that, Angelina?" asked Adelita.

"Right after the swim meet. Maria was smiling and waved at me. It didn't look like anything was wrong. Maybe they went with them to a motel," suggested Angelina.

"You know Maria would never do that!" exclaimed Adelita, shocked at the suggestion.

"Well, I never tell my mother when I do it," sneered Angelina. "You're so old-fashioned. Lots of girls do it."

Adelita was so upset she slammed down the receiver. She immediately picked it up again and called Elaine to tell her what she had found out.

"And she had the gall to suggest they went to a motel with two strange men!" choked out Adelita. "I'm mad at her for even saying that."

"Isn't Angelina the girl that Maria out-swam and bumped off the relay team? She's probably just jealous, you and I both know the girls would never do something like that," soothed Elaine.

Adelita sniffed back her tears. "You're right. She hasn't been all that nice these last few weeks since she lost her spot on the team."

"Thanks for calling, Adelita. I'll let Brandon know. I'm sure he'll want to go over and have a word with Angelina."

"Elaine, I'm getting really scared. You know Maria is a brittle diabetic. She's had to be on insulin since she was six years old," choked Adelita. "She needs her medicine."

"I know. Brandon will do everything possible to find them," promised Elaine. When she hung up the phone, she prayed that what she had said would come true.

***

When Brandon phoned her he didn't get much more from Angelina than what she had told Adelita, except that she thought she had seen the van around the high school earlier in the week. Brandon had police teams checking all the local motels. There was no sign of a white van or the girls. He figured he'd go talk to Angelina in person later and maybe learn more.

While the teams where checking motels, he went to see Melinda. He felt that it would be a waste of time but he didn't want to go home without being able to tell Elaine that he had spoken to the child.

Janice answered the door. "I figured you would come by to see her," she said stepping back to let him come in.

Brandon nodded. "I can't face Elaine unless I do."

"No one has found any sign of the girls yet?" she asked worriedly.

He shook his head. "One of Maria's friends saw them leave the school with two men in a white van right after the meet on Saturday."

Melinda walked up to him and pulled at his sleeve.

"The bad man who took Elizabeth had a white van," she told him, her eyes wide. "Is he going to hurt her?"

Brandon knelt down beside her. "Hi, Melinda. Can you tell me about the dream?"

She looked at him with big blue eyes. He felt that there was more depth in them than there should be for someone so young. She nodded.

Brandon picked her up and carried her to the sofa then sat down beside her.

"Just tell me what you remember from the dream," he coaxed.

She scrunched up her face, trying to remember. "Elizabeth saw him in the parking lot after she was swimming," she looked up at Brandon. "I got to see her swim, too. Mommy took me. She did good. She let me touch her medal."

"That was nice of her," said Brandon. "What else was in your dream, can you remember for me Melinda?"

"There were two men. I think they were brothers. They talked funny."

"What do you mean funny?" asked her mother.

"You know. Like Mr. Lucas talks."

Brandon looked at Janice questioningly.

"Mr. Lucas works at the corner drug store," she explained. "He always gives Melinda a piece of candy when we shop there. He's from Georgia. He has a heavy southern accent."

"So the men in your dream talked like Mr. Lucas. What else?"

Melinda concentrated. "Elizabeth thought he was a nice man. He was cute. But he's not a nice man if he takes her away."

"What else do you remember, sweetie?" asked Janice.

She closed her eyes. "He has green eyes and curly brown hair. Elizabeth was going with him to eat pizza. She loves pizza, like me," she smiled at Brandon. "She says you do, too."

"That's right, we both love pizza," he said patiently.

"Elizabeth and Maria got in the white van with the men. They drove away and now they are far away, I think."

"Why do you think that, Melinda?" asked Brandon.

"Because I can't feel her very well," stated Melinda.

"You can't feel her?"

She looked at him with wide-open eyes.

"When Elizabeth is close, I can feel her. Now it's like she is fuzzy. Like she might be far away from me."

Brandon looked at Janice and shook his head. This was all so strange, yet somehow he was beginning to believe in what Elaine called their psychic connection.

"Is that everything?" he gently asked Melinda.

She nodded.

"Thank you, Melinda. You have been a big help."

She smiled. "You'll find them, right?"

"I plan on it," he promised.

# Chapter 4

Anna Hensley was not looking forward to this visit from Reverend Forester. But then she never looked forward to his visits. The reverend still frightened her even after all these years.

She brushed back her long blond hair that now hung down to her waist. *The Pentecostal Holiness Today* church did not believe in women having short hair. She noticed a few gray hairs around her temples. She smoothed down her long dress, it's hem touched the top of her ankles. She had gotten used to wearing long dresses and not wearing make-up or jewelry since she was brought here twenty-five years ago.

Those things didn't bother her. She had always been modest and never sought to be beautiful. That she was beautiful, went unnoticed by her. The main thing that bothered her about this church, besides her fear of snakes, was this particular pastor's belief that all members must find strangers to marry. Never mind that the kidnapped women weren't part of his congregation, they became part of it when he baptized them.

His congregation consisted of 120 souls who lived in the back woods mountains of West Virginia. They were basically good people, somehow led astray in this one matter of marriage.

It had always been her opinion that everyone should be allowed to worship however they saw fit. Wasn't that basically why this country was formed, to establish freedom of religion?

As a child she had been raised a Baptist. These Pentecostal people also believed that Jesus Christ was the only way to be saved. They believed in baptism by immersion and that infant baptism was wrong. For how could an innocent baby have committed any sin? It was the fact that Reverend Forester made up his own rules when it came to other aspects of his church that always bothered her.

No matter what you thought Jesus taught, there was no place in the Bible that said you should marry women against their will. Not any scripture that Anna had seen anyway. As for handling snakes, she didn't believe that was the only way to prove that you loved God. Although John and her sons often had picked up the snakes, she never touched them.

It was true that the reverend also believed that the government was presided over by Satan and his church members never voted. They believed hospitals were a blasphemy because only God should decide if you lived or died and they used the laying on of hands for healing instead. But she could handle all of that. She had seen a lot of corruption in the government and there were often mistakes made and corruption found in hospitals. That was evidenced by the fact that some doctors performed abortions and wasn't that murder?

Anna had never cared much for television or movies as they were often filled with violence and sex and foul words. She didn't miss any of that at all. But to kidnap a woman and force her to marry a total stranger, that could never be right.

It was true that she had grown to love John and that the two other women who were brought here the year she came had learned to love their gentle husbands. But in her heart she knew that it was still not right.

John said that it wasn't much different than what had happened for centuries to women in other cultures. Some given to enemies to prevent wars between their two groups, some sold by their own fathers who did not value their female children.

Anna sighed. It was useless to fret about her life now, she would never leave John or her boys. She had grown used to the quiet Appalachian mountain life of farming. And she had her sewing to keep her happy. She reached up and touched her face and this scar was not something she ever wanted anyone else to see.

She mourned for the girls her boys were bringing back with them. They were from a different time and life-style. Would they ever learn to accept living here, as she had?

There was a knock on the bedroom door.

"He's here, Anna. Are you ready yet?" John tentatively opened the door. He smiled at her. "Everything will be all right."

She nodded and tied the belt around her waist. "I'm ready."

Reverend Forester stood waiting for them in the living room.

"Good evening, Mrs. Hensley."

"Evening Reverend, would you like something to drink? We have fresh buttermilk, chilled nice and cold the way John likes it," she said politely.

"That would be nice, thank you."

Anna filled three glasses and put fresh cookies on a plate. The Reverend and John were sitting on the sofa talking about crops when she returned to the living room. She handed him a glass and extended the plate of cookies.

"Ah, your famous oatmeal cookies. Thank you," he said as he took three from the plate. "One of these days someone is going to find out your secret for making these so delicious."

John laughed. "She won't even tell me that secret." He took a cookie for himself.

"Maybe she's waiting to give that secret to her new daughters-in-law," said Reverend Forester smiling.

Anna didn't look up at him. She gripped the plate tightly and said nothing.

John coughed. "That's a good idea, isn't it, Anna?"

She nodded. Putting the plate on an end table, she sat down in the rocker.

Reverend took a big drink of buttermilk and smiled at John.

"You two must be proud of both your sons. They have grown tall and strong. Just what you need now that you'll be expanding the farm."

Anna looked up questioningly at John.

"Reverend Forester is deeding us another ten acres. So the boys can each build their own homes and have something for themselves," he looked down at his hands. "My father gave me our land when I married you."

She nodded. "I see."

"Yes, as soon as the boys return, we'll have an old-fashioned barn raising. Well, it'll be more of a house raising. With seven new families being added to my flock, we'll be busy for a few weeks," he smiled at Anna and took another cookie from the plate. "We've been stock piling logs and boards for two years getting ready for just this time."

"Have you heard from the others boys then?" asked John.

"Yes, Paul Andrew's son, Michael, will most likely be back tonight or tomorrow."

Anna held her breath.

"He found a lovely girl in Montana. Came from a ranch there. She actually wanted to come back with him. He said her father was abusive and she was ready to leave home."

Anna looked down at her hands. That didn't sound too bad. A girl like that would probably do just fine here.

"And James Smith's son, Rueben, should be home soon. What have you heard from your boys?" asked Reverend quietly.

"Well, that letter we got yesterday said they were in southern California and had found two good prospects. Both girls are athletic and smart. I haven't heard anything else yet," said John.

"Hummm. Well that's something. No one's heard a thing from Jacob Brown," said the Reverend frowning. "I'm a little concerned about him. I'm worried he may decide he likes living out there in Sodom."

"Oh no, Reverend. I'm sure he'll return. He's basically a good boy," John assured him. "He'll come back. He wouldn't leave his father to tend the farm without his help."

John looked at Anna with a silent warning in his eyes.

She turned away from him. "What about the other two boys?" she whispered.

Reverend Forester didn't seem to notice the exchange.

"I'm on my way right now to visit Elijah Hamilton to ask about his sons, Able and Joshua. Thanks so much for the refreshments, Mrs. Hensley," he said standing up and putting his empty glass on the counter. "Good evening, John. I'll see you at Wednesday night meeting?"

"Of course, Reverend. We'll be there."

Anna's hands were shaking as she washed the glasses. John came up behind her and put his hands on her shoulders. She leaned back into him with a sigh.

He buried his face in her hair and whispered, "Trust in the Lord that it will all work out for the best."

*** 

The San Diego police CSI unit had checked Elizabeth's car for prints but the kidnappers had evidently never touched it. There was no evidence that they had ever been in or near the car. When they finished, Brandon had driven the Mustang back to the house and locked it in the garage.

Now he and Belle were on their way to talk to Angelina. He was hoping she would be able to give them a description of the van or the occupants.

Angelina opened the door when he knocked. She looked up at the huge man in cowboy boots and at the pretty little black woman standing beside him. "Can I help you?" she asked confused.

Brandon assessed the teenage girl with short spiky purple hair and the ring in her nose and wondered if she could really tell them anything useful.

"I'm Elizabeth Franklin's stepfather, Brandon Marcus. I'm a police detective and this is my partner, Belle Aspas," he said showing her his badge. "May we come in and talk to you about yesterday?"

Angelina shrugged and opened the door wider.

"My mom's at work. She's a waitress at Olive Garden. Sunday's are a good day for tips. People eating after going to church feel guilty if they don't leave a big tip," she said sarcastically. She sat down on a chair in the living room but didn't bother to turn down the television where a rap music video was screaming from the set.

Brandon reached down next to her, picked up the remote to shut off the noise.

"Hey, I was watching that," protested Angelina scowling at him.

"This is very important," said Belle sitting down across from the teenager. "We want to ask you a few questions about what you saw yesterday in the parking lot at the high school."

Angelina looked over at Brandon. "You mean about Maria and Elizabeth going off with those two guys?"

"Yes. Angelina, the girls didn't go off to some motel with them," he snapped. "Elizabeth's car was still in the parking lot this morning, and the police have checked every motel in the area. The girls are not here."

Angelina looked up at him and saw the fear in his eyes that he was trying to hide from her by his gruff manner. For the first time she felt sorry for Maria.

"So you think something bad has happened to them?" she asked timidly.

"We don't know that for sure. Just tell us what you saw," said Belle.

"Well, it was after the swim meet and we had all gotten dressed. Maria and Elizabeth didn't want to go with the rest of us to celebrate. We were going to the beach with some of the boys from the team. They knew we were getting some beers," she said defiantly. "They think they're too good for the rest of us. They never want to go anywhere someone will be drinking."

Brandon thought that was smart of Elizabeth, but he didn't say anything.

"OK, go on. Then what did you see?" encouraged Belle.

"I was going out back to put my swim bag in my car because I didn't want to take it with me to the beach and I was riding with some of the other kids. Anyway I saw a white van pulling out of the lot. Maria was in a back seat. The guy driving was really cute. You know, movie star cute. Anyway she waved to me and made a sign, you know, a thumbs-up, like she was really happy to be with this guy. She didn't look scared or anything, I promise," she said earnestly.

"Did you get a good look at the guy driving?" asked Belle.

Angelina shrugged. "I guess so. Maybe."

"What about the other guy?" asked Brandon.

"I couldn't really see him, the sun was reflecting on the window. I saw a girl's blond hair and figured the other girl was Elizabeth because they're always together."

"Do you remember anything about the van?" asked Brandon.

Angelina concentrated for a minute. "Just that it was white. It was one of those with windows on the side, that's why I could see Maria."

"Like a mini van?" asked Belle.

She nodded. "Yeah. And it had a different kind of license plate. Not from California."

"Think hard. What was on it?" asked Brandon.

"It had a sun on it, like a smiley face sun. I don't remember any numbers or what state it was from. But I noticed because it looked funny," she said. "Does that help?"

He nodded. "We can check for any states that have suns on their license plates."

"Do you think you could work with a police artist to help them draw a picture of the driver? It's really important," said Belle.

"When?" asked Angelina, concerned. "My baby brother's asleep in his room, I'm kind of stuck here babysitting him."

"How about if I bring the artist back here?" asked Belle.

"I guess that would be all right, if you're here, too," she agreed. "I'm really sorry I told Maria's mother they probably went to a motel." She looked ashamed and seemed to mean what she said. "I actually know they would never do that. They made a deal with some other girls at school that they would stay virgins until they got married."

Belle patted her shoulder. "I know you wouldn't want anything bad to happen to Maria."

"Thanks for being willing to help us," said Brandon as he stood up to leave.

Angelina nodded, feeling guilty for her earlier comments. "I really do hope you find them soon and that they're all right."

"I'll be back with a sketch artist in a little while," reminded Belle.

"I'll do my best to remember what he looked like, I promise."

Brandon drove Belle to the police station. She got Officer Victor Reilly to go back to see Angelina. Brandon went home to check on Elaine. He hated that he had nothing good to report.

***

Elizabeth opened her eyes and tried to figure out where she was. She was sitting in a car and it was dark outside, so it must be really late. Her head felt weird, like what she imagined you might feel like after you'd had too much to drink.

She turned her head and saw Marie. She was looking the other way out the window and Elizabeth reached over and touched her on the arm. Maria jumped and turned around.

"Oh, Elizabeth, thank God you're awake! I was getting so worried about you."

Elizabeth shook her head. She could see the lights shining on the dashboard and two men looking at a map. The van were stopped on the side of the road.

"Where are we? Why is it so late? Did I fall asleep?" she asked Maria.

"They put something in the soda. Elizabeth, you've been asleep for over sixteen hours. It's Sunday morning," whispered Maria.

Elizabeth was shocked. "What do you mean Sunday?"

"Mark and Matthew drugged us. We're being kidnapped," whimpered Maria.

Elizabeth tried to make her mind wrap around what she was hearing, but that couldn't be right. Matthew was so nice. Why would he do something that awful?

Just then the van started moving again as Mark pulled it back onto Highway 40.

Elizabeth sat up straight and grabbed the back of Matthew's seat.

"Where are we?" she asked. "Tell me right now what's going on!"

Matthew turned around and smiled at her. "So you finally woke up. I was worried I'd given you too much sleeping potion."

"You what!?"

"I gave you something to make you sleep. It's not supposed to hurt you," he said lamely. "Right now we're somewhere in Arkansas."

"Arkansas! You've got to be kidding! Mark, you turn this thing around right now and take us home!" she demanded shrilly.

Mark laughed. "Sorry, sweetheart. You're coming with us to West Virginia to be Matthew's new wife."

Elizabeth's mouth dropped open. "You're kidnapping me to marry Matthew?"

"Yup. And Maria's going to marry me," said Mark smugly as he shifted into a higher gear and increased his speed.

"No way! That is ridiculous! My stepfather's a cop. You are going to be is so much trouble you won't know what hit you! Take us home right now!" she screamed pounding on the back of Mark's seat. "Did you hear me?"

Mark turned around and slapped her in the face. "Shut up!" he yelled hoarsely.

Elizabeth was so shocked by his actions, that she shut up. Her cheek stung from the slap and involuntary tears ran down her cheek.

Maria was crying softly and she reached out and grabbed Elizabeth's hand.

"Don't say anything else, Elizabeth, please," she whispered.

Matthew was appalled with what Mark had done.

"Mark, why did you slap her?" he demanded. "You know our father taught us to never hit a woman. I can't believe you did that."

"She's not a woman," yelled Mark. "She's a screaming bitch right now. And I'll slap her again any time she acts like that!"

Matthew turned to Elizabeth, his face stricken. "I'm so sorry. He's never done anything like that before," he apologized. "Please don't scream again. Sit back and relax. We're not taking you back home and I don't think the cops will be able to find you any time soon."

Mark glanced back at Elizabeth and laughed. "They never found our mother and she was taken twenty-five years ago," he bragged.

Elizabeth was so mad she was shaking. She didn't know what to do. Maria was crying and these men were both crazy. How had they ever gotten in to this mess? All because they were going to get pizza with two cute guys.

***

"Mommy, Elizabeth is awake now," said Melinda as she put her Strawberry Shortcake doll in her little toy baby stroller.

Janice looked up from the breakfast dishes she was washing. They had eaten early because Melinda woke up hungry at six o'clock. "What did you say, Melinda?"

"Elizabeth is awake now."

"What makes you say that?" asked Janice drying her hands on a dishtowel as she walked over to Melinda. She knelt down beside the child. "Is something different?"

Melinda nodded. "She's not fuzzy anymore. I thought it was because she was getting far away, but it was because she was asleep."

Janice pulled the child onto her lap. "Can you tell anything else about her?'

"She's scared but she's also mad. Not at the nice boy with green eyes, but at his brother." Melinda squirmed and tried to get down. "She slept a long time."

"She did?'

Melinda nodded and her brown curls bounced. "Now she's worried about Maria."

"Why just Maria?"

"Well, she needs that special medicine from the little machine she showed me that she has under her clothes," said Melinda innocently. "You saw it, too."

Janice suddenly felt sick. Of course. What would happen to Maria when her insulin pump ran out of insulin? And she was to supposed to eat something regularly because it was constantly pumping small amounts of insulin into her body.

Melinda yawned. "I'm sleepy."

"That's because you got up so early," said Janice picking her up. "Come on and Mommy will tuck you into bed for a nap."

***

Reverend Forester had ordered the men to clean out the old school house behind the church. It had been used as a storage shed for years. Now it was being converted into what he called the "brides' cottage". The young women would be housed there until they settled in and the marriages could all be performed. Anna and the other boys' mothers were asked to donate quilts to decorate the twin beds that had been moved in after the walls were repainted.

"We want the girls to feel special and treasured while they're staying here," the reverend had explained. "It should only be for a few weeks while the new houses are being built for the young couples."

He had later pulled Anna aside while the other women were leaving. He cleared his throat and said, "Mrs. Hensley, I know you had a rough time settling in when you were brought here."

That was the understatement of the century, thought Anna as she stared at him. When had he aged so much? she wondered. His once thick black hair had thinned and now had gray streaks at his temples. But as he looked at her, she saw the same intense dark eyes. He stared back at her, his eyes so dark brown it was almost as if the iris and pupil were one. It gave the impression that his eyes were black marbles and it was very unsettling, as if he could see through your eyes and read your thoughts.

"I'm hoping you'll be instrumental in helping the girls settle in," he said quietly.

Anna felt herself starting to tremble and she stood up straighter and willed herself to stop shaking. She would not let this man know how much he still frightened her.

"Of course, Reverend. I will do my best," she said humbly.

"I want to thank you personally for the lovely quilts. I know you donated enough for your sons and both the Hamilton boys."

Anna nodded. "Mrs. Hamilton doesn't sew much and I was more than happy to share. I seem to always sew more than I can sell."

Reverend smiled. "It was still very generous of you. I know your sewing contributes much to your family's welfare."

Anna nodded. "Twin sized quilts aren't in as much demand right now and it won't take me long to sew more."

He patted her shoulder and she felt a chill run down her arm.

"Bless you for having such a giving and generous spirit," he praised.

As he turned to leave, Anna breathed a sigh of relief. It wasn't until he was gone that she allowed herself to sit down.

As soon as she sat down the shaking started again. The memory of his eyes as he had slashed her face overwhelmed her. Her whole body quivered and it took several minutes before she could gain control of herself. She thought that the reverend wanted her to show the girls her scar to scare them into submission. It made her sick just thinking about it.

*\*\*\**

Maria was starting to feel more nauseated and she had broken out in a cold sweat. Matthew noticed right away that something was wrong.

He looked at Elizabeth and asked, "Is she sick?"

Elizabeth took one look at Maria and knew immediately what was wrong. "Has she eaten anything since she woke up?"

Matthew shook his head. "I tried to give her a sandwich but she refused it.

Elizabeth turned and looked at Maria. Beads if cold sweat dotted her forehead and her hands were starting to shake.

"Maria, you have to eat something right now." To Matthew she asked, "Do you have any kind of juice?"

"We have some orange juice in the back."

He climbed between the two bucket seats where the girls sat and opened one of the coolers in the rear of the van. "Will this help?" he asked handing her a small bottle.

Elizabeth took the bottle of juice and opened the top. She turned Maria's face towards her and looked at her eyes. They were getting glassy.

"Maria, you need to drink this and eat a sandwich."

"I don't feel hungry, I feel sick," protested Maria weakly.

"Of course you do, the insulin pump is still running and you haven't eaten anything for too many hours. Drink some of this right now," insisted Elizabeth.

Maria took a few swallows of the orange juice.

"Drink some more. You'll feel better in a few minutes," coaxed Elizabeth.

After about fifteen minutes Maria's nausea began to fade and Elizabeth got her to eat half a sandwich. Maria had stopped shaking and her eyes cleared but she was weak and she lay back in her seat to rest.

"What was wrong with her?" asked Matthew concerned.

"She's diabetic. She wears an insulin pump to regulate her blood sugar levels, but she has to eat regularly or she gets sick," explained Elizabeth.

"Does she wear it all the time? How does she go swimming?" he asked confused.

"When she swims she can unplug it for a while," informed Elizabeth.

Maria turned to Elizabeth and said, "Thanks. I should have eaten something earlier but I was too mad at them. It was stupid, I know better than that. I just hurt myself. I'm sorry."

Elizabeth smiled. "That's all right. I'm just glad you're better."

Matthew was mentally digesting all this new knowledge about diabetes.

"Back home they call this having *the sugars*," he told them. "I've never heard of insulin before, seems like it can hurt you as much as it helps."

Elizabeth looked surprised. "Doesn't anyone use insulin back home?"

"No," he said shaking his head.

"What do they do when they get diabetes?" she asked bewildered.

Matthew didn't answer but Mark did.

"After a while they die," informed Mark with a shrug.

"It's against our religion to see doctors or go to hospitals," explained Matthew. "Reverend Forester says they are a blasphemy. Only God is the ultimate healer."

Elizabeth was shocked. "He just lets them die?"

"The men can try to heal them with God's help by laying on hands to heal the sick," said Matthew. "Sometimes that works if God wants them to live."

"Dying isn't so bad. It's just the next phase of existence. If you're a good person you go to heaven," interjected Mark. He looked at Matthew and raised his eyebrows.

Matthew knew Mark was thinking the same thing. What was going to happen to Maria if they took her home with them?

Elizabeth sat there with her mouth open. She had never heard such reasoning in all her life. If her father had believed this, she would be dead. It was a miraculous experimental brain surgery that had saved her from an early death at the age of thirteen. Besides, her father had been a brilliant doctor himself, it was nonsense to believe that all doctors were bad. She looked at Maria.

"How long will your pump keep working?" she asked her quietly.

"It usually only lasts twenty-four hours and I have to refill it. I filled it at school after swimming, so I guess it will last until about lunch time today."

"You don't have any more with you?" whispered Elizabeth.

Maria shook her head. "I keep an emergency vial in my book bag. But we left it in your car. We were just supposed to be going for pizza." She looked scared.

Elizabeth reached out and patted her arm. "It's OK, we'll think of something. They'll have to let us get some more insulin for you somewhere," insisted Elizabeth. "I'll make them get you some more."

Matthew was listening as the girl's talked. If they took Maria to West Virginia, she wouldn't be able to get her medicine. Without it he knew she would die.

He had seen it happen with his father's sister. She had gotten the sugars when she was in her forties and after a few years she had died. He wondered why Maria had it when she was so young. How long could she live without this stuff called insulin?

# Chapter 5

The bride's cottage was clean and ready for the first occupant by the time Michael Andrew arrived with his guest. Cynthia Sweet was the girl he had found in Montana three weeks earlier. It had been easy enough for him to convince her that marrying him and moving to West Virginia was a good idea.

Cynthia's mother had died of cancer when Cynthia was only twelve. With her mother gone she had become the one who received her father's blows when he came home drunk.

Her two older brothers treated her like she was their maid. They made her do all the cooking and housework. She had loved school, but never had time to do her homework because there was so much work around the house for her to do. Consequently her grades were poor, but none of her teachers took enough interest in her to try to find out why she did so poorly. She had no friends among her classmates. The ragged clothes she wore to school put her beneath them in their prejudiced estimate.

Michael was like a knight in shining armor who thought she was pretty and told her so. He had met her at the store one evening when she was shopping for the weekly groceries. He could see past the faded dress and downcast eyes.

When he caught her admiring a lovely blue dress at the Wal-mart Supercenter, he bought it for her. She was so surprised that the handsome man with black hair and blue eyes wanted to talk to her and buy her pretty things that she was immediately enchanted by him.

It surprised her at first that he seemed to turn up each time she left the house to run an errand. After a few encounters she realized that he met up with her on purpose and she allowed him to take her to Wendy's for a hamburger. When they talked, Michael actually listened to what she had to say. No one had done that since her mother died.

She told him about her dreams and confided in him how horrible her life was. He told her that he could take her so far away that her father would never find her to hurt her again, and naturally she agreed to go with him.

Anna Hensley and Rachel Andrew were there to greet her that first night in West Virginia. Cynthia was so overwhelmed by the fact that these women actually cared about her comfort that she started crying.

"I'm sorry," she sniffed, wiping her eyes with a tissue. "It's just that you're so kind. Except for Michael, I can't even remember the last time someone cared how I felt about anything."

Rachel gave her a hug and patted her back.

"We are delighted to have you here. Michael told us how pretty you were and that you were a great housekeeper. I take it that you took care of the house back home? Knowing how to do that is a valuable skill around here."

"I never thought of it as a skill," she whispered, sniffing back tears. "It just seemed like something forced on me back home. And no matter how hard I worked, it was never enough."

"It won't be like that with Michael, I promise," said Rachel.

"You have lovely chestnut colored hair," said Anna. "I can teach you how to pull it back into a style more suited to your heart-shaped face."

"I've never learned how to fix it," admitted Cynthia.

Anna sat Cynthia down in front of a mirror and began brushing her hair. She wove it into several braids and twisted them into a bun.

"That does make me look older and a little pretty," said Cynthia shyly.

"We don't use any make up here, but with your pretty creamy complexion, you don't need any," said Rachel smiling.

"Thank you. Before I met Michael no one ever said I was pretty," she said blushing. "The other kids at school just laughed at my old clothes. I left everything behind and Michael bought me all these pretty dresses and shoes. He has been so nice to me, I wanted to run away and marry him."

"How old are you, dear?" asked Anna.

"I just turned seventeen last month, but sometimes I feel really old. It seems like years and years since my mother died." She sniffed again. "I miss her so much."

"Well, all of us will help you make this your home," said Rachel. "And you can think of me as your substitute mother. I've always wanted a daughter."

Cynthia started crying again. "That is so sweet of you."

Rachel handed her another tissue.

"Now I want you to pick out which one of these beds will be yours until the wedding. You'll be staying here until then," informed Anna.

"Soon there will be several other girls staying here with you until they get married, too. We believe that young people should be chaperoned on their dates, and there's no hand-holding or kissing until you're married," Rachel warned teasingly.

Cynthia giggled. "So that's why Michael wouldn't even hold my hand. I thought he was just really shy."

Rachel smiled. "I'm glad to hear that my son listened to the things we taught him even when he was so far away from home."

Anna helped Cynthia unpack her things and put them in the dresser by the bed she had chosen near the front window.

The room had seven twin beds lined up along the walls and there was a small dresser beside each one. The beds looked lovely with the homemade quilts for coverlets. The walls had been painted a soothing shade of apricot. Fluffy white curtains hung in the two tiny windows. There was also a small bathroom with new towels and supplies of shampoo and toothpaste stocked and waiting for the young brides.

"It won't seem so lonely and quiet here once the other girls start arriving. I'm afraid you'll probably find that a few of them won't be as happy as you are to be here," warned Rachel. "But if you keep telling them how nice it is here, maybe that will help them settle in and learn to be happy, too."

Cynthia nodded, eager to help these nice women in any way that she could. "I promise to do everything I can to help them. I know I'm going to be happier here than anywhere else I've ever been," she insisted. "Thank you both for being so nice to me."

"How about you rest for a little while and I'll come get you when it's time for dinner? You'll be eating with my family until you and Michael have a place of your own," Rachel informed her.

"I'd like that very much. And I do feel tired. It was a long trip."

"All the men are building a house for you and Michael and it should be ready in less than a week, according to my husband," Rachel said smiling. "So you won't have to be here very long before you'll have a home of your own."

Cynthia smiled at her soon to be mother-in-law. "Will we really have our very own house? How wonderful."

"It's being built next door to my house so I hope you won't mind that we will be neighbors," said Rachel.

Cynthia nodded shyly. "I think I'll like that a lot." She yawned. "I guess I'll take that nap now. Thank you for being so kind and welcoming to me."

As the two women left the cottage, Anna was grateful that this girl seemed pleased to be here. But she was worried about what would happen when all the other girls arrived.

***

When Jacob Brown left West Virginia he decided that Idaho would be a good place to look for a wife. He knew there were lots of Mormons there, but it didn't have so many that he felt completely out-numbered as he would have if he went to Utah.

He'd heard stories about how Mormon's believed that women were second-class citizens. He figured he could talk a girl into leaving that way of life and accepting his because he would promise that he would always cherish her.

His father had told him he might have to find a way to make a little money on his own while he was away. He only had one hundred dollars in cash to give Jacob for his hunt. Jacob was barely able to make it to Soda Springs, Idaho, before his car was only running on gas fumes.

His sister had packed tons of food for him. Lots of sandwiches and her home canned peaches and pears so he'd had food for the trip. But if he didn't find a way to make money somewhere soon he wouldn't have the gas to get back home.

As he pulled into the parking lot in front of Broulim's Grocery Store he spotted a sign in the window that said "Help Wanted". He went in to inquire about the job and a cashier at the front of the store showed him where to find the manager's office.

The manager, Mr. Bill Robinson, an older man with graying hair, had him fill out some paperwork and everything was going fine until he asked for a social security card. Jacob didn't have one. The Reverend Forester taught that all governments were the evil products of the devil and no one in their church paid taxes or was registered with Social Security. Besides Jacob had written on the forms that his last name was Smith.

"I don't have my card with me right now," lied Jacob.

"Well, just put down your number and you can bring it in later for me to copy. I have to keep everything legal, you know," laughed Bill. "How about if you start working, then we'll worry about the card later? I'm in desperate need of someone to help unload the delivery trucks when they arrive and I'm short handed at the moment."

Jacob had no idea how a social security number was written.

"I don't remember the number off hand," he admitted sheepishly. "Guess that let's me out." He started to hand back the forms, but the manager just smiled.

"That's OK. I can never remember mine either. My wife remembers both of ours, but I never can. Come with me to the back. I've got two trucks waiting to be unloaded and only one other worker right now. I've been helping back there myself and I'm getting too old for this kind of thing. I need your muscles today," he said with a smile.

Mr. Robinson led Jacob through the produce department and out through the back where a tall man was putting boxes of produce vegetables onto a dolly.

"Mitch, I've got you some help," called the manager.

"About time, boss. I'm afraid you're not much help back here," kidded Mitch. He held out his hand to Jacob. "My name's Mitch. I'm happy to have the help."

"I'm Jacob. Nice to meet you."

"OK, guys. I'll even give you each a bonus if you can get both these trucks unloaded by tonight at five o'clock."

Mitch smiled. "Yes, sir." He showed Jacob where another dolly was located and they began unloading dozens of boxes.

Jacob was used to chopping wood and doing heavy farm work so moving boxes was a breeze. He piled the boxes high and moved them quickly.

"You must work out to have gotten all those muscles," joked Mitch when they stopped for a quick break.

"No, I'm just used to working on a farm," admitted Jacob wiping the sweat from his brow.

Mitch handed him a bottle of cold water and showed him where they were kept in the cooler. The water tasted strange and was bubbly. When Jacob made a funny face, Mitch laughed.

"I guess it's an acquired taste. This town is called Soda Springs because we have springs that produce this strange carbonated water. It's supposed to be good for you. It's sold all over the state," informed Mitch.

Jacob frowned. "It sure tastes funny."

"Yeah, kind of like alka seltzer water."

Jacob looked blank. He'd didn't know what alka seltzer was. "Ah, yeah."

"Besides all the springs, we have a geyser that makes this carbon dioxide water. Crystal Geyser is out on the Green River. It's really something. You'll have to go see it." Mitch finished his water. "Well, back to work, I need the bonus."

By that evening the men had unloaded both trucks and were tired to the bone. The manager handed them each a hundred dollars as a bonus.

"This will all be spent right here," joked Mitch. "I've got four kids to feed."

"I guess I'll see you tomorrow," said Jacob as he left.

Jacob used the cash to fill his car with gas, then went to get some dinner. There was a little cafe across the street that looked inviting. His sister's sandwiches were almost gone and he wanted something hot and filling for a change.

In the café he went into the bathroom, washed his face and hands and combed his hair. Unloading the truck had been sweaty work.

He was seated at a small table in the corner. His waitress was a cute blond. She smiled at him and said her name was Susan. He ordered the roast turkey dinner. It came with mashed potatoes, stuffing, green beans and three big slices of turkey breast with gravy. He ate it all.

"Wow," said Susan when she brought his bill. "Most people can't eat all of that. They usually ask for a doggie bag."

"They feed this delicious food to their dog?" asked Jacob incredulously.

Susan laughed. "No silly, that's just what they call the container to take home the extra food they don't eat. Haven't you ever heard of it before?"

Jacob blushed. "I guess I always eat all my food and don't need one."

"From what I just saw you eat, that's probably true." She picked up his empty plate and headed towards the kitchen. "Bye, now," she waved as he left. "Come back soon."

Jacob found a quiet side street behind the town square and settled into the back seat of his car to sleep, but he couldn't stop thinking about the cute waitress. He decided he'd go back there for breakfast.

\*\*\*

Sunday morning Brandon and Belle were canvassing the neighborhood around the high school with a drawing that somewhat resembled Mark Hensley. Angelina had worked for several hours with the police artist, but her memory was sketchy as she had only seen the van's driver for a few seconds as he drove off. She knew his hair was blond, but not the color of his eyes.

No one the detectives talked to remembered seeing him or a white van. They were about to give up when they decided instead to try an apartment building several streets over. There was a handyman out mowing the grass when they approached the complex. Brandon parked the car in the lot. Belle waved at the man and held up her badge. He drove the riding mower to the edge of the lawn and turned off the motor.

Wiping the sweat from his forehead with on old rag he asked, "What can I do for you folks this morning?"

"We're checking the area to see if anyone remembers seeing this man or a white van around here in the last few days," said Belle showing him the sketch.

"Don't recognize him, but there was a white van that parked in our lot three nights ago," he said, studying the drawing.

"A mini van?" asked Brandon.

"Yeah. There were two guys in it but I didn't get a look at their faces. It was here on Thursday night and again on Friday. I was about to check with the renters to see if these guys were visiting anyone in the complex, because they weren't parking on the street but in the lot. Only renters are supposed to park in the lot. But they left Saturday morning and didn't come back," he said with a shrug.

"You didn't notice a license plate number by any chance?" asked Belle.

He shook his head. "No, sorry," he said. "I did notice that they had a lot of stuff piled in the back of the van. You know suitcases and some boxes. That's why I figured they were from out of town visiting someone here."

"Well thanks for your help," said Belle handing him her card. "If you think of anything else, can you give me a call?"

"Say, why are you looking for them anyway?" he asked curiously.

"Two girls from the high school have gone missing. These men might be involved. If you remember anything else, call the number on that card," answered Brandon.

"You know, I did notice something about the license plate," reflected the man. "I don't remember a number, but it had a smiley face sun on it. I don't think I've ever seen a plate like that before."

"Thanks," said Belle as the man left to return to his mowing.

"That's the second person who remembered that sun," reminded Belle. "Let's go back to the station and see if we can figure out what state has a license plate with some kind of sun on it."

Back at the police station it took an hour of searching state license plate sites on the internet to come up with any that had a sun on them.

They were concentrating on southern states because the men had southern accents but they checked some others just in case.

An Oklahoma plate had had a sun belt graphic on it for a few years and Tennessee had a sun rising over the shape of the state. Florida had an orange and it's slogan was *the sunshine state*. Georgia had an orange-colored peach on some of its plates that might be mistaken for a sun. Belle printed them off on the color printer.

Brandon brought up the state site for Kentucky and scrolled through the plates shown there. Suddenly he called out, "Bingo! In 2004 they actually had a license plate with a smiley-faced sun. They only kept it for a few years because it was not very popular," he told Belle as he printed off the picture.

She walked over to look at his computer screen. It was indeed a smiley-faced sun with sunshine rays poking out from its surface. It appeared to be rising over a green landscape.

"OK. Let's take these pictures to show Angelina," she said.

Angelina confirmed that the picture on the plate from Kentucky was the one she had seen on the white van. "That's definitely it," she said. "It's kind of weird looking, don't you think?"

***

It was early afternoon when they reached the Tennessee border. While Mark filled the tank with gas, Matthew took the girls to the bathroom. Each time they stopped for a bathroom break, the men made sure the station they picked only had bathrooms on the outside of the building. They didn't want the girls to have a chance to signal anyone inside who might try to help them. The first time Mark had shown them the small pistol he carried, he warned them about trying to escape.

"A bullet travels faster than you can run," he said solemnly.

Maria nodded, wide-eyed, as he tucked the gun in the back of his jeans.

Now Matthew waited outside the door with the bathroom key in his hand while the girls went inside.

"What are we going to do?" asked Maria as she washed her hands.

"I don't know yet," admitted Elizabeth. "My cell phone is in my book bag and it's back in the Mustang. I'm mostly worried about you now that your pump should be running out of insulin."

Maria shrugged. "If I'm really careful about what I eat, I should be all right for a while." She looked over at Elizabeth with fear in her eyes. "But if they don't believe in doctors or hospitals or medicine, what will happen to me in West Virginia?"

Elizabeth hugged her. "We'll just have to figure out a way to escape before then."

Maria shook her head. "I tried opening the van door but they've fixed the lock so it only opens from the outside. Probably some child protection thing. We'll have to figure out a way to talk them into letting us go."

Matthew knocked on the door. When Elizabeth opened it, he checked to make sure they had not written a message on the mirror or left anything identifiable behind. He walked them to the van then left them with Mark while he went inside to turn in the key and get drinks and sandwiches. Their supply from home had run out now that there were four of them eating. He paid for the tuna salad sandwiches and bottles of water and returned to the van.

As they drove away, Elizabeth found herself getting more determined than ever to do something to help Maria. She wondered if Maria got really sick before they reached their destination, if she might be able to talk them in to at least leaving her at a hospital. She would have to figure out something soon because the way the men where talking last night it sounded like they might be back home by late tomorrow.

Matthew opened two bottles of water and poured a small amount of the liquid the reverend had given them into the water. He handed the girls two sandwiches and the water. "Here. You both need to eat something. I don't want you getting sick."

Elizabeth accepted the food. "Food isn't all she needs. We have to get her some of her medicine," she said. "Her body doesn't process food the way it should."

"We'll think about getting some," said Mark offhandedly.

He wasn't too worried. He thought a lot of Maria's symptoms were an act. She was too young to really have *the sugars*.

The girls ate the sandwiches and drank the water and within thirty minutes they were both asleep. Matthew figured they would sleep for a few hours. During that time he hoped he could figure out what they should do about Maria. He didn't want to take her back to West Virginia only to watch her die. It wasn't right and he felt responsible for her since it was his idea to kidnap her in the first place. Maybe God would give him a sign to show him what he should do about her. He'd never received a direct sign before, but he knew other people had, maybe it was his turn.

# Chapter 6

When Jacob went to breakfast at the cafe on that first Wednesday morning, Susan wasn't there. But he spotted her at one of the back tables when he entered the cafe at lunchtime. When another waitress asked where he would like to sit he said, "At one of Susan's tables."

"Sure, come this way," she said leading the way to the back of the room.

He sat down and she handed him a menu. "She'll be with you in a minute."

He was scanning the menu when a few minutes later Susan approached.

"Hi, you're back." she said, smiling.

He looked up and grinned. "Hi."

"You must like our food a lot. My sister said you were here for breakfast."

He blushed. "Yeah. It's great. So your sister works here, too?"

"She's the redhead behind the counter over there. She handles the customers at the bar for breakfast and lunch while Brenda and I work the tables for lunch and dinner," she smiled. "There are three other waitresses, but basically my sister and I are here a lot. My dad and mom started this place years ago. When we kids starting coming along, mom stayed home and dad hired more waitresses. Now my sister, Beth, and I work here most days."

"It's a nice place and the food is great," said Jacob admiringly.

"Glad you like it. What can I get you for lunch?"

He glanced at the menu. "I'll take the burger basket and a glass of milk."

"OK. I'll put in your order," she said smiling.

After he finished his lunch and Susan brought over his bill, he stammered, "The burger was great. Uh, do you ever get a day off?" That was a dumb thing to say, he thought embarrassed.

"Sure, I don't work on Sunday or Monday. We're actually closed on Sunday."

"Oh, what about evenings? When do you get off in the evening?" he asked looking up at her shyly. She looked at him with what he thought were the most beautiful pale blue eyes he had ever seen. They almost sparkled. He waited for her to say she wasn't interested.

"Are you trying to ask me out on a date?" she asked.

He blushed and felt stupid. "Yeah, I guess so."

"In that case, I'm off at seven o'clock tonight," she said matter of factually.

"I'm finished working at the store across the street by six. I'll be coming back for dinner, so maybe we could do something afterwards?" he said awkwardly. He held his breath waiting for her answer.

"I'll be here. We can decide what we want to do after you're finished eating, OK?"

"That would be great," he said relieved. He stood up and walked out quietly, but he wanted to shout for joy.

Susan shook her head and smiled then walked over to take another customer's order. Jacob was by far the shyest man she had ever met.

Jacob couldn't believe his luck as he walked across the street to the store. She was the prettiest girl he had ever seen and she said she would go out with him. Now he just had to figure out what they could do on their date.

Everything was so different here, not at all like back home. When his mother was alive she had told him a little about her life before she had married his father, but not too much. His father frowned on learning about what he called the "sinful outside" world.

All of a sudden, Jacob missed his mother so much it physically hurt to think about her. She had died ten years ago giving birth to his youngest brother. Jacob had only been twelve years old at the time and they had been very close. Losing his mother had been a horrible blow to him.

He had an older sister and two younger brothers. His sister had been thirteen and she pretty much had to take over the raising of the boys while their father ran the farm. Jacob helped his father with the outside chores, but Esther did all the housework and cared for the new baby, too. Of course some of the women in the congregation had often helped her. Especially that nice Mrs. Hensley. Matthew and Mark were lucky to have such a sweet mother. He wished his mother were still alive now so he could get her advice on courting Susan.

The afternoon dragged by as Jacob helped Mitch unload the delivery trucks. He must have moved a hundred boxes by six o'clock that evening. He was tired but grateful he had a job.

He ordered the turkey dinner again and devoured it all. At seven o'clock, Susan came and sat down across from him at his booth.

"Have you decided what we should do?" she asked. "There's a movie theater just down the street, but I don't know what's playing tonight."

"I'm not much for movies," he admitted.

"Well, we could go bowling."

"I've never bowled. Is it fun?" he asked.

She shrugged. "Yeah. But the alley is usually noisy. I'd really rather go someplace quiet where we could talk."

"Where would that be?" he asked.

"We could just go to the park to walk around. It's across the square and really pretty this time of year."

So that's what they did. They walked around the park and then along the streets. Susan told him about her family. She had an older brother named James, who was on a mission for their Church in Chile. Her sister, Beth, the redheaded waitress he saw at the cafe, was three years older than Susan and she had two younger brothers named William and Ronnie.

"I really miss Jim," she confessed. "He's only a year older than me and we're very close. I could tell him anything and he didn't make fun of me."

"I have an older sister like that," said Jacob. "We got really close when my mother died. It was a hard time for the whole family."

"Oh, I'm so sorry. How old were you when she died?" she asked concerned.

"Just twelve and Esther was thirteen. It was a big responsibility for her to take care of all of us. Especially baby Isaac. My mom died when he was born."

"That was a huge responsibility. Didn't your father get someone to come in and help so she could go to school?" she asked.

"We were mostly home schooled. Our pastor's wife prepares lessons and all the children in our congregation do their work at home. That gives them more time to help their parents with chores and stuff," he shrugged. "Some of the other women in my church helped out when they could. Mostly, Esther did all the household chores and cared for the baby on her own."

"Sounds like a hard life," she said sympathetically. "Don't you get to do anything fun with your friends?"

"Sure," he said smiling. "My two best friends are brothers, Mark and Matthew. We go fishing and hunting and sometimes when it's not time to plant or harvest crops we go camping. There's a great swimming hole we go to in the summer. I live in a pretty small community up in the mountains, but I do have friends," he explained.

"That sounds like fun. My family has gone camping a few times," she said looking at her watch. "It's getting late, I should probably head home. What hotel are you staying in?" she asked.

He blushed and stammered, "I'm not at a hotel."

"Oh, I thought you might be at the Caribou Lodge since it's so close by. I didn't know you were staying with someone around here," she said.

"I'm not. I've been sleeping in my car," he admitted sheepishly.

Her mouth dropped open. "Oh my gosh, you can't do that."

She grabbed his hand and pulled him along the sidewalk back to the cafe. When she told her father about his situation, he insisted Jacob stay with them.

"We have an empty bedroom that is just going to waste. James is gone on his mission and I know he wouldn't mind letting you use it," he assured him.

"Oh, I couldn't do that!" protested Jacob.

"Of course you can," insisted Susan.

Then Beth chimed in, "We can't have you sleeping in your car, our mother would have a fit if she found out we knew about it and didn't intervene."

"I don't know ... " he said. Staying with a bunch of Mormons had not been part of his plans.

"Don't be silly," said Susan. "It's settled then, you're coming home with us."

Jacob finally agreed but felt uneasy. He should have never gotten so involved with this family. How was he going to steal their daughter away when they were all so nice to him?

\*\*\*

The Monday morning after Elizabeth's disappearance, Brandon was checking all the last month's police reports from Kentucky to see if anyone had filed a report on a stolen white mini van. But no one seemed to have had one stolen, or at least they had not reported it. He slammed his fist onto the desk.

"This is a wild goose chase! I need to do something now. There has to be some way to find out where they're being taken," he said in frustration as he began pacing around the room.

"I know you're frustrated, but we've already sent out a bulletin on the van and we really have no idea which direction they're heading," sympathized Belle.

"This is my stepdaughter we're talking about. I need to do more."

"Check for a stolen license plate," she suggested. "Maybe they didn't steal the vehicle, just the plate."

When he ran the check, there had been two smiley-faced sun plates reported stolen last month in Kentucky, one from Lexington and one from Pikeville. He called the Lexington police headquarters and it took the sergeant in charge ten minutes to find the report.

"We don't do much about these things. You know how it is. We just suggest that the owner get a new plate, then we kind of watch to see if the plate gets used during another bigger crime," he said off handily.

"Yeah, I know. Can I get the number? We're following a lead on a kidnapping out here in California," explained Brandon. "What's with the smiley-face sun anyway, isn't that kind of unusual?"

"It was a special license plate issued to help raise funds for *Trooper Island*, a free summer camp for disadvantaged boys and girls operated by the Kentucky State Police on Dale Hollow Lake in Clinton County," explained the officer. "The plate wasn't very popular. Looked too childish, I guess." He paused as he scanned the report. "Ok, the stolen license number was AAA 003. Probably one of the first ones we sold. Belonged to one of the father's of a disabled kid who went to camp."

"Thanks," said Brandon.

"Good luck with your kidnapping, hope this information helps."

When Brandon called the Pikeville police station he was told the stolen plate was numbered AAA 015.

"Wow," said Belle. "I guess they didn't sell very many. At least we can now add those plate numbers to the bulletin. Maybe it will help."

"So now the question is whether the men are from Kentucky, or did they come from another state and just grab a plate there. The closest states to Lexington are Ohio and West Virginia. The closest to Pikeville are Virginia and West Virginia."

"If they came from that far away, we have to face the fact that this isn't a kidnapping for ransom," said Belle quietly. "Elaine hasn't heard a word from them."

Brandon rubbed his eyes. "I know. I haven't said anything to Elaine yet, but I kind of figured that." He looked worried as he entered the plate numbers into his computer.

Belle had never seen Brandon like this in all the years they had been partners. She knew he would be devastated if anything happened to Elizabeth. "Well, if they do call, Detective Wright is at your house and he's the best we have for tracing calls," she reminded him hopefully.

"I know. But it's been over thirty-six hours ... I don't think they're going to call." He looked over at Belle, his face stricken with fear. "You know the first twenty-four hours are the most important in a case like this. What if the girls are already dead?"

"Brandon, I don't think two guys would drive all the way from the east coast just to kill the girls. I know it's scary to think about, but they probably have other plans for them."

"Oh God, I've thought of that too and it terrifies me," said Brandon. "We have to find them soon or it could be too late."

***

To stay clear of cities and the police, Mark had started taking smaller highways as they traveled. He knew that bigger cities would have gotten reports about the kidnapping and would be more likely to notice the van. He felt pretty safe being this far from California, but wasn't going to take any chances. However, staying off Hwy. 40 meant it was taking longer to get home and he was anxious to get back. They had to get gas again soon and he was planning to stop in Lynchburg. Driving across Tennessee seemed to be taking forever.

While Mark was out pumping gas and Matthew was buying food at the gas station, the girls were locked in the van. Elizabeth continued trying to convince Maria that she needed to do whatever necessary escape.

"I don't want to leave you," protested Maria.

"I'll be fine. Brandon will find me eventually. It's you I'm worried about. You're already starting to have symptoms. You're thirsty all the time now, that means your blood sugar levels are way too high," said Elizabeth. "You'll be no help to me at all if you get sicker."

Maria looked up at her with frightened eyes. "I know. I'm not feeling very good right now. My stomach is queasy and my vision keeps getting blurry."

"The last time this happened when the pump didn't work right, you ended up in a diabetic coma," warned Elizabeth. "I'm not going to let that happen again. If you'll pretend to faint, I think I can talk Matthew into leaving you at a hospital somewhere. He seems more sympathetic than Mark. Will you do it for me, please?" she begged.

"I don't want to, but I guess I really don't have much choice," agreed Maria. "It's either fake it now or have it happen for real."

"If we wait until you're really sick, you won't be able to tell anyone what's happening. This way you can tell them to call the police," encouraged Elizabeth. "We don't know where they're taking us, but at least we know it's somewhere in the West Virginia mountains. That has to help a little." Elizabeth leaned over and hugged Maria. "Please do this." Elizabeth could feel the sweat forming on Maria's arms, and she was shaking a little all ready. If they didn't get help for her soon, it might be too late and Elizabeth refused to let that happen to her best friend. "Ok, Matthew is coming. Hurry and lie back in your seat and look sick."

"That won't be hard," whispered Maria. "I really do feel sick."

Matthew opened the back of the van and put several packages of sandwiches and drinks in the cooler, then added another bag of ice. Mark had gone to pay for the gas and Elizabeth knew she only had a few minutes to try and talk to Matthew alone.

When he opened the front door, Elizabeth leaned forward in her seat.

"Matthew, Maria's getting really sick. The last time this happened she was in a coma for two days in the hospital and she almost died," she pleaded. "Please help us. We have to do something to help her soon."

Matthew looked at Maria. She was lying with her eyes closed and her face was pale. He could see sweat beads on her forehead. "She doesn't look very good," he admitted.

"We need to get her to a hospital," begged Elizabeth. "She could die."

Matthew went around the front of the van and climbed into the driver's seat just as Mark returned.

"I'll drive for a while," he said putting the key in the ignition. As he drove away from the station he looked over at his brother. "Mark, Maria's getting pretty sick."

Mark looked at Maria. Even he could tell she didn't look right.

"Yeah, I guess you're right. What should we do?" he asked getting worried for the first time. "I'm not too good at coming up with spur of the moment ideas."

"We probably need to get her to a hospital."

Mark's face clouded. "But she'll tell someone about us."

"She probably will. But she doesn't know exactly where we're going and we'll have a big head start. And you know how hard it is for strangers to find us up in the mountains," he persuaded. "She doesn't even know our last name."

Mark turned around and looked hard at Elizabeth. "I'll make a deal with you," he said as he took her by the arm. "We'll take her to a hospital and you'll promise not give us any more trouble, understood?" He looked her straight in the eyes. "Is it a deal?"

Elizabeth nodded. "I promise, I won't cause trouble and I won't try to run away. She's my best friend. I'd do anything to help her."

Maria started to protest, but she was actually starting to feel faint. She knew she was in trouble and had to get to a hospital soon.

Elizabeth looked over at her. "Maria, you know this is for the best."

Mark let go of Elizabeth's arm. "All right, then. We'll find a hospital."

\*\*\*

Able Hamilton and his brother, Joshua, were the youngest men allowed by Reverend Forester to go on the hunt. Able was nineteen and Joshua had just turned eighteen. Although they were strong hard workers, they were not the brightest men in the group either. With red hair and slender bodies they looked just like their father.

Their parents had moved to West Virginia sixteen years ago when the boys were still toddlers. They had been swayed by Reverend Forester into believing his church was the only true church in the world today. They wholeheartedly supported his views and if he said the boys needed to go elsewhere to find wives, then that was what their boys would do.

The boys had decided to go hunt for wives in Georgia. Their mother was from Georgia and their father, Elijah, said that southern women were easier to manage, whatever that meant. Joshua thought his mother, Rebecca, was pretty outspoken for a woman who was easy to manage. But he loved his mother and if he could find a wife down in Georgia as wonderful as she was, than he was all for it. They'd left home a week ago with high hopes and four hundred dollars in their pockets.

Rebecca had saved for six months to be able to give them money for the trip. They figured that Georgia was close and that they would quickly find what they were seeking and wouldn't need a lot of money. That had proved to be false and they were getting low on cash and food. They needed to find some women quick or go back as failures.

"Look," said Able to his brother. "We didn't have any luck in Atlanta. So let's try a small town. Those city girls were too worldly and ungodly, anyway."

"Well, how was I supposed to know that they were hookers?" complained Joshua. "They seemed nice enough."

Able scoffed. "Of course they seemed nice. They wanted you to give them money for sex. You should have been able to figure that out by the way they were dressed." He shook his head at his brother's simple mindedness.

Joshua blushed. "Yeah, I suppose. They were showing a lot of skin."

Joshua, being younger than Able, knew his brother was smarter than he was. But all the same, he wished Able wouldn't treat him like a dummy. Sometimes their mother would scold Able for doing that.

"Look on the map and see what small town is close by," said Able.

"There are lots of them. You look at the map." Joshua handed him the atlas.

"We'll head north towards home and see what we find heading that way."

Able started the car and pulled out of the gas station. They only had eighty dollars left and it was a long drive back home. Luckily their Volkswagen got good gas mileage.

At lunchtime they stopped in Maysville. It was Sunday and the local Baptist Church was just letting out after morning services. The boys were parked across the street and noticed a family with five daughters walking to the parking lot.

"Look at all those pretty girls," said Joshua between bites of his chili hot dog.

Able was impressed too. The girls all had long wavy hair and they were dressed modestly with hems down past their knees. They looked to range in age from about thirteen to early twenties.

"Come on," he said as he tossed his trash into a nearby can. "Let's follow them and see where they live."

Joshua rushed with him to the car and they followed the green station wagon as it pulled out of the church parking lot. The family lived nearby and it didn't take long for them to get home.

The boys parked their car several streets over and passed the time walking around the nearby Hurricane Shoals Park for the afternoon. They discussed ideas on the best way to kidnap the girls. They felt sure it would be easy as no one in this small of a town probably even locked their doors.

They did decide not to take the oldest daughter because she would probably be the most self reliant and troublesome. The two girls in the middle would most likely be the best to grab.

After a dinner of hot dogs again, because they were cheap, the boys parked in a secluded area of the park and slept in the car for several hours.

It was after midnight when Able woke Joshua. "OK, let's see if we can find a way to sneak in their house and take two of the sisters."

They drove along the street then parked their car under the overhang of a big moss-covered tree. The moss hung down to the top of the car and it was dark under the tree making the car less noticeable. They didn't want to take a chance that someone might spot a strange car in the neighborhood. There was a full moon that illuminated more than they wanted to be seen.

At least the house lots were big and the houses not too close together. The one they walked towards had big azalea bushes around it that almost touched the edge of the roof.

They sprinted to the side of the garage and went around back peeking in all the windows as they went. They could tell by its larger size that one was the master bedroom. The next two windows showed a smaller bedroom with bunk beds and a princess nightlight that led them to believe that the two youngest sisters slept there.

They passed the back door. Around the corner of the house was another window. It was much smaller and turned out to be a bathroom window. Farther along the wall were two windows close together. They saw two twin beds when they peeked in the first window. The last window on that side of the house showed a smaller bedroom with one twin bed, probably the oldest daughter's, they assumed. They had somewhat of an idea of the house layout now and they turned around to go to the back door. As Able predicted the door was unlocked.

Joshua eased the door open and crept into the kitchen. The light from the microwave clock and the moonlight shining in the window kept them from bumping into the kitchen table as they crossed the room. The hallway off to the left was the one that led to the bedroom they were seeking and they crept quietly down the hall.

"Have you got the chloroform?" whispered Joshua.

Able snorted. "Of course."

They poured some of the liquid onto two washcloths.

"Don't get it too close to your own face," warned Able.

"I'm not that stupid," insisted Joshua as he eased open the bedroom door.

Two girls were asleep in the beds, oblivious to the intruders. The men silently walked towards the beds and gently pressed the cloths to the girls' faces. Both girls woke, but their struggles were short lived and silent before they succumbed to the chloroform's fumes.

Able picked up the first girl. "Grab some clothes from the dresser," he instructed. "They'll want something to wear besides pajamas when they wake up."

Joshua grabbed two pairs of pants and a couple of blouses. "What if they wear different sizes, will that matter?"

"They looked close to the same size this afternoon. Just grab something, it will be OK." Able shifted the slight form to his left shoulder and pulled the pillowcase off her pillow. "Here, put the clothes in this."

Joshua shoved the clothes in the pillowcase, and grabbed two pairs of socks and panties out of another drawer. He felt himself blushing as he touched the silky underwear. He got two pairs of tennis shoes out of the closet then handed Able the bag of clothes. Slipping his arms under the second sleeping girl he lifted her out of bed.

"Gosh, she's as light as a feather," he whispered. "Doesn't weigh hardly anything." He grabbed a blanket off the bed and wrapped her in it.

They left the house as silently as they had entered. After putting the girls in the back seat, Able started the car but left the headlights off as they eased away from the curb. They moved into the street and drove quickly away. On the next block they turned on their lights and headed out of town. Joshua looked back at the sleeping girls.

"Both of them are sure pretty," he said. "Which one do you like?"

"I have no idea. Let's just hope they're not too troublesome on the way home. I don't want to get caught before we get them back to our house," said Able. "I'm going to get gas at the next open station and that should last until we get through North Carolina. Keep an eye on them. If they start to wake up give them some more of the chloroform."

"It won't hurt them, will it?" asked Joshua concerned.

"Naw, Reverend said it wouldn't hurt them," assured Able.

# Chapter 7

"Can I go play with Maggie and Martin?" Melinda asked her mother.

"I don't know if that's such a good idea," said Janice. "They're all pretty worried about Elizabeth right now. Maybe we should go and get the twins and bring them over here to play."

"Can they spend the night?" asked a delighted Melinda. It wasn't often that she had children to play with staying at her own house.

"That's a good idea," said Janice. She was ashamed that she hadn't thought of it herself. Elaine was probably beside herself with worry and it would help to have someone else take care of the twins for a while. "Let's go right now and see if they want to come over today."

It was a short drive to the Marcus' house and it only took a few minutes.

"Oh, Janice, hi, it's good to see you," said Elaine when she opened the door.

There were two strange men in the living room. Elaine said they were police officers sent over by Brandon to monitor any calls that might come from the men who had taken the girls.

"I'm getting really worried because we haven't heard anything," said Elaine. "Shouldn't they have called with demands for money by now?"

"I don't know," said Janice.

Melinda tugged on Elaine's sleeve. "Can Maggie and Martin come stay with us?"

Elaine looked at Janice, "Are you sure you want them? They can be quite a handful at times, especially now that they're worried about Elizabeth."

"It might do them good to get away from here," encouraged Janice. "A change of scenery and some distractions. You know how they love Melinda. And I'm sure you can use a break."

"I think you're right. I'll pack up some clothes for them," said Elaine. "Melinda, they're in the playroom, why don't you go tell them."

Melinda went into the playroom. There were lots of toys and games that she usually loved to play with there, but today she just wanted to see the other children.

"Hi, Maggie. Hi, Martin," she called across the room.

They both looked up from where they were sitting on the floor by a big bookcase full of children's games. Maggie had been crying and she wiped her face.

Melinda went over and hugged her.

"I wish Lisbeth would come home," sniffed Maggie.

"Your mom said you can come spend the night at my house," said Melinda smiling at Maggie. "Do you want to come?"

"Me, too?" asked Martin hopefully.

"Of course," said Melinda giving him a hug. "You're my favorite boy."

Martin smiled. "My daddy is trying to find Elizabeth," he said seriously.

"I know," said Melinda. "Why don't you each pick out a toy you want to bring to my house to play with while you're visiting?"

The distraction worked and the twins happily sorted through the toys to pick one.

Janice stood in the door and watched the children. Melinda seemed so much more mature than her age. Watching her leading the littler ones around made it even more obvious.

While Elaine was saying goodbye to the twins, Melinda came up to her and said, "I'll take good care of them, I promise."

"I know you will."

Janice looked at Elaine. "It was her idea to come get them. Sometimes she's smarter than I am. I should have thought of this yesterday."

Melinda looked up at both the women. "Elizabeth is not afraid right now. She's just worried about Maria 'cause she's getting sick. Elizabeth is going to make those two men leave her at a hospital."

Elaine's eyes widened. "How do you know this, sweetie?"

Melinda shrugged shoulders. "I don't know, I just do."

Elaine looked over at Janice questioningly

"It's like she sometimes knows what Elizabeth is thinking. I don't understand it either," admitted Janice. "But she's always right."

*\*\*\**

Because Matthew was driving the van, he was the first one to spot the sign that said *Southern Tennessee Medical Center*. They had just gotten to the town limits of Winchester a few minutes earlier. It almost seemed to jump out at him in glowing letters. This might be the sign he was waiting for from God. He looked over at Mark.

"I think we should take her to this hospital," he said. "We don't know how long it will be before we'll come to another one."

Mark looked over his shoulder at Maria. She was pale, sweat glistened on her forehead, her breathing was rapid and shallow. She didn't look good at all. She didn't responded to his inquiry as to how she was feeling. He looked at Matthew and nodded. "Turn here."

Matthew turned down the street indicated by the sign.

Elizabeth reached up and touched Mark's arm. "Thank you, Mark."

He nodded but didn't look at her.

When they pulled up to the emergency room doors, Mark turned around and stared at Elizabeth. "You stay in the car. What should I say to them in there?"

"Just tell them her full name, that she is diabetic and her insulin pump has run out. They'll know what to do," instructed Elizabeth. She wanted so badly to go with Maria that it physically hurt to see her this way.

Mark lifted Maria out of the back seat and walked through the sliding emergency doors. A nurse immediately rushed over.

"What happened to her?" she asked reaching for Maria's arm and taking her pulse.

"We were camping and she lost her medicine vial. Her insulin pump has run out. We're from California and were afraid to try and drive her all the way back home."

"From the looks of your friend, I think that was a good call," said the nurse.

She beckoned for him to follow her and they took Maria back through automatic double doors into the examining area. He placed her on the stretcher in the room indicated. The nurse pricked Maria's finger and put a drop of blood on the glucometer strip. She called for the resident and immediately began grabbing equipment to start an IV. She told the resident what Mark had said.

"Did you get a blood glucose reading yet?" asked the resident.

"It was 603," she said seriously.

"How much do you think she weighs?" he asked Mark.

Mark shrugged. "I don't know."

The nurse said, "She looks about 110 pounds or so."

"Draw a blood sample for the lab," said the resident. "And start that IV."

The resident began drawing up insulin in a syringe. As soon as the IV was started, he inserted the needle in a port and injected the insulin.

"Hang a bag with insulin and piggyback it into her main line," the resident told the nurse. They were busy with Maria when the unit secretary came and beckoned for Mark to come out into the hall where she started asking him questions about Maria.

"Her name is Maria Gonzales," he told her and she began writing the information on a hospital form. "She's from San Diego, California. I don't know her parents' names or phone number but my brother probably knows. I'll go ask him," said Mark.

The secretary nodded and said. "Do you know if she has any insurance?"

"I'll find out." He turned and walked out of the hospital.

"Drive away now," he told Matthew as soon as he got in the van. "They're taking care of her."

Matthew quickly drove off and Elizabeth gave a sigh of relief.

After a few minutes the secretary started looking for Mark. When she checked the parking lot, the van was gone. She told the resident and asked, " What do you want me to do?"

"We found her Medic Alert bracelet. It has the number we can call to get more information on her," he told the secretary. "Call this phone number and see what they can tell you. They'll have a number to reach her family."

***

Rueben Smith was about to give up and go back to West Virginia when he met Melody Baker. She worked at the library in Hackettstown, New Jersey. Originally, he had wanted to go to Georgia with the Hamilton boys but the reverend had said three men traveling together would attract too much attention.

Rueben had been traveling around the northeast for a week when he stopped in Hackettstown. It was against his religion to drink or go to the movies, which meant no bars or theaters and he was feeling pretty lonely after a week alone. When he spotted the library he figured he could at least go there for a while to be with other people and it wouldn't cost anything.

Melody was sitting behind the desk looking at a magazine when he walked in. Rueben was tall and had shiny black hair and brilliant blue eyes. He didn't even realize it, but with his broad shoulders, square jaw and the deep cleft in his chin, he was quite handsome. Melody smiled and walked over to where he was looking at the magazines. Rueben was a mechanic and he enjoyed reading magazines about automobiles and engines.

"Hi," said Melody smiling up at him. "I haven't seen you in here before. Did you just learn how to read?"

Rueben looked down at the little redhead and stammered, "Ah, no Ma'am. I've been reading since I was five years old."

Melody blushed. "I'm sorry, that was a lame joke. I just meant that I hadn't seen you in the library before."

"No, Ma'am. I've been traveling and was just tired of my own company."

"Well, there aren't many other people in here either. Nowadays it seems no one wants to come to the library. They get their books electronically on a Kindle."

He looked at her blankly.

"You know, one of those computer e-book readers," she explained.

"I'm not much into computers myself," he said. "I kind of like to hold a book in my hands. Books have been my friends since I could first read."

"That's exactly how I feel. I like to actually turn the pages and smell the paper," she admitted. "I love libraries."

He smiled a crooked little grin at her. "Me, too, Ma'am."

"It gets pretty lonely sometimes sitting in this little old library for hours by myself. But it does give me lots of time to read," she smiled back at him.

When she smiled she actually looked kind of pretty. She had bouncy red curls that framed her oval face and a sprinkle of freckles across her nose, but her face was over-whelmed by the thick glasses she wore. Melody was severely near sighted and her lenses made her eyes look awkward and watery. She'd never had a lot of friends in high school and she spent most of her time studying and writing poetry. It was only here in the library where she felt truly at home. The years seemed to be passing her by all too swiftly. Now she was twenty-six and she often wondered if she would ever fall in love or get married and have a family.

"What do you like to read?" she asked Rueben.

"Well, it seems I spend most of my reading time studying books on mechanics. I live in a small town and everyone depends on me to fix whatever machine they have that decides not to work. I'm kept pretty busy. If I have any spare time, I like to read poetry."

"Really?" asked Melody in surprise. It seemed to her that someone so big and handsome wouldn't have much spare time because he would be out with a girlfriend.

"Do you read poetry to your girlfriend?" she asked.

Rueben blushed. "Ah, no Ma'am. I don't have a girlfriend."

"Oh," said Melody with interest.

"My mother's been saying I should be thinking of getting married, but where I live there aren't many available women to choose from," he said shyly.

He seemed so sweet and shy that Melody was enchanted.

They talked for an hour until it was time for her to close the library. He stayed while she locked the doors. When he realized she didn't have a car and was going to walk home alone he offered her a ride.

"I don't live far, I usually walk," she said quickly.

"Then I'll walk you home," he insisted.

Her home was a small apartment a few blocks away. He smiled and wished her goodbye when they arrived. She almost asked him in for dinner, but felt silly even thinking about it. She didn't really know him at all.

Rueben returned to the library every day for the next week. He even brought her lunch one day from the little Italian place in town and they sat outside at a picnic table to eat. He found out that she was two years older than him. That her parents were both dead and that she had no brothers or sisters.

"It must get kind of lonely for you with no family," he said one afternoon.

"It does sometimes. But I do have my cat, Frances," she laughed.

During that week she found out that Rueben was twenty-four, that both his parents were living and he had two older sisters, Dinah and Leah. He still hadn't told her exactly where he lived but she knew it was in the mountains because he talked about how beautiful it was there, especially when the dogwoods bloomed and signaled that spring was coming. By the end of the week she even got brave enough to read him some of the poems she had written.

"How long are you going to be in town?" she asked one evening.

"I don't now. To tell you the truth I should be getting back home, but I don't want to go back alone." As he said it he reached over and touched her hand then drew back quickly and seemed embarrassed.

Melody's heart began pounding and she drew in a sharp breath. She didn't want him to go away alone either. She looked at his face and held her breath.

"Melody, would you come back with me?" he stammered. "I mean would you marry me and be willing to move away from your home?"

Melody smiled at this wonderful man she barely knew and surprised herself by saying, "Rueben, I would be honored to marry you."

She started to give him a hug, but he pulled back.

"Sorry," he apologized. "It's just that I'm not used to having a women besides family give me a hug. I was raised in a very strict religion. We aren't even supposed to hold hands until we're married," he admitted.

"Really?" she said. "Wow, that's actually kind of refreshing given today's standards. What church do you attend?"

"It's called the *Pentecostal Holiness Today* church. Reverend Forester is our pastor. We're all a pretty religious bunch of folks," he informed her seriously.

"*Pentecostal Holiness*, isn't that a snake-handling church?" she asked with a shiver. "Doesn't that scare you, to handle snakes, I mean?"

Rueben shrugged. "I've never been bitten. If you're living righteously, the snakes don't hurt you," he explained. "Does that make you want to change your mind about marrying me?"

Melody looked up into his beautiful blue eyes. "No, not at all."

***

It was Monday morning and Brandon was desperate to find out something that would give them any idea of where the girls had been taken. When he had tracked down the first owner of the smiley face license plate that had been stolen he had hit a dead end. But the man who owned the plate number AAA015 said that the person who stole his plate was seen by the early morning paperboy. He had reported that they were driving a white mini van. Now the police could put out a bulletin for a white mini van with a Kentucky plate license number AAA015.

"At least that's something," encouraged Belle. "That distinguishes them from all the hundreds of other white mini vans."

"Sort of," said Brandon. "But where do we start looking for it?"

Their first real break came when Adelita called a few hours later. She was so excited that at first he couldn't understand what she was trying to tell him.

"Detective Marcus, they let Maria go," she stammered. "I'm trying to find someone to watch my other children so I can go be with her."

"They let her go? Where is she?" asked Brandon excitedly.

"In a hospital in Tennessee."

"A hospital? They didn't hurt her, did they?" he asked concerned.

"No, No. When her insulin pump ran out, she got sick. She went into a coma. It's happened to her before. The men dropped her off at a hospital in Winchester, Tennessee," she explained. "She was unconscious when she was dropped off."

"Then she wasn't the one who called you?"

"No. A nurse at the hospital called me. Maria wears a Medic Alert bracelet because of her diabetes and the pump. Because she's a minor, it lists me as her first contact number. Maria is still in intensive care but she's going to be fine, the nurse said. They've got her stabilized and she's awake. She's been asking for me."

"What about Elizabeth? Did they say anything about her?" asked Brandon.

"No. I'm sorry. The nurse said a young man carried her in and then left. They didn't see anyone else," she apologized.

"Mrs. Gonzales, how about letting me and my partner take you to see Maria? By the time we get there, she might be able to tell us where the men are heading."

"I guess that would be all right. I'm pretty sure my niece is coming to stay with the boys. I'm just waiting to hear back from my sister," she said.

"Fine. We'll be at your house in an hour."

Brandon turned to Belle. "Did you catch all that?"

"I sure did. Take me to my house and I'll throw a few things in my overnight bag. How long do you think it will take to drive to Winchester?" she asked.

"We're not driving. I can get a friend of mine who's a pilot to fly us there. I don't know where the nearest airport is to Winchester, but he'll know. Come on."

Brandon grabbed his cell phone and started dialing.

\*\*\*

The Hamilton boys had made it to Greensboro, North Carolina before the Wilson sisters began to wake up. Abby, the younger sister, was the first to open her eyes. She felt groggy and had a horrible headache. Nothing made sense to her. She was lying on the floor of a strange car wrapped in the comforter from her bed.

Her sister, Bambi, was on the back seat asleep. Abby sat up and tried to see who was driving the car but she wasn't tall enough so see into the front seat. She shifted herself up onto the edge of the back seat next to Bambi. There were two strange men up front and she got scared.

"Who are you?" she said with a quavering voice. "Where are you taking us?"

Joshua turned around and looked into her frightened eyes. Her brown hair was tangled and she looked ready to cry.

"It's OK," he said. "We aren't going to hurt you."

Big tears started sliding down her cheeks and her bottom lip trembled. "Take us home right now. Who are you and what do you want from us?"

"My name's Joshua and this is my brother, Able. Do you want something to drink? Are you hungry? You've been asleep a long time, it's almost noon."

She shook her head. "I feel sick. I don't want anything from you. I just want to go home." She started crying in earnest now.

Bambi woke to the sounds of her sister's hysterical crying. She sat up quickly and felt a wave of nausea wash over her. "What's going on?' she demanded of the two strange men. "Did you hurt my sister?"

"We didn't touch her. She's just scared. I told her we wouldn't hurt either of you."

"Who the hell are you? And how did we get here?" demanded Bambi louder. As sweet and soft as her name sounded, it did not reflect Bambi's personality. She was a fighter and now she was mad. Her brown eyes flashed. "Stop this car immediately!" she yelled punching Joshua in the arm.

"Ow!" said Joshua pulling away from her fists.

"Hey, stop that!" yelled Able. He slowed the car and pulled over on the side of the road. He turned around and faced the girls.

"Now get this straight. You are coming with us and we are not taking you home!"

"But why?" whispered Abby. "What do you want with us?"

"We need wives and we've picked you two. You might as well get used to the idea. And you," he said sternly, staring at Bambi. "You settle down or I'll chloroform you again."

Bambi's eyes widened. "That's how you got us out of the house? You drugged us! That's a hell of a way to get a wife! What's wrong with the old fashioned way of courting a girl?" she asked in disgust.

Joshua looked at Able and shrugged. "That one's yours," he said solemnly.

Bambi tried to open the car door but it was locked and the unlock button had been removed. "Let us out right now!" she demanded shrilly.

Able pulled the car back onto the road and sped up.

"Get out the chloroform!" he told Joshua. "Shut her up!"

Joshua turned around and looked at the girls. Abby was still crying and her face was getting red and her eyes puffy. He felt sorry for her, but Bambi was just plain mad. Her eyes blazed at him, daring him to try and drug her again.

"Look," he said. "I don't want to use that stuff. I know it makes you get a headache and feel sick. If you'll sit back and be quiet, I won't use it. Do you want me to drug Abby again?" he asked Bambi threateningly.

Bambi looked at her sister and some of her anger dissipated. She shook her head. "No, I don't want you to use that stuff again." She sighed and leaned back in the seat. She pulled Abby up on the seat next to her and patted her back. "Stop crying. We'll figure this out when we can all think straight."

Abby wiped her eyes on a corner of her blanket.

Bambi looked at Joshua. "Do you have anything to drink? It might help settle our stomachs. I know mine feels awful."

Joshua handed them each a bottle of water. "Here, it's nice and cold," he said sympathetically. "I'm sorry we scared you. I wish we could have courted you and let you get to know us. We're really pretty nice guys."

Bambi stared at him in disbelief. "Yeah, right."

Joshua shrugged and turned around. "I've got some food up here for you when you're feeling better."

The girls sipped on the water and huddled together in the back seat.

\*\*\*

Jacob had been staying with Susan Smalley's family for two weeks now and the way they lived opened his eyes to what a loving family could be like. Robert Smalley worked hard to allow his wife to stay home with the children and Maryanne was a wonderful housekeeper and devoted mother.

They had what they called *"Family Home Evening"* every Monday night and all the family members had to arrange their schedules to be there. Susan explained that they always had some type of lesson on Christian values and sometimes played games or went to a G-rated movie afterwards they had some type of treat. Each family member had a part in the evening's activities, maybe they read a scripture or gave a prayer or made the snack, but they were all involved. It was so different from his family. Ever since his mother died, all they did was work and try to keep things running as smoothly as possible. His father was constantly tired and often moody. They never talked about religion except in church.

It all seemed so different from how his family operated. His father seemed to just order everyone around and they all did what he told them to do. Jacob and Esther were close, but his father often seemed to be only a hard taskmaster. Although his mother had often told him, Jacob could never remember his father saying he loved any of the children.

This family was very affectionate. Susan's mother, Maryanne, had actually hugged him the day he arrived. She had taken him to her son's empty room and told him to make himself at home. Ten-year old William had shown him his favorite toys and told him how great it was to have him stay with them. Jacob was kind of overwhelmed at first. Now it felt good to have all these people care about him and how he felt.

When he went to work at the grocery store on Tuesday, the manager met him at the door.

"Hey, Jacob. I need that social security number so I can file your paperwork. It's been two weeks and tomorrow is pay day."

Jacob didn't know what to do. He hadn't planned on being here this long and didn't remember that this issue would come up. He looked up at the manager sheepishly. "Can I talk to you in your office?" Jacob asked.

"Sure. Follow me. Is there a problem?"

Jacob closed the door behind them and took a deep breath. "I have a confession to make. A big one," he confided.

Mr. Robinson nodded. "Why don't we both sit down?"

They each took one of the chairs by the desk. Jacob didn't know exactly what to say and he just blurted out the truth.

"My name is really Jacob Brown. I don't have a social security card because the community I come from doesn't believe in getting one and they have as little to do with the government as they possibly can. We all belong to the *Pentecostal Holiness Today* church and our pastor is really strict about it."

"Where do you live?" asked his boss surprised.

"High up in the mountains of West Virginia," said Jacob with a sigh.

"Everyone is supposed to get their social security number when they're born. It's needed to file your tax returns. But no one in your community does that?" Mr. Robinson asked in disbelief.

Jacob shook his head. "No one files a tax return. We don't usually earn much cash anyway, we do a lot of bartering."

"What about school? You seem very educated, didn't you go to a public school in West Virginia?" asked Mr. Robinson, somewhat bewildered by the thought that any legal adult in the United States didn't have a social security card.

"I was home-schooled by mother until I was twelve when she died. The pastor's wife taught all us kids after that," admitted Jacob.

"Well, this does create a problem." Mr. Robinson rubbed his chin.

"I guess I just won't be able to get paid," said Jacob starting to get up.

"No, I'll pay you in cash. You earned it. You're a hard worker." Mr. Robinson opened the safe, pulled out six hundred dollars and handed it to Jacob. "But I'm afraid you can't keep working here. I'm breaking a few laws doing this."

Jacob put the bills in his pocket and stood up. "Thanks. I'm sorry I lied."

Mr. Robinson was shaking his head as Jacob walked out.

Jacob walked out of the grocery store with a heavy heart. He felt bad that he had deceived Mr. Robinson, and that he had lied to the Smalley family. When Jacob walked into the cafe, Beth looked up surprised.

"I thought you had to work today?" she said as she continued filling salt shakers.

Jacob looked so uncomfortable that she didn't ask him anything else. She turned and went into the kitchen to get her father. There were only two customers in the cafe finishing up a late breakfast and Mr. Smalley was able to leave the kitchen.

He walked over to the booth where Jacob sat with his head in his hands.

"Hi, you want to talk about it?" he asked. "Maybe I can help."

"It's kind of a long disgusting story," said Jacob grudgingly.

"I've got some time right now," offered Robert.

Jacob pretty much told him the same things he had told Mr. Robinson.

"So what in the world are you doing so far away from home then?" asked Robert.

Jacob blushed. "The reverend told me to go find a wife."

Robert looked at him amused. "Just like that, huh?"

Jacob didn't answer, he just hung his head and nodded.

"It can take a long time to court a girl and get her to marry you. How did he expect you to get a job and live here that long without a social security card?" asked Robert perplexed.

"It wasn't supposed to take this long. I was supposed to kidnap a girl and bring her home with me," admitted Jacob, feeling awful as he said the words.

"What!? He actually told you to do that?" asked Robert incredulously.

Jacob felt miserable. "I thought that Mormons treated women like second class citizens. I figured a woman would be happy to run away with me if I promised to treat her really nice."

Robert's eyes widened and suddenly he burst out laughing.

Jacob couldn't figure out what was so funny.

Beth heard her father and came over to the booth.

"What are you laughing at? What's so funny?" she asked.

"Jacob thought Mormons treated women poorly. That we didn't respect them." Robert Smalley was laughing so hard he could barely talk.

Jacob blushed when Beth looked at him.

"You've lived with us for over two weeks now. Do you still believe that's true?" she asked seriously.

He shook his head. "No. In fact it seems that women get a great deal of respect in your religion. I guess I was really wrong about that."

Robert smiled. "You certainly were. We expect men and women to treat each other as partners in a marriage. The husband has the responsibility to support his wife and family. The woman cares for him and the children. It doesn't always work out that way, but we try to show respect and love to each member of the family. We believe that we're all spiritual offspring of a loving Heavenly Father who wants us to treat each other with kindness. We're not perfect and we make mistakes and sometimes are rude or troublesome, but we try to live by that concept."

"I've noticed that your family is really good at following that principle," admitted Jacob. "So I guess I'll just have to go home without ... " he stopped and blushed again. He couldn't look Robert in the eye.

"Without Susan, am I right?" guessed Robert.

Jacob nodded.

Robert laid a hand on his shoulder. "Why don't you just stay here?"

Jacob looked up at him in surprise. "How could I do that?"

"I'll go with you down to the Social Security office. There must be some way to straighten this all out. You can stay with us until everything is settled, then if you want, you can get a place of your own," offered Robert.

Beth looked at Jacob. "I know Susan doesn't want you to go away."

"I'll have to think about it. I hate leaving my sister to handle everything at home without me there. My brothers are only ten and fourteen.

They can't help out on the farm as much as I can. I don't know ... " He shook his head and frowned.

"OK. For now you know your options. You can decide later," said Robert. "In the mean time, you can help me here in the kitchen."

***

Anna Hensley opened the front door to find Eve Atkins standing on the porch wringing her hands. "Hello, Evie. Can I help you?" she asked the girl.

"Probably not," gulped Eve. She sniffed and took a deep breath.

"Would you like to come in and talk for a minute?"

Eve nodded. When she was settled in a chair at the kitchen table with a glass of water she looked up at Anna. "Is it true that Mark has gone on the hunt?"

"Yes, he and Matthew went to California."

Eve started crying. "That's what my father told me, but I had to come and make sure. Why did he have to go?"

Anna looked at the girl. She could tell she'd been crying for a while, her eyes were red. She put her hand on the girl's shoulder. "Tell me what's wrong, Evie?"

"But Mark knows I love him," she wept. "We promised each other ages ago that we would one day get married."

"When did you do that, Evie?" asked Anna solicitously.

"When I was thirteen and he was seventeen."

Anna tried not to laugh. "That was a long time ago, dear. Things change. The reverend sent the men out," she shrugged. "I don't like it either. I'm sorry."

"If all the men go out to hunt for wives, who will I marry?" she pleaded.

"I don't know if the reverend has considered that very well. We do have several young women who need husbands. There are two new families that have joined us and they both have sons. What about one of those young men?" suggested Anna.

"If you're talking about the Johnson boys, I'd rather be an old maid!"

"I don't know what to tell you, Evie, I'm sorry," commiserated Anna.

"Thanks anyway," said the girl as she stood to leave. "I guess I really don't know if Mark still loves me anyway," sighed Evie.

# Chapter 8

Elizabeth hoped with all her heart that Maria was all right. She wished she could have stayed with her, but she had made a promise to go willingly with Matthew if they took Maria to a hospital and she always kept her word. She was looking out the van window day-dreaming when she overheard the men talking.

"We just passed Manchester, Kentucky," said Matthew. "We might actually get home tonight if we push it."

"I slept longer than I thought," said Mark groggily. "You've made good time."

"Well, I guess most people are at work by this time on a Tuesday. The roads have been pretty open and I haven't had to go through any construction."

"We'll need to stop for gas and drinks in a little while." Mark turned and looked at Elizabeth. "You promised you wouldn't give us any trouble, do you still mean it?"

She looked up at him and nodded. "I always keep my word."

"OK," he said. "In that case, I'll let Matthew sit back there with you while I drive and you two can spend some time getting acquainted."

She looked at Matthew and shrugged.

Matthew turned into the next gas station and Mark got out to fill up the tank. Matthew came around to the side door and unlocked it.

"I'm sure you need to use the lady's room," he said, opening her door.

She nodded. She was a bit surprised to notice that the restrooms were inside the building this time. They must trust her now, because this was the first time he had stopped at a station that didn't have outside bathrooms. Matthew followed her into the building but left her alone while he went to buy cold bottles of water for the cooler.

Elizabeth used the facilities and washed her hands and face. In a way she was glad they were almost to their destination if for no other reason than she desperately wanted a bath. She had been wearing the same clothes now since Saturday. When she looked in the mirror she noticed that her hair was getting greasy. It needed to be shampooed. She pulled it back with her fingers and held it in a ponytail, but she didn't have any thing to tie it back with so she let it go. When she exited the restroom, Matthew was waiting for her.

"Is there anything you need me to buy for you?" he asked quietly.

"No. Water is fine," she said, noticing that he had at least six bottles in his arms.

He blushed. "No, I mean anything a girl might need?"

It took her a minute to understand that he was wondering if he needed to buy her some Kotex. Now she blushed. "No, it's not that time of month. But thanks for asking."

He nodded, handed her a bottle of chilled water and they walked out together to the van. He climbed in the back to put the water in the cooler then came and sat in the seat next to hers. "Did you want a sandwich or something?" he asked politely.

The water felt good on her parched throat. She swallowed and said, "I am starting to get hungry. Thank you."

"I just bought some ham and some roast beef sandwiches."

"Is there still any egg salad left?" she asked.

"I think there's still one left." He climbed back and opened the cooler again. "Yes, there's one left. Do you want an apple, too?"

"Yes, that would be nice, thanks," she said politely.

By this time Mark had paid for the gas and was getting into the driver's seat.

"Hand me one of the ham and cheese subs while you're back there," he called over his shoulder. "And a bottle of water." He started the van and pulled back onto the road.

Matthew handed him the sandwich and water, then settled back into his seat.

After a few minutes of silence while they all ate, Elizabeth looked over at him. She would keep her word and not cause trouble for as long as it took Brandon to find her, but she certainly hoped it wouldn't be too much longer.

"Why don't you tell me a little about your family," she said. "If I'm going to be your wife, I should learn more about you."

Matthew looked at her a little awed. She was really something special. He figured any other girl would be crying or begging them to let her go. She was brave and smart and he wished he hadn't had to meet her this way.

"Well, my mother's name is Anna," he said by way of introduction. "A man from our church found her in California twenty-five years ago. He ended up deciding not to marry her and my dad married her instead. My dad's name is John. They're really nice people. I think you'll like them both."

She stared at him for a second. "A man found her? Like what you're doing?"

Matthew nodded. "I know it's strange, but that's the way Reverend Forester says we need to add good blood into our small community. He's against the families getting too inbred because it can cause genetic problems."

"But can't you just, I don't know, meet someone from someplace else and start dating or something?" she asked frankly.

"We aren't allowed to leave our community to date. We're always chaperoned on our dates," he admitted sheepishly. "We can't even hold hands until after we're married. The reverend doesn't believe we should spend too much time outside our own community because of all the bad influences in the world out here."

"Then how do you know if you'll even like each other enough to fall in love?"

He shrugged. "My parents did. I guess it's not any different than cultures that have arranged marriages. I've read about those."

"But even those don't usually involve kidnapping," Elizabeth protested.

He looked down at the floor. "I know. I'm sorry about that. But would you and Maria have willingly come away to marry us?"

"Of course not. I was planning to go away to college. I would have wanted to get to know you first and maybe waited a few years before getting married. Lots of couples live together before they marry."

"Oh, no! I would never do that. That's the sin of fornication!" he exclaimed.

She stared at him bewildered. "And kidnapping isn't a sin?"

He didn't answer her. He took a bite of sandwich and looked out the window. Finally he said quietly, "Well, it's not listed in the ten commandments."

She shook her head. "What about thou shalt not covet?"

He didn't answer her at first. "I'm just doing what I was told to do."

"That's what the Nazi soldiers said, too, when they were caught."

He looked puzzled.

"When they were asked why they murdered all those Jews," she explained.

"Oh, yeah." He sighed. "I suppose that's not a good excuse, is it?"

"Not really."

"Well, I hope you'll learn to love me. I'll treat you real nice. My dad is good to my mother and she loves all of us."

Elizabeth shook her head and finished her sandwich. "Thanks for lunch. I guess I should be glad you aren't keeping me gagged and tied up on the floor."

He looked shocked. "I would never do that."

"But putting a drug in my soda was all right?" she countered.

He rolled his eyes. "It didn't hurt you, it just put you to sleep."

"But don't you see, you never learned anything about us before you kidnapped us," she stated. "You didn't know Maria would need her insulin. She could have died."

He nodded. "That's true. We never thought of that because we never go to doctors or hospitals. We're all basically very healthy where I come from."

"That's probably because your community is based on survival of the fittest."

He looked puzzled again. "What do you mean by that?"

"Anyone with the sugars just dies. They probably don't live long enough to have children to pass on the bad genes. It probably works that way with other diseases, too," she stated coldly. "Only the strongest survive."

"Maybe so," he shrugged. "The reverend tries to prevent those kind of weaknesses from occurring by forbidding us to marry into families too closely related. We eat healthy and certainly get a lot of exercise working on the farms. We don't eat all the preservatives that you people get in your food. Our food is all organic. It's really a good way to live," he explained. He wanted so much for her to appreciate what he was trying to tell her.

"Maybe so, but it still seems to be an awfully isolated way to live."

"I've never been sick a day in my life," he bragged. "Neither has my brother. Someone may get hurt in an accident, but we have people who are healers who can patch them up. They use herbs and stuff instead of man-made medicines that have so many bad side effects."

"I guess I'll learn all about it when I get there," Elizabeth sighed.

"My mother will teach you. She's a wonderful cook and she can sew just about anything," he said excitedly. He was glad she was finally coming around to his way of thinking. "I don't have any sisters so she'll love having someone to teach."

Elizabeth nodded. "I have always wanted to learn to sew."

Matthew smiled. It seemed like Elizabeth was going to accept her new life. He finished his sandwich and noticed that she had leaned her seat back and had her eyes closed. He'd talk to her more later, she was probably tired.

\*\*\*

Brandon's friend, Stephen Mann, flew them to Tennessee in his private plane. They landed in the airport at noon on Tuesday. When Brandon flashed his badge it took them exactly thirteen minutes to get a rental car and be on the way to the hospital in Winchester.

Belle was the first one to see the sign for Southern Tennessee Medical Center. They parked in the visitor parking area and hurried to the information desk in the lobby. A nice gray haired volunteer told them that Maria Gonzales was out of Critical Care and now on the Medical/Surgical floor. They took the visitor's elevator and easily found her hospital room.

Maria was sitting up in bed eating her lunch when Adelita rushed over to her.

"I was so worried about you, Maria," she cried. "Are you really all right?"

"Now I am. Oh, Mama, I was so scared, but Elizabeth helped me." Maria started crying as they hugged each other. "How did you get here so fast?"

"I came with them in a private plane," said Adelita turning to the door.

Brandon had held back so the two of them could have a few minutes to themselves. Now he stepped into the room. "Hi, kiddo," he said smiling.

"Brandon, oh, Brandon, I'm so glad you're here," sobbed Maria.

Belle stepped out from behind Brandon. "Hi, Maria."

"Hi, Belle. You have to find Elizabeth," said Maria wiping the tears from her face with a napkin. "They took us because they wanted us to marry them! It was all so crazy, I still can't believe it happened, and all because we agreed to go for pizza. And then I left my extra vial of insulin in Elizabeth's car and my pump ran out." She paused to catch her breath and Brandon was finally able to get a word in.

"OK, Maria, start from the beginning," he said.

She took a deep breath. "These two guys were in the parking lot after the swim meet on Saturday. They came up and congratulated me on winning a first place medal in my race," she said. "They seemed so nice and Mark was really cute."

"He was the one who drove the van?" asked Belle.

"Yes, when we left the parking lot he drove. Anyway, they asked if we wanted to go have some pizza with them. It's all my fault. I told Elizabeth I wanted to go. We weren't supposed to be gone very long and I had just filled my pump, so I left my bag in her car with our swimming stuff. Anyway, we stopped to get something to drink and that's when they put some kind of drug in our sodas."

"They drugged you?" asked Brandon trying to remain calm. "Then what?"

"I was asleep for at least twelve hours. When I woke up we weren't even in California anymore. Elizabeth didn't wake up for four more hours. I was getting really worried about her, but she was fine when she did wake up. She asked them why they had kidnapped us because our parents aren't rich or anything, and that's when they told us they were going to make us marry them!" she ended breathlessly. "I couldn't believe it. It seemed like a nightmare."

"Oh, baby, I know you were really scared." Adelita hugged her.

"I was, but Elizabeth got mad and started yelling at them to take us back home. And Mark slapped her and told her to shut up."

Brandon's fingers automatically curled into fists at this news. He had to deliberately force them to relax. "Maria, did they ever say where they were taking you?"

"Not exactly. They live somewhere up in the mountains in West Virginia."

"West Virginia?" asked Belle. She looked over at Brandon. "They must have waited until they got to Kentucky to steal the license plates. Probably to throw us off the track."

Brandon nodded. "Then what happened after he hit Elizabeth?"

"Well, Matthew got mad at him. He said their father would be upset if they mistreated a woman. He apologized to us. They gave us sandwiches and stuff to eat, but by then I was feeling sick and couldn't eat much. Elizabeth told them I could die and she promised to do whatever they wanted if they would take me to a hospital. At first they didn't want to."

"Was that because they didn't want to get caught?" asked Belle.

Maria shook her head. "No. They said that going to doctors or hospitals was against their religion. That the only true healer was God."

"What religions believe that?" Brandon asked Belle.

"I'm not sure. I'd have to do some research on that," she said.

\*\*\*

Able Hamilton had agreed to let the Wilson girls use the restroom and change out of their pajamas. He stopped the car at a deserted rest stop along the highway. It had one of those outdoor bathrooms with no doors, just a passageway that turned a corner into the ladies' room. He had Joshua stand at the entrance while the girls changed.

Joshua could hear the girls talking because their voices echoed off the concrete walls. Bambi was trying to calm down Abby who was crying again. He couldn't make out all the words clearly, but whatever she said must have helped because a few minutes later they both came out dressed in jeans and t-shirts and Abby wasn't crying any more.

He took Abby by the arm and led them back to the car. "Able is getting us something to eat. I promise that we're not going to hurt you."

Bambi sniffed. "Yeah. I've heard that before."

"I'm only fifteen, I'm too young to get married. I haven't even finished high school yet," whimpered Abby. "Please take us back home."

Joshua opened the car door and made both girls climb into the back seat. He got in behind the wheel as it was his turn to drive. They still had to cross Virginia but he hoped they would make it home by late tonight. Able got in the front and handed the girls some peanut butter crackers, candy bars and bottles of water. "Eat up," he said cheerfully.

Bambi looked at the offering and rolled her eyes. "This looks real healthy."

"When we get back home, you'll have all the healthy organic food you can eat. We grow all our own food and raise our own meat. But for now, this will have to do," said Able. "That's all I could find in the vending machines."

Bambi opened one of the packages of crackers and handed them to Abby. "We have to keep up our strength if we want to escape," she whispered.

Abby ate her crackers and a candy bar. At least the water was cold and tasted good. Her throat was sore from crying and the water helped. She watched helplessly out the window as the scenery passed. With every mile they were getting farther from home. She had never been this frightened in her life. As the middle daughter she had always followed happily along with her older sisters. Now she was relying on Bambi to get them both out of this mess.

Bambi ate all her crackers and racked her brain for a solution to this unbelievable problem. Who in their right mind would abduct two girls and expect them to go along happily and marry them? She would just have to be ready the moment an opportunity arose to escape from these two idiots. They were bound to mess up sooner or later.

The boys were smart enough to stay off the main highways and Bambi didn't see anyone she could signal to for help. Later that afternoon they stopped for gas in the small town of Patterson, Virginia and Bambi asked if they could use the restroom. Joshua held on to Abby's arm as he walked them over to the outside facilities.

The restroom door was unlocked and they didn't need to ask the attendant for a key. This was the mistake Bambi had been waiting for. As soon as the sisters got inside, Bambi closed the door and locked it. There were no windows to escape through, but she had decided that this ridiculous farce was going to end right here. After fifteen minutes, Joshua called to them and knocked on the door.

"What's taking so long? Hurry up you two, Abel's ready to leave," he announced.

"We're not coming out," yelled Bambi through the locked door.

Joshua twisted the doorknob but it wouldn't turn. He knocked on the door again.

"All right now! You two come on out this instant!" he called hoarsely.

"No way," hollered Bambi. "In fact I'm getting ready to start screaming and I'm sure someone in the gas station is going to come out here to see why."

Joshua turned and frantically signaled for Able to come over.

"What's the matter?" Able asked as he walked around to the side of the building.

"They won't come out," Joshua hissed.

"You let them both go in at one time? That was stupid," said Able shaking his head at the naivety of his brother.

"I didn't think about it. They both went in together last time."

Able sighed. "There wasn't a door with a lock last time." He rolled his eyes.

"Now what do we do?" asked Joshua. He peered around the corner of the building but there was no one else in sight. "See if you can get them to come out."

"I can't believe this. We're almost to West Virginia and you let them pull a stunt like this." Able shook his head and knocked on the door. "Please open the door and come out. Bambi, we need to leave."

Bambi hollered back, "You've got to be kidding! You two jerks go ahead and leave. We are not coming out!"

Joshua lost his temper and started pounding on the door.

"I'll break down this door!" he threatened. "Open up this instant!"

Bambi began screaming as loud as she could. The sound echoed around inside the room. "Help! Someone help us!"

"Great!" exclaimed Able. "Come on, let's get out of here."

He grabbed Joshua's arm and pulled him away from the door. As the boys ran towards the car, a big burly mechanic stuck his head out the garage door.

"Hey, what's all that noise? What's going on out there?" he yelled.

Able started the car as Joshua jumped in the other side.

"Hey, you haven't paid for that gas!" hollered the mechanic. He started running towards the car, but the constant screaming from the bathroom distracted him and he turned around. He walked over to the door and yelled in a deep bass voice. "Stop that screaming right this minute!"

Bambi immediately stopped. She recognized that that was not either of their kidnapper's voices. "Help us, Mister. We're being kidnapped!"

Butch Hutching leaned close to the door. "Those two men are gone. Open the door, you're safe now, girlie," he coaxed.

Bambi unlocked the door and peered out. The biggest man she had ever seen in her life stood outside with a concerned look on his face. He had long shaggy black hair and grease stains on his hands and overalls, but to her he looked absolutely wonderful.

Bambi pushed open the door and rushed out.

"Thank you, thank you. You won't believe what happened to us." She stood in front of him and looked up. "You saved our lives, honestly, Mister."

Abby came out cautiously. She was still frightened and this big man looked scary to her. She stood behind her sister and looked at their rescuer with wide-open eyes.

Butch stood there wiping his hands on the rag he kept hanging from his pocket loop. He stared at the two young girls, one of whom had been recently crying. They both looked upset and he suspected they were telling the truth.

"OK you two, come on in the shop and tell me exactly what's been going on."

Abby held on to her sister's arm as they followed him inside. Bambi related the whole story and when she finished Butch shook his head in disbelief.

"That's quite a tale, Miss Bambi. I'll go ahead and call the sheriff." As soon as he finished his call, he handed the phone to Bambi. "Here now, call your parents. They must be worried sick about you two."

\*\*\*

Rueben Smith and Melody Baker arrived at his parent's house in West Virginia around five o'clock Tuesday evening. It had only taken Melody one day to pack up what few things she owned. The apartment she had been renting was fully furnished and she only had her clothes, dishes and some books that belonged to her.

The head librarian had been shocked the day Melody walked in and quit her job. He expected her to spend her life there, after all she was not all that attractive and there were not that many single men in their small town.

When she told him she was moving to West Virginia and getting married he almost passed out in shock. "When did all this happen?" he asked scratching his almost bald head.

"In the last few weeks," she replied as she turned in her badge.

"Isn't that kind of sudden?"

"Yes," she answered cheerfully. "Very sudden."

"Melody, you've worked here for five years and I've never known you to make a hasty decision. Are you sure you want to do this?" he asked in fatherly concern. He had always thought of Melody as another one of his daughters and he didn't want her to do something she would later regret.

"More sure than I've ever been about anything else in my life," she assured him.

"Well, you've got sixty days of paid vacation you have never taken and a small 401 K. What do you want me to do about them?" he asked.

"Can I cash them all out?"

"Yes, it will take a few days, but I've got the paperwork here you'd need to fill out." He went to a special filling cabinet and pulled out the papers.

She sat right down and filled out all the papers. When it was all converted to cash, she had a little over $6,000. She smiled when she got the check a few days later. To her it felt like a small dowry. She would use it to set up a sweet little home for Rueben.

When they pulled up to the house in West Virginia, Rueben's father, Peter, met them at the door. He was a tall thin man with short gray hair and a tiny mustache. He smiled at Melody.

"Welcome to our family, little lady," he said with a grin. "Rueben's already told us all about how special you are. He spent two hours on the phone with his mother and me last week. We're right proud to have you join our family."

Melody felt warmed all over by his reception. She had a lump in her throat as she went with Peter into the house. Rueben followed them bringing in her suitcases.

When Rueben introduced her to his mother, Naomi, she hugged Melody and had such a warm smile that Melody actually felt her eyes watering up.

"Thank you for such a wonderful welcome," she said smiling at them all.

His sisters, Dinah and Leah, both welcomed her with hugs. All the women in Rueben's family were short and he towered over them. Dinah and Leah had their mother's brown hair and hazel eyes.

"He was right," said Leah to Melody. "You do have gorgeous red hair."

"Rueben, honey, don't bring all that luggage in here," said Naomi when she noticed the suitcases. "The brides' cottage is where she'll be staying until your wedding."

"Oh, I forgot," said Rueben setting down the case he was carrying. He looked at Melody and explained. "There are several of us men all bringing new brides back home. The tradition has been that the brides live together for a few weeks until each new couple's house is built and the wedding ceremonies performed. I hope you don't mind." He added sheepishly, "We're all chaperoned on our dates until then."

"How quaint," said Melody, smiling. "I won't mind being away from you if it doesn't take too long to build our house."

"Oh, it doesn't take long when we all get together and have a building party. This house went up in three days," informed Peter. "Of course it takes a little longer to get it all painted and decorated, but Naomi and the girls can help with that."

"That's enough talk," said Naomi. "Let her go freshen up. Dinner's almost ready and we can explain more later."

After dinner Naomi went with Rueben as he escorted Melody to the brides' cottage. Cynthia Sweet was there and she welcomed them in.

"It's been lonely here. I'm glad to have some company. Pick out which bed you want. You'll get to take the bed with you when you leave. Michael told me that," informed Cynthia with a smile.

The beds were of made of different woods and in different furniture styles having all been donated by families for the new couples. Melody picked a bed with a beautiful log cabin quilt done in maroons and greens. The headboard was dark walnut. "I like this one," she said.

Rueben smiled. "That's the bed my father made. Funny you should pick that one. No one told you, did they?"

Melody smiled back at him. "No one told me. I just like the wood and this quilt."

"I'm glad you like this particular style," said Naomi. "Because Rueben and Peter have been making furniture for the past six months and it's all like this."

"I love it. Oh, I can't believe I'm going to have such nice things for my very own."

Rueben brought in her suitcases and put them by her bed. "I'll store the rest of your things in the barn until you need them."

After they left that evening, Melody sat with Cynthia and talked.

"I was worried a little when they told me some of the brides might have problems settling in," admitted Cynthia. "But it looks like you and I will be happy."

"It's been like a dream to me," admitted Melody. "It all happened so fast."

"Me too. But I'm going to do everything I can to make Michael happy."

They chatted for an hour about where they had come from and how they met their soon to be husbands, then they went to bed.

The next morning Reverend Forester came with his wife, Mary and Anna Hensley to meet the newest bride. His stern face softened when he saw that at least these two women were willing brides and they both seemed intelligent and healthy.

"I'm happy to report to you two young ladies that both your houses are under construction as we speak. They should be finished by the end of the week," he said proudly. "The men are all working hard to get them done."

"That's wonderful," said Cynthia. "When can we do something to help?"

"Well, Mrs. Hensley came today to take you to pick out fabrics for curtains and such. She'll show you to our warehouse where extra things are stored. We've been gathering supplies for the last three years knowing that we would be needing them for the new brides," he smiled at them. "You're welcome to take whatever you need."

"Wow," said Cynthia after he left. "It's almost like winning the lottery."

Melody laughed. "Except it also includes a husband."

The women followed Anna down the street to a large wooden building. They both stood in awe when she led them inside where they saw row after row of shelves filled with all kinds of kitchen items, bolts of cloth, blankets, pillows and gardening tools.

"Wow," said Melody overwhelmed. "This is amazing."

"Your grooms and their fathers are supposed to be making some basic items of furniture for your new homes. You're both lucky that your fiancés are good carpenters. Some of the other brides won't be so lucky," Mary admitted. "Each house will be furnished with a kitchen table and chairs, a large bed and a dresser for the master bedroom, and a couch and rocking chair for the living room. You'll get to take the twin bed you're sleeping in now for the second bedroom."

"And depending on your grooms, you might be lucky enough to get a few extra pieces of furniture. My husband made me a lovely sewing table," said Anna. "Each house is made so that rooms can easily be added on to them as your families grow."

Mary laughed, "The Millers have six children, so they now have the biggest house the men have ever built. They even added a second story on part of it."

"I never imagined such nice people existed in this world," said Cynthia in amazement. "To do all this for total strangers is wonderfully giving. My family was never like this."

Anna patted her shoulder. "This little community can do some nice things."

Melody was looking at the bolts of cloth. She ran her fingers over the fabric. "Can I pick whatever I want for my curtains?" she asked.

Anna nodded. "Whatever you want."

"I love this one," she said picking up a bolt of dark green cotton with small maroon roses on it. "These are my favorite colors."

"I'm in charge of helping you learn to sew your own curtains," informed Anna. "Do either of you have any experience with sewing?"

Cynthia shook her head.

"I have a little," said Melody shyly. "I took home economics in high school."

"Well, we'll start simple. Just mainly straight seams. The curtain tops will gather up when they're put on the curtain rods," said Anna.

Cynthia picked out a bolt of blue cotton with tiny white flowers. "This color is my favorite. Do you think Michael will like it?"

Anna smiled, "I'm sure he'll love anything you pick."

"Can you teach me how to make one of the pretty quilts like I have on my bed?" asked Melody. "I think it's lovely."

"I certainly can," said Anna. "As for the curtains, they'll be simple enough because all the window frames are the same size in the houses we build. It makes it easier that way."

They spent the next few hours at Anna's house cutting the fabric and watching her demonstrate how to use a sewing machine.

# Chapter 9

Jacob's father was one of the few people back home who had bothered to get telephone service to his house. Jacob was thankful that he didn't have to leave his message with the reverend when he called one night and spoke with his sister, Esther.

"When are you coming home?" she wanted to know. "We need you. All of us are helping Dad with the spring planting. But it's really hard work."

"I'm sorry. I'm not sure when I'm coming home."

"Why not. Didn't you tell me last week that you had found a girl you liked?"

"Yeah, but there's a problem. I like her whole family. I'm thinking of staying here with them," he admitted sheepishly.

Esther started to cry.

Jacob felt awful. "Please don't cry."

"Jacob, you're my best friend. I need you here," she sobbed. "I can't keep taking care of everything by myself. The boys help Dad as much as they can, but they're still young and sometimes I have to do your job and keep up the house."

Now Jacob felt overwhelmingly guilty. "I'm sorry, Esther."

"Besides, Dad had an awful argument with the reverend this week."

"What was it about?"

"Reverend Forester said at twenty-three I'm plenty old enough to marry one of the Johnson boys. They're that new family that moved here last winter. One of them is thirty and the other twenty-seven and they've never been married," she reminded him.

"I know them. Both those men are kind of mean and domineering."

"Tell me about it. One of them was bullying Isaac last week and I had to yell at him to stop it. He just laughed at me and said he liked a woman with spunk." She shivered remembering it. "They scare me, but I didn't let them know it."

"Isaac is only ten years old. I'd like to teach those Johnson's a thing or two!"

"Yeah, well how are you going to do that if you stay in Idaho?" she whimpered.

"Dad stood up for you with the reverend, didn't he?" asked Jacob worried for her.

"Dad told the reverend he needed me to stay at home and take care of things here. But I don't know if that's the end of it or not. Jacob, I don't want to marry either one of those guys."

Jacob sighed. "Is Dad there right now?"

"He's out in the barn," she sniffed and wiped her eyes.

"Ask him if he can come talk to me for a minute."

"I'll go ask him. Talk to Ephraim while I go get him. He's dying to talk to you."

She handed the phone to fourteen-year old Ephraim and headed to the barn.

"Jake, hurry and come home, please. I miss you," said Ephraim.

"Yeah, I bet you miss how much work I do now that you're doing it for me."

When his father, Aaron, came to the phone, Jacob told him all about the Smalley's. He told him that he didn't want to return home to be under Reverend Forester's control.

"I'm getting pretty tired of it myself," admitted his father. "Ever since your mother died he's been trying to get me to marry the widow Bisher. Not only does she look like a horse, but she's got four kids of her own. Now he wants to take away Esther and make her marry Ricky Johnson. I'd rather cut off my right arm than give her to one of those Johnson boys."

"Dad, you're not a prisoner there. Maybe you should sell out and think about trying a different lifestyle," suggested Jacob. "The Mormons I've met here are nothing like the reverend said they were."

"I don't know. I'll have to think about it. You're mother's buried here ..."

"I know, Dad. But she would never want Esther to be unhappily married. And you aren't all that keen on the reverend's ideas anyway. Mormons believe in family the way we do. They're strong Christians and good people," he coaxed.

"I heard they weren't Christians," said his father.

"That's not true. Anyone who can read should know different. It says right on the front of the Book of Mormon that it is a second witness that Jesus is the Christ."

"I'll think about it. I sure wish you'd come home and help me. I miss you son. I know I've never told you. It's hard for me to talk about how I feel, but I love you."

Jacob felt a lump in his throat at his father's admission.

"I love you too. If you decide to leave West Virginia, I'll come help you move," he promised. "But I don't think I can move back there, Dad."

"I'm sorry you feel that way, Jacob."

"Just seriously consider selling the farm. I'd love to have all of you move out here," said Jacob. "I'll talk to you again soon."

Aaron hung up the phone and looked at Esther. She looked just like her mother. She had the same black hair and blue eyes, even the same dimples when she smiled. He wasn't about to let the reverend make her marry one of the Johnson brothers.

"Esther, I'm going over to have a little visit with Malachi Williams. I want to see if he's still interested in buying our farm," he said seriously.

She ran and threw her arms around her father. "Oh, Daddy. You mean it?"

He nodded and smiled. Somehow this decision seemed very right all of a sudden.

\*\*\*

Belle was scouring the internet looking for information about churches that avoided conventional medicine as part of their creed. There was a small *Fundamentalist Christian* faith group in Massachusetts that referred to their group as *The Body* meaning the Body of Christ. They refused medical treatment even to the point of not wearing eye glasses. They rejected any contact with the government, education, banking, and medicine.

*The Church of the First Born* was active in Colorado and Oklahoma. They believed in the use of prayers to heal. *The Bible Readers Fellowship* was a small *Evangelical Church* in Florida and they shunned medical treatment. The *End Time Ministries* were in several states, *The Faith Assembly* group was mainly in Indiana, the *Full Gospel Deliverance Church* was in North Carolina, and the *Faith Tabernacle Congregation* was based in Pennsylvania but had congregations in several other states. None of them believed in getting medical assistance and had all been charged at various times with lawsuits for allowing some of their members to die without getting proper medical treatment.

Belle shook her head. "I thought this would be easy. I had no idea there were so many churches that refused medical assistance."

"The main one I'd always heard about was the *Christian Science* religion," said Brandon. "They follow that woman Mary Baker Eddy."

"Well, there are a lot more. Here's one called the *Pentecostal Holiness* church. Not only do they not believe in doctors, but they have nothing to do with what they call corrupt man-made institutions such as hospitals, newspapers, television, the radio, and politics," she read from the internet.

"That almost sounds smart to me," said Brandon. "Especially the politics part."

"How are we ever going to find the ones who took Elizabeth?"

"I don't know if we can believe what they told Maria, but find the ones based in West Virginia or states near there. Maybe they were actually telling the truth about where they were headed," he suggested. "I'm still checking for reports of sightings of the van with the smiley faced license plate."

Belle found that the *Pentecostal Holiness* churches were based in West Virginia. Then she read something that really scared her.

"Good grief, the church in West Virginia is a snake handling church!" she told Brandon with a shiver. "I hate snakes! It seems that most states have laws against owning poisonous snakes, but it's still legal in West Virginia. Maybe they really were taking the girls there."

\*\*\*

The Hamilton brothers made it home by late Tuesday night. They were tired and hungry and disappointed. Their father and mother welcomed them back with open arms.

"We lost those girls we told you about when we called the reverend the other day," admitted Able. "I don't think we're cut out to be kidnappers."

"Well, I never liked the idea anyway," said his mother. "You're father talked me into coming here. He didn't have to kidnap me."

"That's different, we both decided to come here after we were already married," reminded Elijah Hamilton. "When we met I had time to court you, Rebecca. Reverend didn't give the boys that option at all."

"I'm not letting them go back and try this again. There are single girls here in our own community that they can marry. It's not like our family has been here for generations like the other boys he sent out hunting," said Rebecca in a huff.

"I'll go talk to the reverend in the morning," agreed Elijah. "Right now I'm just happy to have them both home safe."

"Pa," said Able. "Me and Joshua already know which two girls we like here."

"Yeah," said Joshua. "Maybe we should go talk to their parents?"

\*\*\*

Maria was released from the hospital Wednesday morning. Brandon had arranged for his pilot friend to return and meet them at the airport to fly them back to San Diego. Adelita and Maria took a taxi to the airport and Stephen met them in the lobby.

Maria was still upset about Elizabeth and she was anxious to get back home and find out if Brandon had learned anything new about where she might be now.

When they landed at the San Diego airport, all of her little brothers were there with Elaine and the twins. They all seemed subdued until Elaine nodded to them to go to Maria and their mother. Her brothers raced ahead of the others to greet them.

"Hi, you guys," Maria said when she saw them. Sevando ran up and threw himself at her. She gave him a big hug.

"I missed you and missed you," he said. "Do you feel better?"

"I'm all better," she promised. "I missed all of you guys, too."

Adelita helped herd them all to the parking lot. Everyone was talking at once saying how glad they were to see Maria.

Maggie took Maria's hand and looked up at her. "I bet Elizabeth will be home soon, Daddy promised."

Maria leaned down and hugged her. "I'm sure he's right," she said hopefully.

When they finally got the children settled in Elaine's van, Maria asked her, "Have you heard anything more?"

Elaine shook her head. "Not really. There was a sighting of the van in Kentucky where they stopped for gas after they dropped you off at the hospital. But nothing since then."

"I'm so sorry," said Maria. "I feel like this is all my fault."

Elaine checked the traffic and pulled out of the parking lot. "Maria, don't be silly," she said. "Why do you think it's your fault?"

"Because I'm the one who talked her into going with them for pizza," said Maria.

"If Elizabeth hadn't wanted to go, she would have said so and talked you out of it. You know that, don't you?" Elaine smiled at her. "When have you ever known Elizabeth not to voice her opinion openly?"

"She's right," said Adelita. "Elizabeth has a mind of her own."

Maria nodded. "That's true. But she promised them she would go with them and not make any trouble if they took me to a hospital. So now she won't even try to escape."

"That's because she knows that Brandon will find her," reassured Elaine. "Trying to escape might end up being more dangerous than just staying with them."

"I guess that's true. Mark did wave a pistol at us once," said Maria.

"What did you say?" asked Adelita. "You never mentioned a gun before."

"Oh, I guess I didn't," remembered Maria. "I forgot about it."

"Well, I definitely don't want her doing anything foolish if they have guns," said Elaine seriously. "Who knows what they might do."

"Just one gun, and I don't think he would use it," said Maria.

"They'll still be considered armed and dangerous. We'll need to tell Brandon."

\*\*\*

Anna was the first one to spot the van as it drove into their driveway Thursday evening. She jumped up from her sewing machine and turned to Melody.

"My sons are home. Keep sewing like I showed you, I have to go."

She threw open the door as Mark was climbing out of the driver's seat.

"Hi, Mom," he called when he saw her.

"You're finally home! I was getting worried when we hadn't heard from you since last Saturday," she said as he came up the stairs onto the porch.

"We were trying to keep a low profile. Matthew saw a drawing of me on the television when he was buying supplies at a gas station," he explained. "Someone must have seen me when we left the school with the girls."

Her eyes widened. "Oh, no. That's means the police are looking for you."

"They were broadcasting a description of the van with the license plate we got in Kentucky," he said. "We drove on every back road we could find that headed towards home and it took a lot longer." He gave her a hug. "I'm tired and hungry. Is there anything to eat? We've had nothing but sandwiches for over three weeks now," he complained. "I sure missed your cooking."

"There's leftover fried chicken in the refrigerator. But Mark, where are the girls?"

He turned around and pointed to the van as Matthew was opening the side door for Elizabeth to get out.

"Matthew's bride is coming. I don't have one anymore."

She looked up at him in surprise. "What happened?"

"It's a long story. I'll let Matthew tell you. I'm hungry."

Anna turned around to see Matthew helping a pretty blond girl out of the van. The girl didn't look scared, just tired. She knew her sons had kidnapped two girls from California, but this one walked beside Matthew as if she wasn't afraid.

"Mom, I want you to meet Elizabeth," said Matthew as they reached the porch. "Elizabeth, this is my mother, Anna."

Anna nodded. "I'm pleased to meet you."

"Hi," said Elizabeth wearily. "You certainly live in an out of the way place."

"Yes, we do," she agreed. "You both look tired."

"We are," said Matthew. "We've been on the road since Saturday."

Anna led them into the house and sat them down at the kitchen table where Mark was already eating chicken and a huge slice of homemade bread.

"Are you hungry?" she asked and Matthew nodded. "How about you, Elizabeth? Would you like something to eat?"

"A slice of that bread looks good," answered Elizabeth.

While they ate, Anna went to check on Melody.

"Why don't you finish this tomorrow?" she suggested. "Another bride has just arrived and I would like you to come welcome her."

"I'd like that." Melody turned off the sewing machine and folded the material.

Elizabeth looked up when the women came back into the kitchen.

"This is Melody," said Anna. "She's Rueben Smith's bride. Melody, this is Elizabeth, she's to marry my son, Matthew."

Elizabeth nodded to the woman with curly red hair and glasses.

"It's nice to meet you," said Melody. "I've been learning to sew. Anna's a great teacher. I'm making curtains for my new house."

"All the new couples are getting five acres and a new house," informed Anna.

Matthew smiled. "Did the reverend arrange that?"

Anna nodded. "I guess we should take the girls over to the brides' cottage now."

"Come on, Elizabeth," said Melody. "I'll show you the way and you can pick out which bed you want to have."

Elizabeth looked questioningly at Matthew. "I'll be living some place else?"

"It's the custom here," he explained. "The brides stay in the bride's cottage until the wedding. By then our house will be ready."

John Hensley came in from the barn as Matthew was explaining things to Elizabeth. "We've just about finished Michael Andrew's house and Melody here will have hers finished next," he smiled at Melody. He looked at his sons. "Reverend will be pleased that you two are back. We'll start on your houses next week."

Mark looked up from his plate long enough to inform his father that they would only need one house for now. "I don't have a bride yet."

John looked puzzled and Matthew said, "I'll explain it after the women leave."

Elizabeth looked over at Matthew. "I guess I have to go with them?"

"It will be all right," he said. "Go with Melody."

Anna drove the brides into the village and parked the car in front of a small freshly painted building. "This is it," she told Elizabeth.

Melody opened the car door and said excitedly, "Come on, I can't wait to see which bed you pick."

Elizabeth looked confused. "Which bed for what?"

"All the brides get to pick a bed with a new quilt and that bed goes with them when they move into their house," explained Anna.

"I picked the one that Rueben's father had made and I didn't even know it. And it has the most beautiful quilt," gushed Melody.

Elizabeth followed her into the building. It was one big room with a small bathroom off to the back. There were seven beds lined along the walls. Each looked different and had a lovely quilt on it.

"Mine's over here on the back wall," said Melody as she went and sat down on her bed. "Which one do you want?"

It didn't matter to Elizabeth. She was hoping to be out of here soon. Surely Brandon would be coming for her any day now. She looked at each bed. One of the beds had a quilt that was a grandmother's flower garden pattern with peach and cream colored fabrics. It reminded her of her room back home.

"I'll take this one," she decided.

"That's a nice one," said Melody.

"Well, I guess I'll see you in the morning," said Anna.

Elizabeth looked at Anna. "I don't have any other clothes," she admitted sadly.

Anna looked at Elizabeth's weary face and she felt ashamed. "I'm so sorry, Elizabeth. I should have thought of that. I'll bring you some of mine, we're about the same size," apologized Anna.

"Thank you. I really would love to get a bath and put on something clean."

"I'll go get them right now," said Anna. "You start your bath water."

Poor thing, thought Anna. I forgot that they grabbed her from school. She doesn't have anything. How could I forget what that is like?

Melody looked at Elizabeth. "Why don't you have any clothes with you?" she asked puzzled. "Did you leave your things in the van?"

Elizabeth sighed. "I was kidnapped in my high school parking lot on Saturday. All I have are the clothes I'm wearing."

Melody was shocked. "I'm so sorry. That's horrible. I didn't know. I thought you were like me and Cynthia. We wanted to come here."

Elizabeth shrugged. "I think I'll go start my bath."

Melody watched her go into the bathroom and shut the door. She tried to imagine how she would feel if she hadn't wanted to come with Rueben. She didn't know how to react to this information. Should she try to help Elizabeth adjust to being here, or try to help her escape?

Anna hurried home and went through her things. In a small suitcase she put a nightgown, a package of new underwear she had not even opened yet, a long skirt and a blouse. Then she added a toothbrush and toothpaste, an extra hairbrush and a small bottle of lotion. There was already shampoo and soap at the cottage. When she carried the suitcase downstairs she went into the kitchen. Her men were all sitting around the table talking.

"Tomorrow I'm going into town to buy that poor girl some clothes. She has nothing of her own to wear. I can't believe I was so thoughtless, she had to tell me that she needed a nightgown," admitted Anna.

Matthew looked guilty. "I feel bad about that, too. We kind of just drove off with them and they didn't have anything extra with them for clothes."

"I'm taking some things to her right now. When I get back I want the whole story about why you only have one girl, when on Saturday you had two," insisted Anna.

# Chapter 10

Melinda padded into her parents' bedroom in her bare feet. She climbed in beside her mother. Janice woke up as the child's cold little feet touched her thighs. She looked at the clock on her nightstand. It was only ten o'clock, she must have barely fallen asleep.

"Is something wrong, Melinda?" she sleepily asked the child.

Melinda yawned and shook her head. "Elizabeth isn't in the van anymore."

"Oh, she isn't?"

"No. She's in a new place. There are other girls there. She's not afraid, but she's waiting for her daddy to find her. Why is it taking so long?" asked Melinda looking at her mother with questioning eyes.

"Well, Brandon doesn't know exactly where she is. She was riding in the van for a long time and she's traveled a very long way from us."

"I can still feel her though," said the child. She yawned again and smuggled down deeper under the covers.

"I know you can," said her mother as she tucked the covers around her. "I just wish you were old enough to tell us where she is."

"She doesn't know where she is, Mommy. Maybe if she can figure it out, she can let me know, too," mumbled Melinda drowsily.

\*\*\*

Reverend Forester was exasperated with the Hamilton boys. They had completely failed in their mission to find wives. And now their parents wanted him to break his own rules and let them marry two of Seth Willis' daughters.

"How do you think that would look to the rest of my flock if I let your boys do that?" he asked Elijah sternly.

"Well, those girls have to marry someone! We've been here a long time, but we're still first generation members. Our blood should still be considered untainted enough for your precious gene pool," insisted Rebecca fighting for her sons. They were both too young in her estimation to have a stand off with the reverend.

"Now, Rebecca," said Elijah putting his hand on her arm. "There's no need to be rude. We can all be sensible about this."

Rebecca exhaled and nodded. "I'm sorry, Reverend. I just lost my temper for a minute. Can you forgive me? I know your rules are important, but it is true that our blood has not ever mingled with others here in your flock."

Reverend Forester smiled at the feisty little woman. "I forgive you."

"And we have always been contributing members since we moved here," reminded Elijah. "That shows how community minded we feel."

"That is true, too. Have your sons said anything to the Willis girls about marrying them?" asked the Reverend.

"Oh, no. They would never do that with out your permission," said Elijah.

"All right then. I will talk to Seth tonight. His daughters are both of marrying age. If he is agreeable, then I will talk to his daughters."

"If I might suggest, Reverend," said Rebecca. "My Able fancies Ruth and Joshua says he likes Hulda."

Reverend Forester nodded. "I'll see what I can do."

"Thank you, Reverend. Thank you," said Elijah shaking his hand. "We really appreciate you doing this for the boys."

***

It was Thursday afternoon before Brandon could convince his department head that he was the one who needed to go east to look for Elizabeth.

"I think you're too close to this one," the chief had said. "After all, she is your stepdaughter. The FBI is searching for her and I've got some of my best officers working on this case day and night."

Brandon shook his head. "And just what have they accomplished?"

Chief Reynolds rolled his eyes and conceded that Brandon had a point. "All right. Go to West Virginia. Take Belle and see what the two of you can find out."

"Thanks, Chief. I need to do this because she is my stepdaughter."

"Yeah, yeah. You would have gone anyway, wouldn't you?"

Brandon nodded. "Yes, I was about to hand you my badge."

Reynolds waved his hand at the door. "Get going. Try to keep your expenses to a minimum, if you can."

"Don't worry, I'm covering those myself."

The airport was packed when they got there that evening. They took a redeye flight, but with the plane changes and layovers, it was Friday morning before they landed in the Charleston, West Virginia airport. Brandon paid for a rental car and they carried their luggage out to the rental car lot.

"It's that blue one over there," he said as he led the way to the car. Belle followed close behind and they put their luggage in the trunk and climbed in the Nissan.

"I've got the maps with the locations of the three churches we want to find," said Belle. "Two of them are Pentecostal and one is a Faith Tabernacle church. There's one in a little town about twenty miles from here."

She gave him directions and they drove along some beautiful back roads through hills and forests. The little town was situated between two mountains in a narrow valley. The church building was the biggest one in the center of the hamlet. There was also a grocery store and a gas station. A few houses could be seen behind a stand of large oak trees.

Brandon parked in front of the store and they went inside. There were two men sitting on stools at the soda fountain. Both of them turned and looked over at the newcomers. The man behind the counter looked at them too, but no one said a word as Brandon walked up to the counter. They all just stared at him.

"Morning, gentlemen," said Brandon. "We're looking for the town preacher. Is his house anywhere nearby?"

A scrawny man on the stool closest to Brandon snickered. Brandon turned and looked at him. He had a scraggly beard and greasy brown hair that hung down to his shoulders.

The man glanced at Belle and said, "Our preacher ain't gonna marry no white man and colored girl if that's what you're aiming to ask him." He leered at Belle and smiled. He was missing at least two of his front teeth and the rest didn't look too healthy. "Even one as pretty as this here girl."

Brandon reached over and grabbed the man by the bib of his overalls and lifted him off the stool. The man's feet dangled a foot above the floor and he let out a squeal.

"What business is it of yours?" asked Brandon.

The man grinned up at Brandon. "I'm the head deacon in the church."

Lord have mercy, thought Belle. If Elizabeth is here with these people, Brandon will kill someone before we leave this place.

The clerk behind the counter moved closer and said to Brandon, "Don't mind him. He's also the town drunk."

Brandon gently placed the man back on his stool. He pulled out his badge and held it out for them all to see. "I'm Detective Marcus and Ms.

Aspas is my partner. Maybe one of you nice fellows would like to answer my question?"

The clerk said, "Pastor Riley lives in the yellow house just beyond that stand of oak trees. He's usually at home this time of morning."

"Thank you. You boys have a nice day," said Brandon patting the scraggly man on the back a bit roughly.

As they left they heard the man behind the counter say, "Jeb, you're an idiot."

Brandon was cussing under his breath as they walked along the road to the pastor's house. "Bunch of backwoods hillbillies," he said out loud.

"It's all right, Brandon. I don't let that kind of stupidity bother me."

Brandon smiled down at the petite woman.

"I wish they knew you like I do. If they saw how quickly you tossed that street junkie on his backside last month they wouldn't dare make snide remarks about you."

She laughed. "That junkie was a bit surprised, wasn't he? Coach says I'm the smallest and best street fighter he's ever had in his class."

The pastor's house was the first one on the dirt road behind the oak trees. Brandon stepped up on the porch and knocked on the door of the small yellow house. A rosy-cheeked older woman answered his knock.

"May I help you?" she asked pleasantly.

Brandon showed her his badge. "We'd like to speak to Pastor Riley."

"My husband is just finishing up his breakfast. Come inside and I'll go get him."

She led them into a small living room and they sat down on the sofa. Belle noticed several photos of children and three pictures of Jesus on the walls. The pastor came in the room a few minutes later.

"Morning," he said extending his hand. "My wife says you'd like to talk to me."

They shook hands and all sat down back down.

"We're from the California police department and we're looking for this young girl." He held up a recent photo of Elizabeth. "We wondered if you might have seen her. Elizabeth's been missing since Saturday."

"What makes you think she would be way out here in West Virginia?" asked the pastor. "Seems pretty far from California."

"The men who took her had stolen license plates from Kentucky. One of the other girls they kidnapped heard them say they lived in West Virginia," said Belle.

"So this other girl must have escaped from them?"

"It's a long story. She's diabetic and she got sick. They dropped her off at a hospital ... "

"That wouldn't be anyone from my congregation then," interrupted Riley. "We don't believe in hospitals."

"That's what the men told this girl, too," said Brandon. "But Elizabeth told them that she would go with them willingly if they left her friend where she could get medical attention."

"Did the men say why they kidnapped these girls?" asked Riley puzzled. "Were they after money?"

"No. They were after wives," said Belle.

Pastor Riley shook his head. "Not anybody from here then. We don't allow our folks to marry anyone outside our flock," he said earnestly.

Brandon pulled out the drawing of Mark. "Does this man look familiar to you?"

Riley studied the drawing and shook his head. "Sorry. I don't know this man."

"Well, thank you for your time," said Belle as they got up to leave.

Back in the car she asked Brandon, "Do you believe him?"

Brandon nodded. "But that sort of explains the narrow minded attitudes around here, doesn't it? Where to next?"

"There are two Pentecostal churches west of here," she said, looking at the map. "Both of them are in small towns up in the mountains."

"It's almost like we're on another planet up here," observed Brandon as he started the car. "The air even smells different. Must be because there's no smog."

"It certainly is different from California," agreed Belle.

***

After Matthew had explained to his parents what happened with Maria, Anna said, "You did the right thing. The girl could have died before you even got her here and we wouldn't have been able to help her."

"I know and I just couldn't let that happen," said Matthew.

"Mark will just have to wait to find a wife," said John.

Mark looked at his dad, then over at his mother. "I really want to marry one of the girls from here," he said. "I know the reverend has all those rules, but she and I love each other. I only went with Matthew because I had to."

John looked stricken. "Oh, Mark. I don't think he would allow it."

But Anna asked, "Who is she, Mark?"

"It's Thomas Atkins oldest daughter, Eve. Mom, I think I've loved Evie since I was seventeen years old." He bowed his head. "And she said she loves me."

"She came to me a few weeks ago and confessed she loved Mark. She was terribly upset that he had gone on a hunt." Anna looked at John. "Isn't Thomas your second cousin?"

John nodded. "Yes, he is."

"Well, that means Mark and Evie are only third cousins. Marriage shouldn't be a problem. They're not that closely related and it would be legal," insisted Anna.

"It's the reverend's policy, not mine," said John with a shrug.

"But if they love each other ... maybe we could go and talk to Thomas and see what he thinks about it," Anna suggested.

John sighed. "I guess we could go this evening and see what he thinks."

John and Anna went with Mark after supper that evening to visit the Atkins.

Thomas Atkins was just heading back from the barn. "Evening cousin John, Anna. Can I do something for you?"

Anna nudged Mark and he stepped forward.

"Evening, cousin Thomas," he said shyly. "I was wondering if I could talk to you about something important."

"Sure thing, come on inside."

They followed him back into the house.

Eve was helping her mother clean up the kitchen but when she spotted Mark her eyes widened. "Hello Mark, Mr. and Mrs. Hensley." She left the kitchen and came over to sit next to her father on the sofa.

Mark looked at his mother for support then cleared his throat.

"Well, you see, Mr. Atkins. I've come to ask for Evie's hand in marriage," he said boldly.

Thomas looked at his daughter. "What's all this about, Evie?"

She shrugged and shook her head. But she looked at Mark with hope in her eyes.

"I thought you went to California to hunt a bride," said Thomas.

Mark nodded. "I did, but only because I thought I had to. It didn't work out, thank goodness, because I love Evie," he admitted. "Mr. Atkins, I've loved Evie ever since I can remember. We once even promised each other we would get married."

"We did," smiled Eve. "Please, Papa. You know I love Mark, I'll never be happy with anyone else," insisted Eve. She took her father by the hand. "Please say yes."

"I don't know, Evie. The reverend has some pretty strong ideas about this sort of thing."

"Evie and I are only third cousins," said Mark. "Will you allow me to talk to the reverend about us getting married? I would like to have your blessing."

Thomas was skeptical, but Eve was his favorite and he always gave in to her. "I guess if she wants to marry you, I won't stand in the way."

Eve hugged her father around the neck. "Oh, thank you, Papa."

Now they just had to convince Reverend Forester.

Reverend Forester threw his hands in the air when Mark told him that he and Eve wanted to get married. "You're the second family to come to me with this kind of request!" He looked over at John. "How closely are they related?"

"They're only third cousins. And you have to admit that both our families are all a healthy bunch. No stillborns from either side as far back as I can remember. No simple minded souls or handicaps," informed John. He and Mark held their breath while Reverend Forester considered the request.

"Her father agrees with this? You've already spoken to him?" asked the reverend. He was pacing around his den trying to decide. "And Eve agrees, too?"

"Yes, sir," said Mark. "I'll make her a good husband, I promise. You know what a hard worker I am."

"That is true," agreed the Reverend. "But I seem to recall that you can have a bit of a temper at times."

Mark hung his head. "I'm working real hard to control that, Reverend. I would never do anything to hurt Evie. I promise."

"I want to talk to Eve. Have her come see me tomorrow and then I'll make my decision. I promise to pray about it to learn the Lord's will, then I'll let you know."

They left happy that he hadn't rejected the idea immediately.

"I think he'll come around," said John.

Mark looked over at his father and smiled. "He will if Evie has anything to say about it."

\*\*\*

It was a beautiful spring afternoon when Michael Andrew picked up Cynthia and drove her in a horse drawn buggy to see her newly finished house.

"My grandfather built this buggy," informed Michael. "Mom thought it would be a romantic way to take you to see the house."

Cynthia laughed as she settled herself on the worn leather seat. "She was right."

It was a short mile to their land. The little log house was nestled at the edge of a stand of trees. It was the first one to be finished for the new couples and the men had done a wonderful job. It had a front porch that stretched the full length of the house. Michael's father waited for them in one of the rocking chairs outside.

Michael stopped in front and helped Cynthia out of the buggy. He tied the horse up to the porch rail and took her by the arm.

"I was so excited about finishing it I couldn't wait to show you," he said. "I hope you like it. I know I do."

As they climbed up the front steps Michael asked his father, "Where's Mother?"

"She had one of her bad headaches," informed Paul. "She's resting up for your wedding tonight and couldn't come with me."

Michael nodded. He opened the front door and ushered Cynthia inside. "It's not a big house," he apologized. "But it's made so we can add more rooms later as we may need them." Then he blushed.

Cynthia laughed at him. "You mean for our future children?"

He nodded.

She stopped and stood in the middle of the living room gazing in awe at her new home. She couldn't believe that by this evening she would be able to start her new life with Michael in their own house. Her parents had never had a home of their own and had always rented apartments. To her this was absolutely amazing.

He walked her over into the kitchen area. It wasn't fancy but there was a new refrigerator and stove. There were no dishwasher or microwave or other modern conveniences, but there were lots of cupboards and a lovely table and chairs stood to one side of the room.

The living room and kitchen were one big room and at the far end was a stone fireplace. A small hallway led to the two bedrooms. The smaller one was empty.

"Is this where my bride's bed will go?" she asked him.

"Yes, and Michael's already working on a cradle," joked Paul.

"Dad, that was a surprise," scolded Michael blushing again.

"Sorry, son."

Cynthia laughed at the two of them.

The bathroom had an old-fashioned claw foot tub and a sink with a wooden cabinet for towels. A pretty oval mirror hung above the sink.

Cynthia walked from room to room caressing the furniture. No one would ever know that it had all been handmade in a few short weeks. The floor was freshly finished oak and it shone where the sun came through the windows and touched it. Her blue and white flowered curtains billowed out from the windows in the warm breeze. She could smell the scent of honeysuckle carried inside on the wind.

She turned to Michael. "It's the most beautiful house in the world. Thank you for making all this for me." Her face glowed with happiness.

"Well, I didn't make it all by myself," he said humbly. "My Dad and all the men here helped me. Especially with the furniture. My Dad is really good at that."

"It's the nicest thing anyone has ever done for me," she said and her eyes filled with tears. "I never dreamed something this wonderful could ever happen to little old me." She sniffed and wiped her eyes.

Michael thought she was the most beautiful thing he had ever seen and right now he was happier than he had ever been. He reached over and brushed a strand of chestnut hair from her cheek and tucked it behind her ear.

"All right you two," said Paul. "Time to go. Cynthia has to get ready and your Mother will kill me if we're late getting her back to the cottage."

"Oh, my gosh, I better hurry," said Cynthia looking at the time.

They were due to get married in a little ceremony at the church in less than hour. When they dropped Cynthia off at the bride's cottage Mary Forester and Anna were waiting for her. Cynthia hurried to get changed.

"Have you decided what Biblical name you would like to have?" asked Mary as she laid out the wedding dress. "I mean, if you want to choose to change your name."

"I think I want my name to be Lydia," she said as Anna braided her hair. "She was the first Christian convert from the New Testament. She wanted to change her life and follow Jesus and I do, too. I've been thinking about it ever since the reverend baptized me last week."

"That's a good choice," said Mary as she slipped the dress over Cynthia's head carefully so as not to disturb her hair.

In her new ankle length white dress and with white daisies in her hair, Cynthia looked lovely as they walked the short distance to the church.

Elizabeth and Melody followed the others a few steps behind.

"My house will be finished in a few days," confided Melody. "Then it will be my turn to get married. I can hardly wait. Rueben is working day and night to finish everything."

"I'm happy for you," whispered Elizabeth as they entered the little chapel.

Michael was standing by the altar with Reverend Forester. His father walked Cynthia, soon to be called Lydia, down the aisle. Rachel was beaming as her son took his bride's arm and turned to face the reverend. The ceremony was short and the guests all clapped when Michael kissed his bride for the first time.

Someone started playing the fiddle and someone else joined in on a trumpet. The pianist pounded out music with gusto as the whole congregation rose to their feet and started dancing. Elizabeth had never seen such a wild wedding. Everyone seemed to be enjoying themselves immensely as they twirled and laughed.

Rueben came over and grabbed Melody by the hand.

"This is the only time we are allowed to touch until we get married and I plan on making the most of it," he laughed as he whirled her out onto the dance floor.

Matthew came over and stood by Elizabeth. He smiled and handed her a cup of punch. "Do you want to dance?" he asked.

She shook her head. "No, thank you."

"Have you been looking at the list of names the reverend gave you?"

She nodded.

"Have you found one you like?" he asked.

"I want to keep my own name. Elisabeth was the mother of John the Baptist. Do you think it would be all right if I didn't change my name?" she asked.

"I like Elisabeth, too. I don't think he'll make you change it since you already have a Biblical name," said Matthew. "My mother didn't have to change her name when the reverend baptized her."

Elizabeth looked up quickly. "That's right, mother wasn't born here."

"No, she was born in Texas and brought here."

"I remember Mark saying that was twenty-five years ago."

Elizabeth started to ask more questions, but Matthew's father called him away. She stood against the wall watching all the people dancing and waving their arms around and she shivered. "Please let Brandon find me soon," she prayed softly.

***

Brandon and Belle were lost. In the last two days they had driven over so many side roads through the mountains they were no longer even sure where they were. When they finally spotted a small group of buildings they pulled over and went inside a grocery store to ask for directions.

"Excuse me, sir," said Brandon to the store clerk at the front register. "Can you tell me what town this is?"

The clerk laughed. "You're in Grundy, Virginia. Got lost in the mountains, did you? It happens all the time. Where are you headed?"

"We're trying to find Jolo, West Virginia."

"Well, you've come a little too far south. If you go back out on route 83 and head northeast it's just back over the state line. If you get to Bradshaw, you've missed it."

"Thanks," said Brandon.

"Brandon, it's getting late," said Belle. "Maybe we should find a place to stay for the night. At least this town is big enough for that. And I'm getting hungry."

"There's a Comfort Inn just up the road near the Appalachian School of Law. And the Italian Village has good food," informed the store clerk. "You don't want to be driving the mountain roads to Jolo in the dark. Most of the cliff roads don't have guardrails and we've lost tourists there before," he warned.

"Thanks, I think we'll take your advice," said Brandon.

Back in the car Belle said, "A law school out here in the middle of the mountains. I never would have imagined. These are some pretty hardy people out here."

Brandon sighed in disgust. "I can't believe we're not even in West Virginia any more. There were no signs that said we'd entered Virginia."

As they rounded a bend in the road that ran next to the river, they saw a Wal-mart Supercenter that was built on top of a two story parking garage.

"Would you look at that!" said Belle. "I'll bet you won't find any place else that has a Wal-mart like that. I guess it's built so high off the ground because this little valley is in a flood plain."

"How in the world do you know that?" asked Brandon looking at her questioningly.

"It says so on that sign by the river," she answered pointing to a road sign.

"Oh. OK, then."

"There's the Italian Village. I'm starved," said Belle.

"Let's eat and get some sleep. We'll find Jolo in the morning," agreed Brandon with a sigh. "I'm beginning to feel like those men with Elizabeth have dropped off the face of the earth."

Belle looked at him sympathetically. "I'm sorry this is turning out to be so hard. But we'll find her," she said.

\*\*\*

On Sunday morning the Hensley's picked up Elizabeth on their way to church.

"It's a little scary at first," warned Matthew. "But if you're going to live here you might as well see it now as later."

A chill ran down her spine as she remembered that Mark had mentioned that they belonged to a snake handling church.

"Will there be snakes at church?" she asked.

"Usually. But they aren't always out of their box."

"You won't let anything bad happen to me, will you Matthew?" she asked.

"Of course not. Nobody is forced to pick up a snake. It will be all right, I promise."

The church services were the strangest that Elizabeth had ever seen. There was loud music as well as hymns, and the people sometimes got up and danced, waving their hands over their heads and spinning around calling out prayers in what they called speaking in tongues. It was all so foreign to her, but that was nothing compared to when the reverend brought out the snakes. Elizabeth thought she was going to faint when Matthew walked over and picked up a rattlesnake. He held it out and talked to it as it curled around his arm.

"It's all right," said Anna putting a comforting hand on Elizabeth's arm. "Just sit still and watch. You don't have to do it."

Elizabeth slid over on the bench closer to Anna and hid her face in a songbook.

"It takes a lot of getting used to," said John. "I've seen it since I was a boy, but it sure frightened Anna when she first came here."

"Do people get bitten?" whispered Elizabeth.

"Sometimes they do."

"But don't they die?" she asked worriedly.

A young woman walked by the end of their pew with a snake across her shoulders and Elizabeth cringed away.

"Sometimes they die, sometimes not," said John with a shrug.

Elizabeth looked around and noted that thankfully there were very few children in attendance. The youngest looked to be about twelve years old. It seemed even more horrible to her if a child was bitten and died. She leaned closer to Anna.

"Where are the little children?" she asked.

"There aren't very many young ones right now. Aaron Brown's youngest child is ten, but I don't see them here today. Now that we'll have young married couples in our group, we'll soon have babies again," she said smiling.

"Doesn't that frighten you?" asked Elizabeth horrified at the thought.

"Reverend doesn't let small children handle the snakes," said John.

"But there are some just crawling around," she said. Elizabeth lifted her feet as one slithered past under their bench.

Anna shrugged. "You get used to it."

Elizabeth looked over at Cynthia, now called Lydia. She was watching with fascination as Michael held up a viper. It curled around his hand as he caressed its back. Elizabeth doubted she could ever get used to this.

Anna followed her gaze. "I wonder if Rachel's not here because she still has that bad headache," she said. "Last night she said it was the worst one she's ever had."

"But she won't go to a doctor, will she?" asked Elizabeth.

Anna shook her head. "Granny gives her some arnica potion to help with the pain. Sometimes it does help. They usually go away after a while."

Elizabeth wondered if Rachel's headaches were migraines or a symptom of something much worse. These people seemed unconcerned that someone could die if they didn't see a doctor. Then she remembered what Mark had told her, dying was just the next step. No one seemed afraid of it at all.

The bizarre scene at the church lasted for thirty more minutes with people singing, praying and dancing with the snakes. Finally Reverend Forester had them put the snakes back into some decorated boxes. A final prayer was said and everyone started leaving.

Anna was going to Melody's new house to help put up her curtains and she didn't want Elizabeth to be alone in the brides' cottage. She dropped her off at Granny Hensley's cabin.

"I'll come back for you after lunch," said Anna. "You don't mind helping Granny get her lunch, do you?"

"No, I'd be happy to help," said Elizabeth as she looked at the little old woman sitting in a rocking chair by the fireplace. There was a small fire burning even though it was a warm spring day and the old woman wore a shawl over her shoulders.

"Come on over here, child," said the woman in whispery voice. "My eyesight ain't so good these days and I gots to sit by the fire most days now as it always feels right airish to me."

Anna noticed at the puzzled expression on Elizabeth's face.

"Airish means chilly," she explained. "Granny was born and raised in these mountains and she uses a lot of local folk words. I'll be back shortly."

Elizabeth nodded and walked over to the old woman.

"I be ninety-three years old now," said the woman. Her hair was white and thinning and her face as wrinkled as an old apple doll's. But she wore a bright smile and her eyes twinkled when she peered at Elizabeth. "You be the girl Matthew found?"

"Yes," said Elizabeth pulling up a chair to sit by Granny.

"Don't be shy, it's always chancy when the men goes hunting wives, but peers Matthew done real good a choosen you," she laughed and Elizabeth noticed that she was missing all of her teeth. "What did you think of the church service?"

"It was certainly different," said Elizabeth.

Granny laughed. "That it be, but you'll get used to the snakes."

Elizabeth couldn't help but smile at the old woman. "I'm not so sure about that," she said softly. "And I really miss my family."

"That can be right discomforting, that's true." Granny nodded as she rocked.

"Especially Elaine."

"That be your mother?" asked the old woman. She stopped rocking and patted Elizabeth's hand. "How old you be girl?"

"I just turned eighteen."

Granny laughed and her eyes twinkled. "I had three younguns by the time I turned eighteen. I guess times have changed."

"Elaine is my adopted mother. My mother died when I was a little girl. My father was murdered when I was thirteen. Elaine was my nurse and she adopted me," explained Elizabeth. "Then she married Brandon, so I have a stepfather, too."

"How come you had a nurse when you was thirteen? Seems a bit old for that."

"She wasn't like a nurse maid. Elaine's a Registered Nurse. I was really sick and my father hired her to help me," explained Elizabeth. "Actually, I was dying."

"You be lying to me girl? You don't look dead to me," said Granny skeptically. "You must think I'm plum crazy to believe a story like that."

"No. It's true. My mother died of a brain disease. I inherited it. My father was a doctor and he did experiments and found a way for me to have an operation that fixed my brain," insisted Elizabeth. "I wouldn't lie to you, honest."

Granny Hensley thought for a minute. "That be a big problem then," she said seriously.

"Why? I'm perfectly fine now, " said Elizabeth. "I'm not sick at all."

"That be true. But what about your babes? Couldn't they be borned with that same problem in their brains?" asked Granny.

"That probably would happen. The disorder is a dominant gene, mine just showed up earlier than it does in most people. My mother was almost thirty, but I was only thirteen," she shrugged. "My doctor fixed it so I couldn't have children. I'll have to adopt when I want a baby."

Granny sucked in her bottom lip. "I reckon that would work out in your world. But that be a problem here. Reverend won't like having a girl with bad genes who can't have no babes."

Elizabeth stared at her. "Does that mean he might let me go back home?" she asked hopefully.

Granny shook her head. "You been here. You seen our home. You could tell folks how to find us. Outsiders don't like the snakes and our strange ways, especially the hunt."

Elizabeth didn't like the way that sounded. Did that mean they would keep her prisoner or even kill her to keep her from showing others where this little community was located?

Granny reached over and patted her hand. "Don't look so scared. Nobody's a going to hurt you. But Matthew will have to find his self a different bride."

Elizabeth held her breath and didn't say anything. If Brandon didn't find her, and she would never be able to leave this place, what would become of her here?

"I thinks I'll have lunch now. Go fetch that cornpone a setting on the table. Cut me a big piece and put lots a butter on it and a little of that jam Anna made for me," Granny instructed Elizabeth.

Elizabeth cut a piece of the cornbread and put it on one of the plates sitting on the table. She buttered it and spread strawberry jam on the top then carried it to the old woman. She handed her the plate and sat back down.

"You git yourself one too," said Granny. "Nothing better in the world than warm cornpone. And it don't take no teeth to eat it." She smiled and took a bite.

Elizabeth didn't feel like eating anything. In fact she felt afraid and sick to her stomach wondering what would happen when the reverend heard about her illness. "I don't feel very hungry right now," she told Granny.

Granny patted her hand. "Maybe later," she said as she munched on her lunch.

Anna came and picked Elizabeth up a few minutes later.

"Do you want to come home with me?" asked Anna.

Elizabeth shook her head. "I think I need to rest. I don't feel very well."

"Too much excitement," said Anna. "What with the wedding last night and church services this morning." She walked her the few blocks to the brides' cottage. "You get some rest and I'll come get you when it's dinner time."

The cottage was quiet and Elizabeth fell asleep on her little bed after a few minutes. She had horrible dreams about snakes and being kept as a prisoner. After an hour she woke up with a headache, drenched in sweat. She got out of bed and took a bath hoping it would make her feel better. She was going to have to tell Anna and Matthew her problem. Maybe they would help her escape or maybe Brandon would come and find her soon.

***

Melinda woke up screaming. Her mother ran into her room and turned on the bedside lamp. Melinda was shaking. Janice picked her up and carried her to the master bedroom and put her in the bed. Bill pulled her over next to him.

"What's wrong, Honey? Did you have a bad dream again?" he asked.

Melinda started crying. "It's Elizabeth. She's afraid of the snakes."

Janice climbed into bed next to the little girl.

"It will be all right. Brandon will find her, I promise."

"But Mommy. There are snakes at the church and Elizabeth is afraid of snakes. Will they make her touch one?" sniffed Melinda.

"I don't know, honey."

"I hope they don't make her touch one," said the child. Melinda put her head on her father's pillow beside his head.

Bill looked at Janice and mouthed, "A snake-handling church?"

She nodded. "Elaine told me that Maria said the men belonged to some snake-handling church in West Virginia."

Bill shook his head. "I didn't even know those still existed." He pulled the covers up around Melinda and looked at Janice.

"So much for sleeping late on Sunday," he complained.

She smiled and climbed back out of bed. "I'll go make pancakes."

\*\*\*

Jacob had gone to The Church of Jesus Christ of Latter-day Saints with the Smalley family that morning and he was impressed with the Mormon speakers who had given talks that day.

Susan explained to him that there were no paid clergy in their church. Their leadership was all volunteer and the men were "called" to the position. They worked at jobs just like anyone else and took care of their congregations, called Wards, in their "spare" time. It all seemed strange to him, to not have a paid preacher.

The speakers that day were a youth speaker and a woman and her husband. Susan said sometimes they were assigned topics by the Bishop who was over the Ward, and sometimes they prayed about which topic they should pick on their own. The speakers that day talked about Christ's atonement and of God's love for all his children. The talks were all well presented and thought provoking.

"Seems to me that it would be frightening to get up and have to give a sermon in front of all those people," Jacob told Susan after the service was over and they were walking to the car.

"No one is forced to speak. But if you're raised in the church you get used to it. I've given short talks since I was four years old," explained Susan. "Those were just in front of the other children in what we call Primary. But it gets you practice for giving talks later in front of the adults."

"I've given talks, too," added Will. "But it was a little scary," he admitted.

"I think it would scare me more than handling a rattlesnake," said Jacob thoughtfully. "In fact, I'm sure it would."

Susan's eyes widened. "You handle rattlesnakes?"

He nodded. "And vipers and other snakes."

"In church?" she asked surprised.

"Most Sundays," he admitted.

# Chapter 11

Reverend Forester opened the door and faced the Johnson boys. He figured he knew what they wanted before they even spoke a word. "Afternoon."

Randy Johnson was the first to say something.

"Afternoon, Reverend. It was a nice ceremony you did Saturday evening for Michael. Real nice," he complimented.

"Thank you. What can I do for you two fellows?"

"Well," hemmed Ricky Johnson. "We was wondering, since you announced the decision to let the Hensley boy marry Evie, if you'd help us find wives?"

The Reverend cleared his throat. "Well, Ricky. I talked to Esther Brown, but she wasn't too keen on getting married just yet," he apologized. "You fellows have any other women in mind for me to talk to? Anyone ready to get married?"

"Yes, sir," said Randy. "I'm kind of partial to Deborah Wilson."

"Have you spoken to the young lady yet?" asked Reverend Forester.

Randy blushed. "Kind of. She don't know me too well, but she didn't run away screaming or anything."

The Reverend was having trouble keeping a straight face. "I could talk to her father for you and see how he feels about it."

Randy smiled. "Thank you kindly."

"How about you, Ricky?"

"I've really got my heart set on Esther," he said earnestly. "She's real spunky."

The Reverend sighed. "All right. I'll talk to her father again. What have you two got to offer these brides?"

"Asides the five acres and house you all would be givin' us, Pa said we could each have a milk cow and ten chickens," said Randy.

"And we both been making furniture like you told us. Ma has made us quilts and such. And she's put together a mighty fine stock of kitchen gadgets," informed Ricky.

"Well, that sounds like a good start. I'll see what I can do."

The Reverend watched out the window as the men walked away. He turned to his wife and said, "I guess the old way of hunting wives is going out of fashion."

She nodded. "You didn't have to 'hunt' me," she reminded.

"True, I loved you the minute your family moved here more than fifty years ago," he said smiling at her. "I guess I've just wanted to keep my flock healthy."

"Seems to me that the Andrew and Smith boys did all right. They found sweet young wives without having to steal them," she said looking up from her knitting.

"You're right on that," he nodded. "I'm worried about the pretty young thing Matthew brought here. She seems to be settling in, but she doesn't seem too happy."

"Anna Hensley wasn't happy when she first came here either. But she loves her family with all her heart now," reminded Mary.

The Reverend nodded and looked out the window at the trees surrounding his house. As he reflected on his wife's statement, he felt guilty. Anna only gave up trying to escape after her face had been cut. He still felt horrible about that every time he saw her scar. After the third time Anna had been caught in the woods trying to escape, he had brought her here to his house and threatened her life. He never would have really harmed her, but he wanted to scare her with the knife.

Back then, she hadn't seemed to realize how dangerous it was out in the woods by herself or how far she was from civilization. He had worried that she would die out in the woods if she didn't stop running away. But when he had waved the knife threateningly at her, she had jumped up to push past him. He had lost his balance and the knife slashed her cheek. The blood had splattered everywhere and she fainted. He still shuddered thinking about the scene even now. Mary had sewn up her wound and done a wonderful job. It had healed and never gotten infected, but the scar was forever visible.

After that, the young man who had kidnapped Anna decided she was too much for him to handle. John Hensley had nursed her back to health. He had loved her and helped her find peace here. The Reverend sighed. It was no use worrying about the past. There was nothing he could do to change it.

Reverend Forester looked over at his wife. "I think I'll take a little walk and go visit Brother Brown. I promised the Johnson's I'd talk to him again about Esther."

"All right, dear," she said. "Whatever you think is best."

It took thirty minutes for the reverend to walk to the Brown farm. Aaron Brown was in the yard playing catch with his two younger boys.

"Afternoon, Reverend. You boys go play on the other side of the barn while I talk to the reverend," he said tossing the ball to Isaac.

"Aaron," said Reverend Forester reluctantly. "I promised Ricky Johnson I'd come talk to you again about Esther marrying him."

Aaron's face clouded. "I thought we had all ready told you how we felt about that, Reverend. She's not inclined to marry that man. I'm sorry."

Reverend Forester sighed. "Indeed you did. But Ricky really fancies what he calls a spunky girl and you have to admit Esther is spunky."

"He calls her that because she stood up to him when he was bullying my young son Isaac," informed Aaron. "Those two men can be right mean when they get a mind to be, Reverend. Esther deserves better than that."

Reverend raised his eyebrows. "I wasn't aware of that fault in them. I'll have a good talk with them both and let them know we won't have that kind of behavior in our community. It's not the Christian way I want us all to live."

"And forcing girls to marry someone they don't love is Christian?" asked Aaron in disgust. "Just to let you know, I've sold my farm. Jacob's on his way back here to help us pack up. Me and mine are moving to Idaho to be with him."

"You're moving away to live with Mormons?" asked Forester shocked.

"Jacob tells me they're real nice people with good family values."

"I'm right sorry to hear you'll be leaving us." The Reverend held out his hand.

"If you decide to come back, you're family will always be welcome."

Aaron nodded. "Thank you, Reverend. I'm sorry it's come to this." Aaron shook his hand and watched as Reverend Forester walked away. There was an obvious new weariness in his step.

***

It was midmorning Sunday when Brandon and Belle finally found Jolo, West Virginia. The local gas station attendant answered their questions while Brandon filled up the car.

"If you're looking for *The Church of The Lord Jesus With Signs Following* it's just up the road," he told them. "It's the only snake-handling church in town. Just keep following this road and look for the church building on your left."

"Thanks," said Brandon as he paid for the gas.

The church turned out to be a small, wood framed building on the lip of a ravine. They could hear voices as they parked the rental car next to a battered truck. Brandon led the way and opened the door to the most bizarre church service he had ever witnessed.

Inside the building, Church members were singing in loud voices accompanied by electric guitars, a piano, an organ and tambourines. Three women in brightly flowered skirts were twirling around with hands raised over their heads. Every one was clapping and dancing and singing.

Brandon and Belle stayed close to the wall out of the way of the dancers as they walked further into the room. The music was catchy, with a kind of Appalachian Pentecostal rockabilly musical sound. Belle found herself smiling and tapping her toes as she watched the frenzied dancing. Everyone seemed to be deliriously happy singing about the Lord Jesus. As the two of them crept closer to the pulpit they noticed several boxes sitting on the floor. One box had a cross carved into the lid and "Jesus saves" written on the end.

One of the men danced over to the box and lifted the lid. Belle jumped back as he pulled out a four-foot timber rattlesnake. He danced away with it in his outstretched hands crooning softly to the snake.

A woman whirled by with a snake stretched across her shoulders and beatific smile on her face as she spoke a gibberish language.

"That must be what's called speaking in tongues," said Brandon leaning over closer to Belle so she could hear him over the loud music.

Both of them pressed their backs to the wall as more worshipers came forward and lifted snakes from the boxes. Brandon identified vipers and diamond back rattlesnakes being carried around by men and women as if they were harmless toys. The music blared and the dancers swirled in front of them for several more minutes, then one of the pastors indicated that it was time to stop. All the snakes were returned to the boxes and the chairs replaced in rows as the music died down.

"Salvation is something that makes you feel good!" said the pastor loudly.

"Amen," came the chorus from the congregation.

"Let us now close with a prayer."

The pastor offered a simple prayer and the people began to leave. Some stared at the newcomers standing against the wall, others blithely passed them by.

The pastor came over and introduced himself. Belle noticed a bandage on his right hand as he extended it for a handshake.

"Name's Dewey Chaplee, assistant pastor of *The Church of the Lord Jesus*. How may I help you fine folks?" he asked.

Brandon made introductions and showed the pastor his badge.

"We're trying to locate a young woman who was abducted from California. From what we've learned so far she was brought to West Virginia by someone from as snake-handling church such as this."

"Oh, well, I can assure you it wasn't by anyone from my congregation. I see all of them just about everyday and no one's done any traveling lately," said Chaplee.

Belle pulled out the drawing of Mark. "Do you recognize this man?"

Pastor Chaplee carefully studied the drawing.

"It looks kinda like the oldest Hensley boy. It's hard to tell from a drawing though," he admitted. "I saw him and his daddy at one of the revivals a few years back."

Brandon felt a surge of hope. "Do you know where they live?" he asked.

"Don't know exactly, but they go to a church led by Reverend Forester up in the mountains about a six hour drive from here."

"Further in the mountains than this?" asked Belle incredulously.

The pastor chuckled. "Afraid so, little lady."

"Why does your church believe in handling snakes?" she asked respectfully. "I don't mean to be disrespectful or anything, I'm just curious."

"We believe that all the words in the Bible should be followed," he explained. "The gospel of Mark in chapter 16 says that *'these signs shall follow them that believe; In my name shall they cast out devils; they shall speak with new tongues; they shall take up serpents; and if they drink any deadly thing, it shall not hurt them; they shall lay hands on the sick, and they shall recover.'* Now that doesn't mean that no one will ever get hurt by the snakes or poison, but we believe it is a way to show God we trust in Him and will follow whatever is His way."

Belle nodded.

"I myself was bit last week. But I'm still here, so I guess it wasn't my time to leave this earth yet," he chuckled as he extended his bandaged hand.

"You believe in faith healing, not in doctors and hospitals, is that correct?" she asked. "And you don't celebrate holidays?"

"Most holidays elevate men, not God. We try not to do that."

"Could you give us some idea of how to find this Reverend Forester?" asked Brandon. "It's very important that we find this girl before she is forced to marry one of the men who kidnapped her."

"Are they doing that again?" asked Chaplee shaking his head. "Forester had them do that about twenty-five years ago. I hadn't heard about it since then."

"They've done this before?" asked Belle shocked.

"Back then his following was smaller than mine. He didn't want too much intermarrying. Seems a poor thing to do to me. My folks find their own spouses and we haven't had too many problems," he told Belle.

He turned to Brandon. "If you follow route 83 to Bradshaw and go north on 80 to Logan, I can give you the name of a man who can help you find Forester's church."

While the pastor told him the man's name and where he lived, Brandon wrote down the information. "Thanks for all your help."

Belle smiled. "I don't think I'll ever forget seeing your service today."

The pastor chuckled, "I imagine you will remember it. Good luck. Hope you find the girl you're looking for."

***

When Anna went to check on the girls in the brides' cottage that evening she found Elizabeth lying on her bed crying. She walked over and sat on the edge of her bed. "Elizabeth, I know it's hard being away from home, can I help?" she asked sympathetically.

Elizabeth sat up and wiped her eyes. "How did you stand it when they first brought you here, Anna? I'm so homesick."

Anna sighed. "It was horrible at first. My parents were both dead, but I missed my older sister terribly. I had been living close to her and her family when the man who kidnapped me took me away from my dorm room at college."

Elizabeth looked at her. "My parents are both dead, but I love my adoptive family so much it hurts being away from them like this. Knowing that I may never see them again is impossibly hard to bear."

Anna put her arms around her. "I'm so sorry this happened to you. I never wanted my sons to hurt anyone. I hate that the reverend has so much influence over them that they would do this to you."

"When you were brought here, did you try to run away? I've thought about it."

Anna nodded sadly. "I did run away, several times. I always got lost in the woods and they found me and brought me back." Anna turned her head and traced the scar on her cheek with her finger. "Trying to escape is what got me this."

"Someone deliberately did that to you?" Elizabeth said horrified at the thought.

"Not deliberately, I've come to believe it wasn't intentional. But the reverend did it. I think he was only trying to scare me. When I overreacted, this happened," she explained. "I sometimes still have nightmares about it even after all these years."

"Is that why you stopped trying to go home, because you were ashamed?"

"No. My family would still have loved me even if I was wounded. It was while I was recovering that I met John. He helped take care of me. He has what they call a healing touch. He was so gentle and kind, I fell in love with him." She brushed Elizabeth's hair back from her wet cheek and lifted her chin to look at her face. "I hope you can learn to love Matthew. He's gentle like his father. After I fell in love and had my babies to care for, I never wanted to leave."

Elizabeth started crying again. "That's another big problem," she sobbed. "I can't ever have any children and I shouldn't have them."

"Why ever not?" asked Anna taken by surprise.

Between sobs, Elizabeth explained about her mother's death and her subsequent illness. "My father found out I had the same genetic brain disease. If it hadn't been for the brain surgery I had, I would be dead, too. I could pass that on to any children I have. I told Granny Hensley about it and she said that I wouldn't be allowed to leave now that I know where this community is located. Is that true?"

Anna stared at her for a minute. "I had no idea and of course Matthew didn't know about any of this either."

Elizabeth tilted her head forward and pulled aside her hair. A thin white scar left from the surgeon's incision was obvious along the edge of her scalp.

"It took me years to grow all my hair back after it was shaved off. That's why I keep it so long ... to cover the scar," she said as she smoothed her hair in place. "So was Granny right? Will they keep me here even if I can't marry Matthew?"

Anna nodded. "They may try. And there is no way you can find your way out of these wooded mountains on foot. I'll talk to John tonight. We'll think of something, I promise. I'm so sorry about your mother and about all of this."

Elizabeth wiped her eyes and hugged Anna. "Thank you for understanding. Have you ever had any news about your sister?"

"Once. John found out she died about ten years ago in a car accident. But that's all the news I've ever gotten," said Anna.

"I'm so sorry."

"Don't worry about me. I'm fine now. I would never want to leave John and the boys. This is my home and my life and overall it has been a good one, filled with love," she said. "Don't say anything to Melody about any of this. I don't want her to accidentally tell anyone about your illness or my plan to help you leave," warned Anna.

"What about Granny Hensley?" asked Elizabeth.

"She won't say a word to anyone. She's not overly fond of the reverend's ideas either. She's actually related to George Went Hensley, one of the founders of the first snake-handling church. He never taught that the men in his church should practice what they call here 'the hunt'. That all started with Reverend Forester," explained Anna. "So don't worry about her."

"But why does the reverend feel the need to teach that?" asked Elizabeth.

"I haven't heard the whole story, but rumor has it that he had a cousin born blind and crippled because his uncle married a first cousin."

"But isn't that against the law?"

"It is now. But back then there weren't many people living in these mountains and it was a common practice," said Anna. She stood up to leave. "I'll come see you tomorrow. Try and get some sleep."

***

Brandon slammed his fist into the steering wheel. "Damn it!" he swore. The dirt road they had been driving on for the last thirty minutes had come to a dead end. "This is another logging road. How many of these blasted things do they have in this forsaken place?" he asked Belle.

She shook her head.

Sunday afternoon they had driven to Logan to look up Seth Winchester, the man Pastor Chaplee had told them about. Turned out Seth had been a hunter and tracker in his younger days and knew the mountains better than anyone around. The problem was he was now ninety years old and having problems with his memory. They'd found him in a rest home sitting in a wheel chair eating dinner with three other old timers. Obviously he couldn't come with them, but he had tried to draw them a map. The trouble with that was that he was no longer up to date on the number of logging roads in the area they were searching.

It had been too late Sunday evening for them to start looking and they'd had to wait until Monday morning to try and follow Seth's map.

Belle handed him a bottle of water. "Here, have a drink and see if we can get turned around. It's almost lunchtime. If we stop and have a sandwich while we study the map we'll be able to think better."

After several attempts Brandon got the rental car turned around.

"It's a good thing this car has four wheel drive," said Belle.

They drove back to what could be called the main road, at least it was paved, and he pulled off to the side and parked in the shade of a big pine tree. While they ate the ham sandwiches they'd purchased from the little cafe where they'd had breakfast, Brandon studied the hand drawn map again.

"Ok, add another line right here for a logging road Seth didn't know about," he said pointing to a spot on the map. "If we update it as we go maybe we'll be able to find our way back out when it's time to leave Forester's compound."

"I'm sure it's not a compound," corrected Belle. "You make this sound like that episode that happened in Waco, Texas back in the '90's."

"Well, I'm starting to feel that way," said Brandon as he finished his sandwich.

"Sounds to me more like this Reverend Forester is just some mixed up religious leader trying to do what he thinks is right for his people," said Belle.

"That's what David Koresh said about the Branch Davidian group he was leading," scoffed Brandon. "He caused the death of twenty children and I don't remember how many adults before that conflict was finished."

Belle was silent for a few minutes. "I hope no one gets hurt when we find Elizabeth," she said somberly. "That would be awful."

Brandon started the car and pulled back onto the road. He had no idea where they were exactly, but he could see another dirt road off to the left up ahead.

"I guess we won't know about that until we find Elizabeth and this guy, Reverend Forester," said Brandon.

# Chapter 12

Jacob had five hundred dollars left from his pay and he used some of it to buy his plane ticket back to West Virginia. He had flown in late Sunday night and this morning he used the rest of his paycheck to rent a small U-haul truck to drive home and help his family move. When he drove the truck in the driveway at the farm his little brother, Isaac, ran out to meet him, his face streaked with tears.

Jacob jumped down from the truck and picked up the boy. "What's the matter?"

"Jacob, that mean Johnson man took Esther!" Isaac sobbed softly.

"What? Where's Father?" asked Jacob as he rushed towards the house with the boy in his arms.

"He's inside loading up the shotgun," informed Isaac between sobs.

"Dad! Where are you?" hollered Jacob throwing open the front door.

His father appeared in the hall doorway, the loaded shotgun in his hands.

"That SOB Ricky Johnson stole Esther right out of her bed sometime last night! I'm going right now to bring her back," Aaron stated as he held up the gun.

"Wait, I'll go with you, but we have to get the reverend first," insisted Jacob.

Aaron sighed. "I suppose we must or I'll probably kill that man."

Jacob pulled Ephraim aside and told him, "I want you to take Isaac and go to the Hensley farm. Tell John what happened. Now go!"

Ephraim grabbed Isaac by the hand and pulled him to the front door. "We'll take the back way," he shouted over his shoulder. "It's closer."

"You two stay there until we come for you!" yelled Aaron after them.

Jacob walked with his father to the reverend's house and he knocked on the door. "Now Dad, let me do the talking, OK. You're too riled up right now."

Aaron reluctantly nodded agreement.

Reverend Forester opened the door and smiled.

"Morning Jacob, you're father told me you were coming back to help with the move," he looked puzzled for a moment. "Are you two going hunting?" he asked indicating the weapon.

"Damn right!" said Aaron hotly.

"Dad, let me handle this," said Jacob putting a hand on his father's arm. "Reverend, it seems that Ricky Johnson stole Esther right from her bed last night."

Reverend Forester gasped. "He what!"

"I know he wanted her to marry him, but you never told him he could, did you?" asked Jacob.

"I certainly did not!" stated Forester. "In fact I informed him Sunday evening that he would have to set his sights on some other girl because she was moving away with her family." He paused and took a deep breath. "That's probably what set him off, the fact that she was moving away."

"You'll go with us to talk to him?" asked Jacob.

"Of course," he said. He called back over his shoulder to his wife. "Mary, I have to go over to the Johnson place. I'll be back shortly."

They all rode in the reverend's car the two miles to the Johnson farm. Bertha Johnson met them at the front door.

"Oh, Reverend, I'm so glad you're here! That stubborn girl's been crying all morning. Maybe you can talk some sense into her," she said hotly. Bertha peered over his shoulder and her eyes widened when she saw the shotgun in Aaron's hands.

"Talk sense into her!" bellowed Aaron. "I'll knock some sense into that boy of yours! Let me pass, Reverend."

Jacob grabbed Aaron's arm before he could push his way into the house. "Wait, Dad. Hold on a minute."

"Mrs. Johnson," said Reverend Forester calmly. "Esther doesn't want to marry Ricky and she is going to be moving away with her family. Now please let me speak to your son for a minute."

Bertha put her hands on her hips and her face got red. "Well, you change your tune when it's a girl you know, don't you, Reverend? I'm sure all those other girls that you sent the boys out to find were all happy as clams to join your little congregation!"

Reverend Forester sighed. "I am beginning to change my thinking on that. Now let us in before there is more trouble than you want to deal with, Mrs. Johnson."

She reluctantly opened the door wider and the men filed into the room. When Esther saw her father she ran over to him and he threw his arm around her.

"I knew you'd come for me," she sobbed into his chest.

Aaron patted her back then gently pushed her behind him. "Now stay right there out of harm's way, Esther, and let us talk to Ricky," he said soberly.

Ricky Johnson stood across the room glowering at the three men. "I have a right to go on a hunt like the others, don't I? Seems to me that's only fair," he stammered.

"Sit down, Ricky, and you too, Mrs. Johnson. Where is your husband?" asked Reverend Forester. "I'd like him to hear this, too."

"I'm right here, Reverend," said Amos Johnson. He came in the room and sat down beside his wife. "Now, Bertha, let's at least hear him out," he advised soothingly.

"Thank you," said the Reverend as he reached over and carefully removed the shotgun from Aaron's hands. "You won't be needing this," he said softly.

Aaron and Jacob stepped back and let the reverend have the floor.

"Now, as for the hunt, starting today I am officially stopping all such activity," said Forester calmly. "I have finally come to see that it is probably no longer necessary or desirable. Michael and Rueben both found decent young women willing to marry them. Evie is going to marry Mark and Deborah has agreed to marry Randy," he cleared his throat. "Now Ricky, I spoke with Ishmael Rollins and his daughter, Hannah, seems to have a terrible crush on you. I know she isn't as pretty as Esther here, but she's capable of some of the best cooking I've ever tasted. I'm sure these other men here will agree with me that looks fade, but good cooking lasts forever."

The reverend paused and let his audience absorb this news.

Ricky looked up hopefully. "Hannah has a crush on me? Really? You wouldn't lie about something like that, would you Reverend?"

"I certainly wouldn't," said Forester solemnly.

"I do fancy a good meal. Ma will tell you that. And she may not be beautiful, but Hannah is a right sweet person, isn't she Pa?" asked Ricky.

"She is that," said Amos. "I recollect that she brought that delicious apple pie to welcome us when we first moved here last year."

"It was right tasty," agreed Ricky. He stood up and walked over to Aaron with a sheepish look on his face.

"Mr. Brown. I'm truly sorry for scaring Esther that way." He peered over Aaron's shoulder at Esther. "No hard feelings, Esther?"

Esther wanted to slap his face, but she looked at the Reverend who was nodding to her. "All right. I forgive you, this time," she said politely.

Reverend Forester began herding his little group to the door.

"Well, we'll let you folks get on with your day. I expect to see you all at Sunday services. And Ricky, if I was you, I'd start courting Miss Hannah right away."

Ricky nodded. "I will do that startin' today, Reverend."

"Good day, Mr. and Mrs. Johnson. We'll be leaving now."

There was a collective sigh of relief as they all climbed into the reverend's car.

Forester handed Aaron his weapon and suggested, "You might want to unload that before you pack it up."

Aaron nodded as he took the gun. "Thank you for not letting me do something I would regret forever, Reverend."

"I seem to be regretting a lot of things myself lately, Aaron," admitted Forester as he turned the car around and started driving to the Brown's farmhouse.

"Reverend," said Esther tentatively. "Thank you for helping me." She paused then said, "I am a little worried about Hannah, though. Ricky can be kind of mean sometimes."

Reverend Forester looked at her and laughed. "Don't you worry a minute about Hannah," he said. "Haven't you noticed how well she keeps those three older brothers of hers in line?"

***

Melody Baker was happier than she could remember ever feeling before. She was madly in love with Rueben and tonight they were getting married. Their home was finished and the curtains she had sewn were hanging in the windows.

Anna had helped her make her own wedding dress. She didn't want white and had chosen a pale green brocade. It was a simple A-line, calf length dress with short cap sleeves and she was proud that she had helped make it for herself.

Melody stood in front of the mirror and smiled while Mary put a few pale pink rose buds in her curls. Anna straightened the hem of the dress and admired the finished product.

"Thank you both," Melody said with a sigh. "Tonight I feel beautiful."

"You are beautiful," said Mary. "And you are blessed with an inner beauty that never fades with age."

While the women had helped Melody finish getting ready, Elizabeth stood back and watched. She was a little envious of Melody's happiness. Maybe one day I can feel that way about someone, she thought hopefully.

Anna walked over to her and whispered. "You're coming back to my house after the ceremony tonight. Matthew and I are going to talk to you about getting back home." She squeezed Elizabeth's hand. "Come on, it's time to go."

All four of them walked the short distance to the chapel. All of Rueben's family and friends were in attendance to wish the happy couple well. It was pretty much the same ceremony that Elizabeth had witnessed for Michael and Cynthia, with one exception. Melody had written a poem for Rueben, which she read with trembling lips and tears. Afterwards everyone danced and ate the wonderful foods brought by the guests. Elizabeth was thankful that no snakes were invited.

It was almost nine o'clock when Anna took her by the hand and said, "It's time to leave, come on."

Elizabeth rode in the back seat with Anna while Matthew drove them to the farm. Mark had elected to stay for a while longer as this gave him another chance to dance with Evie. Elizabeth wasn't sure where Mr. Hensley was as she had not seen him all evening.

The three of them sat alone in the living room and Anna kept her arm around Elizabeth's shoulders while she explained what they planned to do.

"John is over at the Brown's helping them pack to move away," she said. "But he is in agreement with Matthew and me about our plans for you."

Matthew hung his head and said, "I'm really sorry for doing this to you, Elizabeth. I hope you can find it in your heart to one day forgive me. I'd like to make it up to you a little by helping you get back home safely."

Elizabeth smiled at him. "I forgive you already, Matthew. You were the one who convinced Mark to take Maria to the hospital. I'll never forget that."

He nodded. "Thank you."

Anna was proud of Elizabeth for being so kind. She almost wished things could have been different and Matthew could have married this sweet girl. She cleared her throat. "Early tomorrow morning, Matthew is going to drive you down the mountain and to the Charleston airport. John has already called and reserved your passage to fly home. Here is the money to pay for your ticket." Anna handed her five hundred dollars. "We all wish you the very best life," she said blinking back tears.

Elizabeth was overwhelmed. She knew how hard it was for them to earn cash. "Thank you," she said sincerely. "I wish we had met each other another way."

Anna nodded. "Me too. You are exactly the kind of daughter-in-law I would love to have become a part of our family." She hugged Elizabeth.

"I'm supposed to drive you back to the bride's cottage so no one will become suspicious of anything," said Matthew. "I guess Hannah Rollins and one other girl are moving there tonight, so at least you won't be alone."

As they were getting up to leave, there was a knock on the door. Elizabeth looked at Matthew questioningly, but he just shrugged. "We're not expecting any one."

When he opened the door, there stood Reverend Forester.

Elizabeth gasped and quickly sat down beside Anna. She hoped he wasn't suspicious of their plans for her to leave.

"Hello, Reverend," said Anna.

"I apologize for coming by so late," he began. He held his hat in his hands and he was nervously twisting the brim. "I had a hard time getting away from the wedding. Elizabeth, I'm pleased to see you are here, I need to talk to you, too."

"Come have a seat, Reverend," invited Anna. She was puzzled to see him acting so humble.

He sat down and put his hands together in his lap. Taking a deep breath, he said, "Anna, I just want to say how sorry I am for everything that happened to you twenty-five years ago. I have come to realize how wrong I was to ever start the hunt."

Anna looked at his face and could tell that he meant what he was saying.

"I have done you and others a grave injustice by forcing you to come here and marry men you didn't even know." He cleared his throat. "And I am especially sorry for causing your injury. I hope you believe that it was an accident." He bowed his head.

"Reverend, I realized that a few years ago. When I saw how much you loved your people, I began to believe that you wouldn't have done this to me on purpose. I was so rebellious. You were just trying to frighten me so I would stop running away."

He looked at her and nodded. "You didn't understand then how dangerous these mountains can be. I was worried you would get hurt out there alone."

Anna smiled. "I know that now. As for my wound, if that had not happened to me, I would never have met John. I fell in love with him when he cared for me so tenderly. So in a way, I think of it as a favor."

Reverend Forester looked surprised. "Oh, no! Don't say that. What I did was an accident, but it could never be considered a favor."

"Yes, to me it turned out that way. I love my husband and boys with all my heart. I would never want to leave this place now," she said sincerely.

The Reverend felt a lump rising in his throat. "Mrs. Hensley, I believe you must be the most forgiving woman I have ever met." He cleared his throat and turned to Elizabeth.

Elizabeth shrunk back into her seat and leaned into Anna, afraid to hear what he would say to her. She expected him to tell her that one day she would be happy here, too. She almost fainted when she heard what he really had to say.

"Elizabeth, I am so sorry I caused this to happen to you. If you want to leave, I will personally drive you back home," he told her. "I'm going to announce to everyone that there will be no more hunts, ever."

Elizabeth felt such relief that she couldn't speak. She nodded to him.

Anna squeezed her arm. "Thank you for the offer, Reverend. But I think that Matthew should be the one to make sure she gets home safely."

Reverend Forester nodded. "Well, if that's what you want, that's settled then. I'll be on my way. Thank you all." He stood up and left them all mulling over his words in relief.

***

"Mommy," whispered Melinda shaking her mother's shoulder.

Janice rolled over in bed and looked at her daughter.

"Did you have another bad dream, honey? Come get in bed with me."

"No, Mommy," said the child. "I'm not scared. Elizabeth is coming home. She's not afraid anymore."

Janice sat up sleepily. "She's not?"

Melinda shook her head causing her curls to bounce. "That man who took her away is going to help her come home. And Elizabeth isn't afraid because she doesn't have to touch the snakes."

"Well, I'm glad you think she's coming home. I'll call Elaine in the morning to see what she's heard from Brandon."

"No, Mommy," said Melinda stamping her foot. "Not Brandon. The man who took her away is taking her to a place so she can fly home."

Janice blinked. This was the first time that Melinda had been so adamant about Elizabeth. "But she can't fly, honey."

Melinda rolled her eyes at her mother. "In an airplane, Mommy."

"Oh, of course, how silly of me," said Janice. "Come to bed." She reached down and pulled Melinda into bed with her. "I'll call Elaine in the morning and give her the good news."

Melinda patted her mother's cheek. "OK," she said as she snuggled down in the bed. "Go back to sleep, Mommy."

Janice looked at her daughter. Sometimes this child seemed much too mature for her age.

\*\*\*

Brandon was beyond frustrated, now he was despondent. Everything including the weather was plotting against him and keeping him from finding Elizabeth. He and Belle had spent an entire fruitless day searching for the ubiquitous dirt road that would lead to Reverend Forester's community. As the evening approached, a heavy ground fog began to envelope the mountain. Now he could barely see three feet in front of him. When he almost hit a deer that jumped in front of the car, he slammed on the brakes and sideswiped a tree. The crunch of metal echoed through the fog.

Belle got out and looked at the damage. Shaking her head, she climbed back into the car. "It's only the back fender," she said looking at his ashen face.

Brandon put his head down on the steering wheel. "Belle," he said in a choked voice. "I'm not going to find her in time, am I? It's been ten days, who knows what has happened to her by now."

Belle fought back tears of her own as she looked at this big, gruff man she had come to love as a partner and friend and she felt a lump choking her. She swallowed and said as cheerfully as she could, "Sure we will. We'll just start again tomorrow when the fog is gone and we're both rested. Let's head back to the main road. Let me drive for a while."

They changed places and while Belle eased them back around and started slowly down the road, Brandon rested his head against the side window and closed his eyes. He was exhausted and he fell into a troubled sleep.

As they descended the mountain, the fog cleared a little and Belle made it safely to the nearest paved road. After about an hour they found Hwy. 85, and the town of Wharton, elevation 958 ft. according to the sign. Much of this area of West Virginia was devoted to coal mining and Wharton was no exception. She pulled the car into the lot in front of the Miner's Market Grocery store. She went in and bought sandwiches and bottled drinks.

Belle talked with the girl at the register then walked back to the car. "There doesn't seem to be any hotels in this town," she said. "Should I keep driving?"

Brandon nodded and stared out the window. "I don't think Seth remembers the area as well as he thought he did," he complained.

"Well, he is in his nineties and he said it had been twenty years since he was out this way." She handed him a sandwich and started the car. After a few miles she noticed a small sign in a yard that said "Rooms for Rent".

She stopped the car in front of the small white house with a big front porch. "I'm tired. I'm going to see if we can rent rooms for one night."

The tiny middle-aged lady who answered the door agreed to let them stay for the night. "I'm Miss Millie. I don't 'spose it will hurt to have you stay only one night. I usually let rooms out to miners who come for a few weeks at a time. We don't get many folks from the city down in our little holler," she told Belle. "'Specially not any of color." She smiled at Belle and the words didn't have a sting to them.

"Thank you so much," said Belle. "We're police detectives from California working on a case. It's been horrible trying to drive around on the mountain roads."

"Well, you 'uns come on in and rest a spell. I'll just fix us a snack," she said before she disappeared into the kitchen.

Brandon wearily sat down on the faded sofa and leaned his head back against the wall. "What time is it?" he asked Belle.

"Almost nine," she said. "We've been driving around since six this morning. I'm so tired I could fall asleep in this chair."

Miss Millie returned with a pot of tea and a plate of cookies.

"These are my specialty," she said proudly. "My homemade oatmeal cookies won a prize at the county fair." She poured the tea and passed around the cookies.

Belle took a bite and sighed. "These are the best oatmeal cookies I've ever eaten. There's something a little different about them." She sniffed the cookie and took another bite. "I've got it," she said. "You put nutmeg in them."

"Yup, that's the trick. Everyone else uses cinnamon, I use nutmeg and currants instead of raisins," she said smiling. "What business are you two lookin' into up in these mountains?"

"My stepdaughter was kidnapped by one of the snake-handling church groups somewhere up in these mountains," said Brandon wearily.

"Goodness, is Reverend Forester doin' that agin?" asked Miss Millie.

Brandon sat up straight. "Do you know Reverend Forester and where he lives?"

"Course I do," said Miss Millie. "I, myself, was almost taken twenty-five years ago by Alma Jeffry. But when I told him we was first cousins, he changed his mind. I've been up there for meetings a couple of times. My grandpa lived there 'til he passed fifteen years ago."

Belle looked at Brandon. "Maybe our luck is finally going to change."

"Miss Millie, could you show us how to find Reverend Forester?" asked Brandon. "I don't think we're ever going to find the place on our own."

Miss Millie patted his arm. "I kin draw you a map that will take you right there. First thing tomorrow morning after the fog lifts, you uns can try agin."

\*\*\*

It was almost ten o'clock when Matthew dropped Elizabeth off at the bride's cottage. Hannah, Eve and Deborah had all moved into the cottage that evening and they were happily chatting away about their new homes that were now beginning to be built, about their upcoming weddings and about the men they would marry.

Elizabeth listened quietly from her side of the room. She hoped that Matthew would find himself a bride as willing to be with him as these girls were to be with the men who had proposed to them. And deep within herself, she hoped that one day she could be this happy about getting married. She was anxious to go home and get on with her life, to finish school and go to college, but she was a little envious of their happiness.

As she lay in bed after they were all asleep, she found it hard to believe that she had only been gone from home for ten days. It seemed like a lifetime. She wondered how Maria was doing and why Brandon had not found her yet. She was thinking about all the homework she would have to catch up on when she finally fell asleep.

It was five o'clock in the morning when she was awakened by someone gently shaking her shoulder. She opened her eyes to see Matthew standing there. He had his finger to his lips indicating for her to be quiet. She sat up in bed. The other girls were all still sleeping and she didn't want to face any awkward goodbyes.

"Are you packed?" he whispered.

She nodded. "I'm only taking the few things that your mother bought me. Can you help me fold this quilt? I do want to take it."

He folded the quilt while she went into the bathroom and got dressed. He carried the cloth bag with her things and she followed him out to the van.

She climbed in the passenger side and buckled her seat belt. It was a strange sensation getting back into this van. There were no longer boxes and coolers inside. Matthew wasn't living in the van as he had for three weeks while on the hunt and the back was empty. All of that seemed so long ago.

As he pulled away from the cottage he handed her a paper bag.

"Here's an egg and ham sandwich for your breakfast. Mother didn't want you to be hungry. We already ate breakfast before I came."

"I'm sorry you had to get up so early to take me to Charleston," she said as she opened the bag hungrily.

He laughed. "I'm always up this early. Taking you to Charleston got me out of having to milk the cows. It will take over four hours to get to the airport and your flight leaves at eleven. Mark's having to do all the milking."

She smiled. Inside the bag was a big sandwich on homemade bread and a cinnamon roll. "I'm going to miss your mother's cooking," she said taking a bite. "I wish I'd had more time to learn how to make some of her recipes."

Matthew nodded. "Mother did want me to tell you some bad news."

She looked over at him questioningly.

"Rachel Andrew died last night," he said sadly. "She was having another one of her bad headaches and she just passed away."

"I'm sorry to hear that," she said. "It's too bad she couldn't have seen a doctor about them. Something might have been done to help her."

Matthew shrugged. "Maybe."

They traveled in silence as Matthew drove along the twisting dirt road down one mountainside and up another. She hadn't remembered how long it had taken to get to the farm or how curvy the roads were. If she didn't look straight out the front window she started to feel motion sickness. The road ran along the edge of the mountain with the steep granite rock on one side and a straight downward drop on the other side. The one time she looked down over the edge she felt dizzy seeing how far they would fall if the van left the road.

An hour later Elizabeth had finished her food and fallen asleep by the time they came to the first paved road. It was little wider than the previous one and it had no guardrails either. Matthew drove carefully not wanting to take any chances of having an accident and making her miss her flight. She woke up at seven o'clock down in a small valley between two steep mountains as the van stopped at an intersection with four way stop signs. Neither of them paid much attention to the car that was also stopped at the intersection. A Nissan car was sitting at the stop sign to their right as Matthew pulled the van across the road and drove on.

Brandon's eyes widened. "Belle, look at that van!" he exclaimed excitedly.

Belle looked up from the hand drawn map she was studying. "I think you're supposed to turn left here," she said vaguely.

"Belle, look at that van!" he said again as he turned right and followed in the direction the van was going.

"I said left, Brandon."

Then Belle saw the van. It was a white van with a smiley-faced sun license plate. "Did you see the number on the plate?" she asked.

"Yes. It's AAA015."

Brandon pushed down on the accelerator until he was almost on the van's back bumper. "This is the van that they drove when they took Elizabeth," he said.

Brandon eased the car forward then sped past the van. The road was narrow, but he didn't see any other cars coming. As they passed, Belle saw a young man with curly brown hair driving the van and a passenger in the other seat.

"It's not Mark," she said. "Maybe it's the other man. Didn't Maria say he had brown curly hair and his name was Matthew?"

Brandon didn't answer. He raced forward several hundred yards, then stopped the car across the road to block the van's passage. He pulled his weapon out of his shoulder holster and started to open the car door.

Matthew hollered as a car raced past them on the narrow road. "What is that crazy driver trying to do, cause an accident?" he asked as he pulled the van further to the right to avoid being hit.

Elizabeth looked up just as the car turned and blocked the road ahead.

"Is this some kind of attempt to rob us?" she asked frightened. "Can you see who is getting out of the car up there?"

Matthew was slowing down trying to figure out if he could get past the other car, when a man jumped out and pointed a gun at them. He slammed on the brakes and started to back up.

"Wait!" screamed Elizabeth grabbing his arm. "That's Brandon. That's my stepfather!"

Matthew stopped the van and Elizabeth opened her door to jump out.

"Be careful," warned Matthew. "He might not know it's you. Hold your hands up." He opened his door and slowly got out with his hands raised above his head.

Brandon recognized Elizabeth as she ran towards him, her blond hair flying out behind her. He opened his arms and she rushed into them. He held her with one arm and kept the revolver pointed at Matthew with the other.

"Brandon, I can't believe it's really you!" cried Elizabeth as she hugged him.

When she noticed that he still had his weapon aimed at Matthew she reached up and pushed his arm down. "It's all right. He was taking me to the airport so I could go home."

Brandon lowered his gun and hugged her with both arms.

"I've been driving all over these mountains for days trying to find you," he confessed. "It's like a maze of dirt roads up there." He buried his face in her hair and gave her a squeeze. "I was afraid I would be too late or that I'd never find you."

Belle had arrived by then and put her arms around them both.

Matthew held back unsure of what to do. He was certain that he was about to be arrested by Brandon for kidnapping.

Elizabeth pulled herself free and walked back to where Matthew stood waiting. "I guess you don't have to take me to Charleston after all," she said smiling.

Matthew shrank back as Brandon and Belle walked over to where they stood in the middle of the road.

Elizabeth looked at Brandon. "Dad, this is Matthew, my almost husband."

"Elizabeth, are you all right? Why aren't you upset with him?" asked Belle.

"It's a long story," she said brightly. "Right now all you need to know is that I don't want him arrested."

"But he kidnapped you," argued Brandon. "He needs to pay for what he put us all through these last few days."

"He was the one who took Maria to the hospital even though it was against his religion," informed Elizabeth. "How is she by the way? Is she back home?"

Belle nodded. "They called her mother after they got the information off her medic alert bracelet. She was home a few days after you left her."

"I figured they would find the bracelet. That's why she always wears it."

"Elizabeth, I have to arrest him," stated Brandon stubbornly.

"No you don't," insisted Elizabeth. "I've lived around policemen long enough to know that if I say I went willing with him, you won't have a leg to stand on in court. I'm eighteen now and that's legal age to leave home."

Brandon sighed and rubbed his chin. Suddenly he noticed that he had a lot of stubble and reminded himself he needed to shave before he went home. "OK. You're right," he admitted as he slowly put the revolver away.

"Of course I am." Elizabeth turned to Matthew.

"Thank you for everything you did to help me. And thank your parents, too." She reached into her pocket and brought out the five hundred dollars. "I want you to take this back to them. I won't be needing it now."

He shoved the money into his jeans pocket. "Elizabeth, I'm so sorry for doing anything to hurt you. I wish things had been different, you'll always be special to me."

She reached up and gave him a hug. Matthew blushed, but he hugged her back.

She watched as he walked back to the van, then she turned to Brandon. "Have I got a story to tell you!" she said with a smile.

"We have one, too," said Belle. After they were settled in the car and Matthew had driven off, Belle said. "You won't believe what we saw at a snake-handling church on Sunday."

Elizabeth laughed. "Oh, yes I will. I went to a meeting on Sunday, too."

Brandon looked at his stepdaughter in awe. He had been so worried that she would be traumatized by her experience and here she was laughing at Belle as if she had been away on a holiday vacation.

"I was so worried about you," he said shaking his head. "But you look just fine."

Elizabeth nodded. "I was pretty worried myself for a while. But I've learned that sometimes things can turn out all right even if it seems like there is no way for them to. I really liked some of the mountain people I met."

"We've met a few really nice ones, too," said Belle.

"What time was that flight leaving from Charleston?" asked Brandon.

"Eleven. Can we still make it in time?" asked Belle.

Brandon smiled. "Certainly. I'm sure we can get three seats without a problem."

"I know, all you have to do is flash your badge," said Belle. "It works every time."

Elizabeth shivered and wrapped her arms around her chest. "I can't believe I'm actually going home."

# Chapter 13

Janice was fixing breakfast when Melinda came into the kitchen with her new kitten cuddled in her arms.

"Mommy, Elizabeth is coming home," she said looking up at her mother. "Do you think I can show her my new kitten? Maybe she can help me pick out a name for her."

Janice looked at her daughter but before she could come up with an answer, the phone rang. She wiped her hands on a towel and picked up the receiver. "Hello?"

"They're on the way home!" said Elaine excitedly.

"They are, right now?"

"I just got a call from Brandon. He found Elizabeth and they will be boarding a plane in a few minutes. Their flight leaves Charleston, West Virginia, at eleven."

"I can't believe it," said Janice. "Melinda told me last night that Elizabeth would be flying home. She barely told me just now that she was on her way. Then you called. I can't figure out how she does that."

"They'll be home by this evening if the next flight isn't delayed. You can't imagine how relieved I am," she admitted. "When I talked with him yesterday afternoon he was so discouraged, he was afraid he would never find her."

"Keep me posted," said Janice. "I want to hear the whole story when they get home. I just hope Elizabeth will be all right after all she's been through."

"She one of the strongest people I've ever known," said Elaine. "Brandon told me that she seems fine. I'll talk to you later, I've got to feed the twins."

"Bye," said Janice. As she hung up the phone she looked at Melinda. "Well, you were right again. Elizabeth is flying home today," she said shaking her head.

Melinda looked up with wide eyes. "I already knew that Mommy. I told you last night. Can I have Kix for breakfast?"

"Nope. I'm making French toast."

"Yeah. That's my favorite!" Melinda put the kitten down by her dish of food. "Here's your breakfast, too," she said. "We'll play more later."

\*\*\*

Jacob turned the truck and followed his father's station wagon off the highway into the rest stop. He parked the U-haul beside the car and got out to stretch his legs. It was a little after noon on Wednesday and they had already made it through most of the state of Tennessee.

"I think we'd better stop here for lunch," said his father through the open car window. "The boys both say they're starving. But then I think they're always hungry."

They found an empty picnic table and spread out the map. While Esther got the sandwiches out of the cooler in the back of the car, Jacob and Aaron checked their route again.

"We should make it to Oklahoma by tonight," said Jacob. "Of course the truck can't travel as fast as a car, but that's were I stopped when I was hunting. There's a big rest stop there where I stayed for the night."

"That's fine for one person, but we probably better find a motel for this bunch," said Aaron. "Come back to the car for a minute while Esther's getting lunch ready. I have something I need to show you."

Jacob followed his father back to the car and Aaron pulled a small metal box out from under the driver's seat. "I want you to see what your mother put in here," he said handing Jacob the box.

When Jacob opened the box he saw a small stack of documents inside. He pulled one out and looked closely at it. It was an official copy of his birth certificate. He looked questioningly at his father. "I thought we didn't believe in government institutions and getting registered with them," he said.

"Reverend Forester doesn't. But your mother had enough foresight to want her children's births registered. There's a birth record for all four of you in there. We went to the county seat and registered our marriage, too," he explained.

"That will make it a lot easier to get the boys registered in public school now," said Jacob. "And we can all get social security cards. Robert Smalley was going to try and help me get one, but I left to come help you move before we could check in to it. I already have a job but I needed a social security card to get paid legally."

"Well, you hold onto the box now," said his father handing it to him.

Esther called them over to the picnic table where she had spread out a big lunch for everyone. Aaron looked at the sandwiches, homemade pickles and potato salad.

"I swear you put on a spread as good as you mother did," he said with a smile.

Esther blushed. It was good to see how much happier her father was becoming now that they had left the farm. She didn't think he had ever really enjoyed farming.

"I fixed everything I could think of to use up as much food as I could before we left. It seemed such a shame to leave so much behind," she said.

"Well, I think the Johnson's appreciated all the things you took over to them. They haven't lived there long enough to build up a good supply yet. After this harvest, I imagine they'll do just fine," said Aaron sitting down beside Ephraim and taking the plate she handed to him.

He glanced over and saw that the boy was reading more than he was eating, which was very unusual. "What are you looking at, son?" he asked between bites.

"It's one of those pamphlet things that Jacob brought with him," said Ephraim. "It's called 'For the Strength of Youth'. It's written for Mormon teenagers." He held up the pamphlet.

"I guess I better read this before I let you get indoctrinated by it," said Aaron taking the pamphlet. He looked inside and read:

> "OUR DEAR YOUNG MEN AND YOUNG WOMEN, *we have great confidence in you. You are beloved sons and daughters of God and He is mindful of you. You have come to earth at a time of great opportunities and also of great challenges. The standards in this booklet will help you with the important choices you are making now and will yet make in the future. We promise that as you keep the covenants you have made and these standards, you will be blessed with the companionship of the Holy Ghost, your faith and testimony will grow stronger, and you will enjoy increasing happiness.*" It was authored by The Church of Jesus Christ of Latter-day Saints and published by Intellectual Reserve, Inc. in 2012.

"This looks interesting," he said after swallowing a bite of sandwich. "I think I'll read it while Esther takes her turn driving this afternoon."

Ephraim sighed. "It talks about being honest and virtuous and kind and all the things you've already taught us, Dad. And it says we should all work hard and do what's right. You probably don't need to read it at all."

Aaron laughed and ruffled Ephraim's hair. "That statement just tells me there's something in here you don't want me to know about, young man."

Ephraim rolled his eyes. "I was hoping I would be able to do some new and exciting things now that the reverend wasn't watching over me. But it looks like the Mormons are almost as strict as he is. I won't be able to get away with anything," he complained.

Jacob playfully punched Ephraim in the arm. "I wouldn't let you get away with anything anyway. You didn't stand a chance," he laughed.

"Well at least Mormons go to movies and watch television. They just don't watch anything with bad language, sex or too much violence. But I wonder if that leaves much of anything to watch?" he pouted.

"I've seen all kinds of interesting shows on the Smalley's BYU channel," said Jacob scooping up a second helping of potato salad. "Their church has it's own TV channel and Mormons make movies, too. I think you'll love the one I saw called 'Joseph and the Amazing Technicolor Dream Coat'. It had lots of music and dancing."

"You mean there are Mormon movie stars?" asked Isaac wide-eyed. "Won't they all go to hell like the reverend said?"

Jacob laughed. "I don't think so. Everything I've seen was clean and wholesome. And they make a lot of movies about Jesus and other people you've read about in the Bible. The movies I've seen were really good."

"Wow," said Isaac delighted. "I can't wait."

They finished eating and cleaned up their trash. Aaron rode with Esther and took the opportunity to read through the youth pamphlet. He was impressed by the high standards the Mormons encouraged their teens to follow.

"Looks to me like Jacob ran into some nice folks," he commented when he finished reading the pamphlet and handed it back to Ephraim.

Esther glanced over at him. "We'll soon find out for ourselves," she said.

\*\*\*

Elizabeth watched out the window as the lights on the San Diego airport runway came in to view. It was already dark and they had been traveling since eleven o'clock that morning. The layover in Denver had given them enough time to get something to eat and they had been back in the air. She looked over at Brandon who was asleep. He was exhausted from his frantic search for her. She almost felt a little guilty that she was feeling so good. When the plane's wheels touched down the jolt woke him up. He rubbed his face and looked down at her.

"I promised I'd bring you home," he said drowsily as he patted her arm. "I don't think Elaine would have let me in the door without you."

She leaned over and gave him a hug. "I knew you were looking and that always made me feel better. Thanks, Brandon."

It was fifteen minutes before they were allowed off the plane and it was almost nine when they headed for the baggage claim area. As they were walking down the corridor, they suddenly heard squealing. Elizabeth looked up to see Maggie and Martin running towards them down the corridor with Elaine close behind.

"They wouldn't go to sleep so I finally gave up and we drove to the airport," she told them breathlessly. "They've been dying to see Elizabeth ever since you called this morning."

"Oh, Lizbeth, we missed you so much," lisped Martin.

Elizabeth leaned over and scooped him up into her arms. "I missed you, too."

He patted her cheek then hugged her around the neck.

Maggie was jumping up and down hollering, "Me, too, Lizbeth. Pick me up, too."

She grabbed her up and spun around with them both in her arms. "Wow, I think you've grown since I left. You're getting too heavy to carry." She set them back on their feet and took them each by the hand. "I think you'd better walk before I drop you on your heads."

Brandon grabbed the suitcases and Elizabeth's cloth bag off the conveyer belt and they headed for the parking lot.

"I'm sure glad to be home," he said when Elaine slipped her arm through his. He stopped and gave her a kiss. "I missed you."

Martin saw the kiss and laughed. "Daddy's back and now it gets kissy. Ugh!"

"One day you'll like that," teased Belle.

"Miss Belle are you coming home with us, too?" asked Maggie wide-eyed.

"No, honey. I'm going straight to my house and collapse. I might not get out of bed at all tomorrow, even if the chief calls," she declared.

Maggie's mouth dropped wide open. "You must be very tired."

"Yes, I certainly am. And so is your daddy. Promise me you'll both let him sleep in the morning. I've heard about your early morning raids on daddy's bed." Belle looked sternly down at the twins. "Will you promise me?"

They both looked up solemnly and nodded. "We promise," they chorused.

***

Melinda climbed up into her chair at the breakfast table. "Hi, Daddy. Do you have to work today?"

Bill smiled. "I'm afraid so. I'd rather stay home with you," he said as he reached over and tickled her under the arm.

"That's OK, Daddy. We'll probably go and visit Elizabeth today now that she's back home again," said Melinda off-handedly. "Right, Mommy?"

Janice looked at her husband. "I promise you, I didn't tell her. Elaine called last night after Melinda was already in bed to tell me they were home."

"I already knew," said Melinda looking at her mother. "When Brandon found her that man who took her away was already bringing her to the airport."

Janice threw up her hands. "See Bill, she just knows things. I have no idea why she is so connected to Elizabeth."

Bill shook his head and shrugged. "I guess it doesn't really matter. It doesn't hurt anything," he said turning back to his paper.

Janice looked at Melinda. "After Daddy leaves and you eat your breakfast, we'll go and see Elizabeth."

"Ok, Mommy. I'd like that," said Melinda. "Can I bring my kitten?"

***

Melody Baker was now legally Miriam Smith or Mrs. Rueben Smith according to Reverend Forester. She stood in the middle of her living room and looked around. The curtains she had made hung in the windows. She was amazed at the furniture Rueben and James had made for her. She stroked the arm of her rocker and felt the silky smoothness of the highly polished wood. This is my home, she thought with a smile, and I have never been happier.

She had fixed lunch for her new husband and kissed him goodbye as he left to plow the four acres behind the house with the tractor he had borrowed from his father. The new barn that was finished last night was visible out her kitchen window where she watched several of their chickens scratching at the dirt in the yard.

She sighed, as happy as she was she still felt a little bit like there was something missing. Almost every day for the last six years she had gone to her job at the library where she enjoyed helping patrons find interesting books. When there were no patrons she enjoyed reading whatever interested her, or she spent time writing her poetry. Now she was alone at home and after only two weeks she was getting bored. How many times could she dust the same clean furniture anyway? she wondered.

As she started to open the door to let in the fresh spring air, she was startled to find Reverend Forester and Mary standing on the porch.

"Hello," said Mary. "We were just going to knock."

"May we speak to you about something we consider very important?" asked Reverend Forester seriously.

"Certainly, come on in." Miriam led them into the living room where they all sat down and faced each other.

"Your home is lovely," said Mary looking around the room.

"Thank you," said Miriam. "Rueben and his father did a wonderful job on the furniture." Then she sighed. "But I kind of feel rather useless sitting here all day."

Mary's face brightened. "You do? That's good. Oh, I didn't mean that the way it came out. What I mean is that we're here to see if you would be willing to help out with the group of children I've been home schooling."

"Really?" said Miriam excitedly. "What do you need me to do?"

"I've kind of reached my limits as to what I can teach the older children. I've done fine with them on an elementary school level, but these teenagers are looking for more than I can give them," confessed Mary. "I could really use some extra help."

"I would love to help," agreed Miriam. "What kind of library do you have here?"

"Only a small one in the school house. Mostly lower level reading. I've been teaching the children for ten years now and they've read everything we have, several times in fact," admitted Mary.

"Actually," said the reverend. "We were wondering if you could suggest other books that would be appropriate for us to purchase for the library. We don't approve of anything with a lot of violence or sexual themes or bad language. We'd rather the children not be exposed to all that," he explained.

Miriam stood up and walked to her bedroom door and beckoned for them to follow. "I don't think you'll need to purchase much of anything if you'll allow me to donate the books I brought with me," she said as she lead them into the room where there were seven boxes full of books stacked in the corner of the bedroom.

Mary looked at the boxes and smiled. "That's wonderful. You brought all of these with you from home?"

Miriam nodded. "I didn't own much in the way of personal possessions but I've always had lots of books. These were the ones I couldn't bear to leave behind. Rueben complained when I couldn't narrow down my choices any more than this. I have everything from the 'Anne of Green Gables' series to 'The Adventures of Sherlock Holmes'. I've never liked books with what I considered objectionable themes either and I think all of these would be quite appropriate for your library."

"You'd be willing to loan them out to the students?" asked Mary hopefully.

"Books are meant to be read. I'll donate them to your library," said Miriam.

"Oh, how wonderful! You don't know how much this will help."

"Rueben will be glad to get them out of our bedroom. And I can always borrow them back when I feel like reading them again," she said smiling.

"There's one other thing we would like to ask of you," said Mary. "Would you be willing to teach a class on literature for me? You know so much more about books and authors than I do."

Miriam's face lit up. "I would love to teach literature. I could help them with book reports and poetry writing and oh, a million things!" she said excitedly.

"Thank you very much. I'm so relieved. I was afraid you wouldn't be interested," said Mary giving her a hug. "Teaching can sometimes be overly challenging for me."

"I promise you, I would love to help."

"I'll send a man with a truck to get the books," said Reverend Forester. "I don't think we could fit them all in our car. Thank you for being so willing to help out."

"No, thank you for giving me this opportunity," said Miriam. She waved goodbye as they drove off, then hurried out back to tell Rueben the good news. She was all ready feeling useful again.

***

The last few weeks had been extremely busy ones for Elizabeth. Her teachers all worked with her to catch up on the schoolwork she had missed. Then it seemed that graduation preparations rushed at her.

Even with all that to keep her busy, she still felt a little bit like something was missing. She finally figured out what it was, she missed Matthew and Anna. They were so much a part of her life for those few days that it felt like they still should be involved in it now. It seemed strange that she should care about people that she barely knew and had met under such bizarre circumstances, but it was true.

Anna had been such a comfort to her when she was distressed. And she had felt touched by how much Matthew seemed to care about her and how he was so sorry for putting her through the ordeal. She wished she had a way to keep in contact with them, but she didn't have any idea what their address would be. Mail was never delivered to their homes and was probably sent to a post office box down in the nearest town. The only phones she knew about were at the reverend's house and the home of the head deacon and when she tried to find out the phone numbers they were unlisted.

Sadly, she decided that she would have to close that chapter in her life and get on with this one. But it was funny how some of their values stayed with her.

When Elaine took her shopping to buy a new dress for graduation Elizabeth didn't like any of the short sleeveless sundresses.

"This one is cute," said Elaine holding up a brightly printed dress with thin shoulder straps. "It would look nice on you."

"I think I like this better," said Elizabeth. "She held up a long skirt and a ruffled blouse with cap sleeves. If there is one thing I learned in West Virginia, it's that modesty can be beautiful and I think I like that idea."

Elaine smiled. "You can wear whatever you want. It's your graduation."

Graduation night was thrilling. To be finished with high school made all the seniors completely giddy. But as Elizabeth looked out into the audience seeing all her family members, there were two other faces she wished were in attendance. When her name was called, she proudly walked across the stage and shook hands with the principal. Her favorite English teacher gave her a hug before Elizabeth moved the tassel on her cap to the opposite side representing that she was now officially graduated.

Afterward graduation when Elizabeth was in her room studying the information packets that three of the colleges had sent to her, she kept coming back to the one from Southern Virginia University. It was in the Shenandoah Valley at the base of the Blue Ridge Mountains in Buena Vista, Virginia. The photos reminded her of West Virginia and she was drawn to it.

"Still studying the pamphlets?" asked Elaine looking in the door at her. "You know I would love to have you close by in San Diego, but I want you to go wherever you decide is best for you. I would never want to hold you back."

Elizabeth looked up and nodded. "All of these schools have something that would work for me, but I like this one best." She held up the brochure from Virginia. "It's a smaller school with around 800 students so they have a really good student to teacher ratio. And they have a fantastic music department." She sighed. "I've been accepted to all three, but Southern Virginia is also offering me the best music scholarship."

"What about the one that offered the swimming scholarship?" asked Brandon as he came in and sat beside her on the bed. "You're not interested in that one?"

She shrugged. "I prefer music to sports. Look at this," she said handing him the letter she had received offering the scholarship from Southern Virginia University.

"Wow. They would cover just about everything. It says they want to meet with you and have you play the piano for them," he noted.

"I'd have to fly out to do that next month," explained Elizabeth.

"We could handle that," said Elaine. "If this is where you want to go, we'll arrange whatever is needed."

"I like their philosophy about music, too. Listen to this," she read out loud from the brochure.

> "Students who participate in SVU's music program understand that music is a priceless and irreplaceable component of human life, occupying a unique position in our culture. It speaks to the intellect, emotion and human soul in an essential way. The music program has a dynamic and varied music concert and performance schedule, presenting numerous concerts each year, including recitals and ensembles. We offer a broad range of courses, including music theory, music history, composition and performance practices." (Published by Southern Virginia Univ; One University Dr.; Buena Vista, VA in 2012)

"It certainly sounds like they take music seriously," said Brandon.

"You both know how much my music means to me," said Elizabeth. "Some of the other colleges and universities put so much emphasis on sports that the cultural arts get second billing."

"Well, it sounds like you've all ready made up your mind on this one," said Elaine handing back the brochure she had been studying. "I say go for it."

Elizabeth smiled. "And you'll like this part," she said. "I think it's supported by The Church of Jesus Christ of Latter-day Saints. At least it says that 93% of its students are Mormons. And you know that would mean no wild parties or drinking or drugs."

Brandon stood up. "Ok, that's the one I'm voting for. I remember how immoral I was as a male college student and I'd prefer you not associate with guys like I was back then." He ran his finger around his collar as if it was too tight fitting. "If Elaine had met me back in my younger days she would never have consented to marry me, you can bet on that." He cleared his throat.

Elaine laughed. "You're probably right. I was very conservative in college. The nursing school I went to was practically like a nunnery. We even had a ten o'clock curfew in my dorm."

"You're kidding," laughed Elizabeth. "Really, a curfew?"

Elaine nodded. "I was taking a full load of classes at the University and courses at the Nursing School as well as working weekends as a CNA at the hospital. I didn't have time for parties. It was the hardest thing I've ever done."

Brandon reached over and pulled her into a hug. "Harder than taking care of me and the twins?" he asked.

She rolled her eyes. "Barely. Between the three of you, I hardly have time to breathe. But nursing school was harder."

"Wow, it must be really hard if its worse than taking care of us," he laughed as he pulled her from the room. "When's lunch?"

When the two of them left her room, Elizabeth continued to page through the brochure. Just looking at the photos somehow made her feel closer to West Virginia. She couldn't explain it, but what had started out as a horrible experience with Matthew had turned into something completely different.

***

Jacob Brown could not believe how drastically his life had changed over the last few weeks. As soon as his family had arrived in Idaho, they'd been welcomed into the community. Maryanne Smalley helped them find a house to rent and Robert went with them to the Social Security office to get everyone cards. Jacob was back working at the grocery store with Mitch. Because it was summertime both of his brothers would have been home alone but Maryanne insisted they spend the day at her house with Will and Ronnie. Their only problem was that his father had not had as much luck finding a job. He was out for hours every day and had applied almost everywhere.

One evening after dinner Robert came by to help his father work on writing up a better resume'. "What work experiences do you have?" he asked Aaron.

"I've spent most of my life working on a farm. I haven't done much of anything else. Leastwise I've never worked for anyone else," he confessed.

Robert nodded. "That's most likely the problem then."

"But he's a really good carpenter," interjected Esther. "He made almost all of the furniture we brought with us."

Robert looked around. "You made all this furniture?"

Aaron nodded. "Most of it. I made the dining room table and chairs, the coffee and end tables, and the bedroom dressers and such. I love working with wood. I'd rather do that than anything else," he admitted.

Robert ran his hand over the surface of the table where they sat. It had inlaid wood in a checkerboard pattern across the top and the chairs had carved flowers on the backs. "This is very good workmanship. Perhaps we could find you a job making furniture."

Aaron shook his head slowly. "You know what? I'd rather start my own business making furniture. Do you think that would be possible?" he asked.

"Well, it would take start up money to rent a location and buy tools," said Robert.

"I brought all my tools with us and I have money from the sale of my farm," informed Aaron. "Do you think this town could support a business like that?"

"It certainly would as soon as people see what a fantastic product you turn out."

Jacob smiled at his father. "Everyone back home said his creations were the best of anyone's and they all make some furniture of their own. I think opening a shop is a great idea."

Robert stood up from the table. "It's settled then. Tomorrow after the lunch rush is over I'll go with you to look for a location to set up this new business," he told Aaron.

"Thank you. I would appreciate that. You and your family have made us so welcome I don't know how we'll ever repay you," said Aaron.

"Just let my wife see some of your handiwork and she'll think of something for you to do!" laughed Robert. "I can just hear her now ... "

*\*\**

In May Matthew had watched with a touch of envy as Mark kissed his new bride, Eve. They made a striking couple, both blond and blue eyed.

Now in September, of the seven men sent out to find wives, Matthew was the only one still single. Even the Johnson brothers had gotten married.

His mother had encouraged him to consider courting Elijah Jeffery's daughter, Bathsheba. She was pretty enough, he agreed, but she didn't compare to Elizabeth.

Elizabeth was so smart and courageous. When she had offered herself as a sort of ransom for her friend Maria, it had touched his heart to think that she would care that much for her friend. He wanted to find a woman like that. One who would give her self to protect the ones she loved. He sighed. Maybe he was doomed to be single forever. There was no one else like Elizabeth.

He had worked hard helping to build the house for his brother, but all the while he was wishing it for himself and Elizabeth. Now here it was fall and he was still living with his parents, helping his father harvest the crops and thinking that he may never have a wife or home of his own.

He was sitting on the porch moping about one evening when his mother came out and sat down beside him on the steps.

"You're still mooning about over Elizabeth, aren't you?" asked Anna.

"I'm not mooning!" he protested. Then he sighed. "Yes, I guess I am."

She hugged him briefly. "It's probably better that she's gone, you know. She could never give you children what with that genetic thing she has," she reminded.

"Would you have stopped loving Dad just because you couldn't have children?" he asked looking at her. "Think about it."

She shook her head slowly. "No, I guess not. I would have loved him with or without you boys." She patted his shoulder and left him to sit alone on the porch as the sky darkened.

Matthew put his head in his hands. Maybe this was his punishment for going out to kidnap a wife. He had fallen in love with a woman he couldn't have.

# Chapter 14

The summer had sped by as Elizabeth waited for September when she would be leaving. Elaine had flown with her in July to audition for Southern Virginia University. She had done so well with her recital they offered her an advanced placement in their music program.

After that she had taken the twins and Melinda to the park several times a week because she knew she would miss them terribly when she moved away. They were spending a day at the beach at least twice a week and she even took them to the San Diego Zoo. But it seemed that no matter how busy she was she kept finding herself thinking about Matthew. She wondered how he was doing. Had he found a bride yet? She missed his sense of humor and his honesty.

After a few dates with some boys she knew from high school, she stopped saying "yes" when they asked her out. They all seemed so juvenile. They talked excitedly about themselves and their plans to party at college. They talked about sports or video games, nothing serious. None of them asked her about her own plans for the future.

All they were interested in was drinking and sex and she didn't enjoy having to fend them off. One young man had seemed more promising than the others until he had asked her if she'd had sex with the man who had kidnapped her.

"Of course not!" she said shocked at his impertinence. "He was more of a gentleman than you'll ever be!" She'd slapped his face and walked home from that date completely offended by his attitude.

By the end of August she had pretty much resigned herself to devoting her time to her music and studies with the vague hope that she might meet more mature guys at the university. If not, then fine. Right now she wasn't interested in dating anyway and she would need to apply herself to the rigorous program she had signed up for this coming year.

Melinda watched as Elizabeth packed her suitcase. After a few minutes she looked up at her. "Are you going far away again, Lizbeth?"

"Yes, I'm afraid so." Elizabeth stopped packing and sat down on the edge of her bed. "Come sit by me, Melinda."

Melinda climbed onto the bed and Elizabeth put her arms around the child. "Melinda, now that you're almost six years old I have a favor to ask of you," she said.

"My birthday is September 19th. You'll be gone away," pouted the child.

"Yes, I'm afraid I will. Can you do something important for me?"

Melinda looked at Elizabeth, her face serious, and nodded. "OK."

"While I'm gone away, I need you to help look after the twins. They're still little and I won't be here to help. Can you do that for me?" she asked seriously.

Melinda nodded, her curls bouncing. "I can be like their other big sister."

Elizabeth smiled at the little girl who seemed too mature for her age. "Yes, you can be like a big sister. You and I will always feel this special connection wherever we are, won't we?"

Melinda smiled. "I can always feel you, Lizbeth."

"Right. So you can be like me. You can help people littler than you are."

Melinda slid off the bed. "I'll go watch out for them right now." She happily skipped out of the room to go find Maggie and Martin.

"That was a nice way to get her mind off your leaving," said Elaine with at smile as she watched from the doorway. "I wish it could be that easy for me."

Elizabeth sighed. "It isn't easy for me either. But I somehow feel that this is what I should be doing for right now. I don't know why."

"Of course it's right. You have to grow up and get on with your life. College is the next big step. And you can call whenever you want. I'm just going to miss you terribly. You and I have been through a lot together, haven't we?" noted Elaine.

Elizabeth walked over and gave her a hug. "Yes, we have. I don't know what I would have done if you hadn't been there for me after my father died."

Elaine blinked back tears. "You helped me, too. I loved your father and I needed you to give me a purpose after he was gone."

Just then Brandon walked up behind them and put his arms around them both.

"Now ladies, let's not have too much crying here. If you get me started, how will I keep up my image as a big tough guy?"

*\*\**

It was after church services on Sunday afternoon in late September and Jacob was playing catch with his brothers in the yard. Aaron watched them for a few minutes. "Hey Ephraim, can you play with Isaac for a few minutes while I talk with Jacob?"

"Sure, Dad," answered Ephraim.

Jacob walked over to his father. "Did you need me to help you with something?"

Aaron shook his head. "Come sit with me on the porch. I just have a few questions for you."

Jacob followed his father on to the porch and they sat down in the rocking chairs Aaron had made. "Questions about what, Dad?"

"Well, you and Esther have been going to the Mormon church for months now and I was wondering if you could tell me a little more about what they believe."

Jacob thought for a few minutes. "Well, I'll try."

"What exactly is the Book of Mormon?" he asked.

"Susan calls it the history of the Indians. Basically it tells about a group of people who left Jerusalem and traveled by boat over here. I guess they landed somewhere in South America. They had prophets who told the people about Jesus and how he would be born to Mary and die to save us all," said Jacob. "Part of the book even tells about how Jesus came and visited these people after he was resurrected. He taught them all the same things he taught the people over in the Bible lands."

Aaron nodded. "So I suppose that's how the Indians got the legend of the great white God who would someday return?"

"Most likely," said Jacob. "It caused them a lot of problems when the Spanish sailors landed in South America. They thought their god was returning."

"But what makes this church different from other churches?" asked Aaron.

"Well, for one thing, they believe in divine revelation," said Jacob.

Aaron looked puzzled. "You mean that God answers prayers?"

"Not just that, but that he speaks to prophets just as he did in Bible times. They have a prophet who directs the church today. His name is Thomas Monson. And they have twelve apostles just like Jesus did."

"Where are they?"

"They live in Utah, but they travel all over the world to speak to members of the Church. And they even have broadcasts on television to let the members know how God wants them to live," explained Jacob.

"You mean there is actually something good on television?" asked Aaron teasingly.

Esther laughed as she came out of the house onto the porch. "So, you're finally asking questions about the church?"

Aaron scowled at her. "Just because I haven't been going with you to their church doesn't mean I haven't wondered about it. It seems to make everyone here so happy and helpful, I just wanted to know why."

"In answer to your question," said Jacob. "The Church has lots of good things on television. It's the same with anything else, television can be used for good or evil."

Aaron nodded. "So they have a prophet. I would like to know what he talks about, then I'll judge for myself if what he says is from God."

"That's also what their church teaches," responded Esther. "Everyone is supposed to pray and find out for themselves if something is good and true. No blind obedience expected here. Susan said that there is something called General Conference this weekend and there will be two days of meetings shown on television. Come and watch it with us."

"I think I will," agreed Aaron nodding his head.

"It really makes sense to me," said Jacob. "If God loved people back in Bible times then he probably loves us today and wants to tell us how to live so we can be with Him again. Surely he wouldn't just love them and never talk to us."

"Susan told me that we lived with God before we came to earth," said Esther. "And that for us to be living here now we had to be on Jesus' side during the war in heaven with Satan. Otherwise we would have been cast out with Satan and the spirits that followed him. I'd never thought about it that way when I read about the war in the Bible. It makes me feel good that I was smart enough to know what was right even before I was born." She smiled. "It seems funny to think about it that way, but it makes sense."

Aaron nodded. "OK, I'll watch this conference thing with you this weekend. But don't expect me to jump right in like you two have." He got up and walked back into the house leaving them both on the porch.

Jacob looked over at Esther. "Do you think we told him too much? I don't want him to think we're crazy believing all this stuff," he said worriedly.

Esther laughed. "Jacob, you think that was too much? Wait until I tell him that they believe angels still appear to people!"

"Oh gosh, I didn't think about that," laughed Jacob.

\*\*\*

Elizabeth's first semester at college had flown by. She was packing to go home for Christmas vacation when she got a phone call. Thinking it was from Elaine, she hurriedly answered her cell phone. "Hello, Elaine."

There was a pause. "Hi, Elizabeth. This is Matthew."

She sat down hard on her bed. "Matthew? Oh, my gosh! I usually only get calls from home on my cell phone. How did you get this number?"

"I called Brandon at the police station," he confessed.

"I'll bet he was a little ambivalent about that!" she exclaimed. "How are you?"

"Not too well, I'm afraid."

Her heart skipped a beat. "Why? Is something wrong? Is someone sick?"

"No, nothing life threatening," he admitted. "It's just that I can't seem to get over this ache that I have in my heart."

"I don't understand," she said puzzled.

"I can't seem to get over you," he said. "Everyone at home is married except me, and I can't find another woman like you anywhere."

She laughed. "You're kidding, I hope. Of course you can find someone else. I'm really not that special."

"Oh believe me, you are."

"So Mark married Evie?" she asked trying to change the subject.

"Yes, about a week after you left. Would you believe she's already expecting a baby? Actually she expecting twins," he informed her with a laugh.

"Well, I bet Mark's proud."

"As a cock rooster," he chuckled. "Even the Johnson brothers are married. And Lydia and Michael Andrew are expecting a baby, too."

"It's sad that Rachel won't be there to see her first grandchild," she said.

"Yeah, it is."

"Sounds like Reverend Forester's flock is going to start growing," she said trying to get back on to a happy note.

"It will."

There was a long pause as he tried to think of something else to say.

"Where are you, Matthew? I thought the only phone around there was at the reverend's house," she said. "Did your parents get a telephone?"

"No, they didn't, but I'm not at home," he said quietly.

"Where are you then?" she asked perplexed.

"I'm at the campus bookstore," he said sheepishly.

"You're here? In Virginia, at my university?" she asked excitedly.

"Yeah. Brandon told me which school you had decided to attend and after thinking it over, I decided to drive up here."

"I don't believe it. Wait right there and I'll come find you. Don't you dare leave!"

She rushed out of her dorm room and ran down the stairs. It took her ten minutes to cross campus and get to the bookstore. During that time she kept him on the phone, afraid that if she hung up he would somehow disappear.

Then she saw him. He was standing by a pay phone with his back to her. She slowed to a walk and studied him from behind. He looked even better than she had remembered, his broad shoulders seemed broader and his brown hair curlier.

She tapped him on the shoulder and he turned around and hung up the phone.

"Hi," he said with a big grin. "You look prettier than I even remembered."

"I was just thinking the same thing about you," she grinned popping her cell phone in her pocket. "I can't believe you're here. You look great."

Matthew blushed. "I'm just the same big jerk who tried to kidnap you."

She looked up into his beautiful green eyes and laughed. "No you're not. That guy was just some misguided idiot to think he could kidnap me."

"Do you have time to have lunch with me?" he asked shyly.

"I do. There's a little cafe near here. Come on, I'll show you."

Over lunch she told him about her plans to go home for Christmas. "I'm flying out tomorrow morning. I wish you'd called earlier in the week."

He nodded. "I figured you'd be heading home for Christmas. We don't usually celebrate holidays as commercialized as they are. But I'll let you in on a little secret," he leaned close and whispered. "Years ago, my father carved a little nativity scene for my mother because she missed having a tree and all the things she had had as a girl. She puts it out every year. Reverend Forester has actually seen it, but he didn't say a thing to her about putting it away."

Elizabeth smiled. "We always center our holiday around Jesus and our family. I wish you could come and see how we do it. We make a lot of our own gifts and ... " she paused and her eyes lit up. "Matthew, come home with me for Christmas!"

He looked at her concerned and started to shake his head. "I don't know. What would your family think about you bringing me home with you?"

"They would see how happy I was to have you there and they would love you as much as I do." She blushed. "Matthew, I do love you. I don't know how it happened given how we met, but it's true." She reached over and took his hand.

He looked down at her small hand nestled in his and he smiled. "Are you trying to corrupt me? I'm not supposed to hold hands until I'm married."

She started to pull back, but he held on tightly to her hand. "I think I like holding hands and being corrupted that way," he grinned.

"Will you ... come home with me?"

"But I don't have any money for a plane ticket," he protested.

She thought for a minute. "Come on," she said pulling him from his seat.

At the travel agency where she had gotten her ticket, the agent refunded her money on the spot. "I have three people who need a seat on that plane to fly to California for Christmas. Everything's booked solid. I won't have any trouble reselling your ticket," he said.

Elizabeth held out the five hundred and fifty dollars and looked up at Matthew.

"Do you think your van can make it all the way to California again?" she asked with a grin. "I've got gas money."

\*\*\*

Reverend Forester knocked on the Hensley's front door. It was late, but he knew they would want the message.

John opened the door and invited him inside. The Reverend brushed the snow off his coat and walked inside. He stood in the doorway with his hat in his hands. "Evening John and Anna. Sorry to come by so late," he apologized. "But I got a phone call from Matthew and knew you would want his news."

"Come sit down, Reverend," said John. "Anna's baking cookies."

The Reverend smiled. "I thought I smelled cinnamon."

Anna wiped the flour off her hands and sat down beside John. "The cookies will be cooled in a few minutes," she said.

"Matthew said he's driving to California with Elizabeth to meet her family," informed the Reverend. "Did you know he had gone to Virginia to see her?"

John nodded. "He mentioned it."

Reverend nodded. "Well, I guess she invited him home for the holidays." He shrugged. "I know he has been pretty moody since she left. Maybe this will help him."

Anna smiled. "He's pretty much taken with her. I can't get him interested in anyone else since she left."

Reverend Forester nodded again. "I figured as much. I've done a lot of praying these last few months and I now know that I haven't been the best religious leader that I could have been." He looked at them and shook his head. "I'm trying to let people use a little more free will in their lives. So, whatever those two decide is up to them."

I'm glad you feel that way, Reverend. We've kind of come to that way of thinking ourselves," said Anna as she stood up. "I'll bet those cookies are cooled by now."

\*\*\*

Eve looked at her bulging belly and smoothed her sweater down as far as it would go. She looked over at Mark and said, "If these babies don't stop growing, I won't have anything to wear that will cover my belly."

He grinned at her and winked. "Are you sure there are only two babies in there?"

She picked up a sofa pillow and threw it at him. "The midwife said she felt two heads and two butts. I know you think this is funny, but I'm getting tired of being so fat. What if I always stay fat after they're born? Will you still love me if I'm fat?" she asked moodily. "Really fat?"

He walked over to her with a frown on his face. After walking around her and looking at her new figure from all angles he finally said, "I guess there will just be a lot more of you to love if you stay fat."

She hit him with the other sofa pillow. "You're mean!"

He scooped her up in his arms and carried her out onto the porch. After gently setting her in the rocking chair he had made for her, he kissed her cheek.

"There, rock those babies to sleep so they stop kicking you and I'll make us some hot chocolate," he said lovingly.

She looked at him with stars in her eyes as he went back into the house. How did that big tough-talking man turn into such a gentle husband? she wondered as she began to rock back and forth. He was right, though, rocking seemed to quiet them down. He came back with two steaming cups and a warm blanket.

"Are you warm enough with just that sweater on?" he asked.

"It's wool and plenty warm. Besides it's got to be at least forty-five degrees out today, the snow is melting," she observed as she sipped her cocoa.

"It is unseasonably warm today. According to Granny Hensley and those fuzzy caterpillars we saw last fall, it's supposed to be a hard winter."

"Those ones that are brown and black? I can never remember if it's going to be cold if they have more black fuzz or more brown fuzz," she complained.

"Me either," he admitted as he sat down in the other rocker. "But Granny says all the signs point to a lot of snow and cold weather by January. Anyway, the point of my bringing it up is that my father and I are going to spend a couple of days up on the mountain cutting down dead trees to stock up on firewood. I can't have my favorite wife and babies getting cold, can I?"

"Your favorite wife! I better be your only wife!" she scolded.

He leaned over and kissed her cheek. "Until death do us part," he laughed.

"Don't kid about that, it's bad luck," she said reaching up and grabbing his hand. "I don't even want to think about living without you. You know, I've had a crush on you since I was eleven years old."

"I figured it out. But at fifteen, I wasn't interested in such a skinny little girl." He poked at her belly. "Guess no one would call you skinny anymore."

She reached over and punched him in the arm. "That wasn't nice!"

\*\*\*

"That Mormon Tabernacle Choir Christmas Show was fantastic, wasn't it, Dad?" asked Esther when they got home from the Smalley's. "I love Christmas carols."

The boys were upstairs getting ready for bed and Jacob had gone in the dining room with Susan to set out the eggnog and cookies.

"I didn't think you knew any Christmas carols," mused Aaron.

"Just because we didn't have a big Christmas tree or decorations, didn't mean that mother didn't sing Christmas carols to me," informed Esther.

"I didn't know she did that," he said sadly. "I guess I never realized how much she missed celebrating Christmas. We never celebrated when I was growing up and I never missed all that holiday business."

"How old was she when you found her in Mississippi?" asked Esther as she moved closer to him on the sofa.

"Only sixteen. Her parents had died in a car accident and she was living in some kind of homeless shelter. I thought she was the most beautiful girl I had ever seen. You look a lot like her, you know," he said fondly.

"I do, really?"

Aaron nodded. "You have the same coloring and pixie nose," he said touching her upturned nose.

She pushed his hand away. "I remember mother's black hair, but I'm sure I don't remember that she had a pixie nose," she said annoyed.

He smiled. "You also get the same frown line across your forehead when you look at me like that."

She made an over exaggerated smile then stuck out her tongue. "Tell me how you two met, please," she begged. "No one has ever told me."

"Well, it's kind of embarrassing now," he said. "But I guess no worse than Jacob going off to steal a wife and getting converted instead." He winked at her.

She smiled and glanced over where Jacob and Susan were talking quietly. They were sitting on the floor and had started playing a game of Scrabble on the coffee table.

"It was in July," said Aaron, remembering. "I was in Jackson, Mississippi. It was a pretty big city even back then. I saw your mother standing outside a grocery store. It was blazing hot that day and she had on the shortest pair of shorts I'd ever seen. And she had great legs," he smiled.

Esther eyes widened. "That must have been a shock after growing up around modestly dressed church women."

"It was. But I'd never seen anything so pretty. She had long black hair down to her waist and she was begging for spare change from the customers coming out of the store," he said shaking his head. "She'd have a fit if she knew I told you that."

Esther grinned. "I bet she would."

"Anyway, I told her I'd left my wallet in my car, but if she would come with me I'd give her ten dollars."

"And she went with you?" asked Esther.

"She was reluctant at first. But I was a clean-cut guy and I guess I looked trustworthy. Sorry to say she found out I wasn't," he said sheepishly.

"You weren't trustworthy?"

He shook his head. "Not at all. When she got to my car, I'm ashamed to say that I chloroformed her."

Esther looked shocked. "You didn't!"

"I did. That was what the reverend told us to do to get a wife."

"What happened next?"

"When she woke up, we were two hundred miles from Jackson," he chuckled. "Boy, did I get an earful from her."

"She wasn't scared?" asked Esther.

"Probably she was. But she knew how to sass," he said smiling as he remembered the scene. "Anyway, I told her what I was doing. That I wouldn't hurt her or anything but that I thought she was beautiful and I wanted to marry her."

"You told her that? What did she say?"

He smiled. "She looked at me like I was crazy, then she started laughing."

"Really? She laughed?" asked Esther, incredulous.

He nodded. "She stared at me for a while. Then she said I was kind of cute and if it meant she didn't have to go back to the shelter she would marry me," he said.

"Just like that?"

"Just like that. And neither one of us ever regretted getting married," he said wistfully. "I wish she were here now. I still miss her so much sometimes it hurts."

***

Matthew put Elizabeth's suitcase in the back of the van. When he climbed in and started the engine he looked at her and smiled. "You're sure it doesn't bother you to ride in this van?"

She laughed. "Well, it does bring back memories, but they're not all bad. I see you still have a cooler in the back. How long have you been living out of the van this time, may I ask?"

"Just one day so far," he answered sheepishly. "I didn't know if you would even want to see me when I called but I was prepared to stay for a few days."

"Well, this time we have enough money to sleep in hotels and take baths. These seats are not that comfortable for sleeping," she complained.

"Are you ridiculing my van?"

"Definitely. But it is nice to have this much space when we're traveling," she said. "Just not for sleeping."

"What did your parents say when you called and told them I was bringing you home? Were they upset that you weren't flying?" he asked worriedly.

"No. Elaine was fine about you coming. She said she wanted to meet you."

"What about your father?" he asked nervously.

"He said to remind you that he has a gun, so I better be there soon," she grinned at Matthew's expression. "I'm kidding. He was fine with it. They both just want me to be happy and you make me happy."

"Just so you know," he said as they reached the interstate. "I sent the stolen license plate back to the owners with an apology."

"That was decent," she said skeptically.

"Well, I could have just thrown it away, but that didn't seem right. And this way I won't be stopped by the police." He looked over and grinned. "Not this time, anyway."

She laughed. "You're a piece of work, you know that?"

"Well, I'm giving up my life of crime forever and going straight."

"That's a relief to know," she chuckled at him. "Not to change the subject, but how long do you think it will take us to get to San Diego?"

"If we drive hard and don't hit bad weather I'm hoping to arrive two days before Christmas," he said as he passed an eighteen-wheeler.

"Just get us there in one piece, please," she said as she held on to the armrest.

***

Melinda looked at her mother. "Elizabeth is coming home for Christmas holiday, isn't she?" she asked.

"You tell me," said Janice. "You always know everything before I do."

Melinda smiled. "Not always, Mommy."

Janice put another colored ball on the Christmas tree. "Her mother said she would be flying home tomorrow. Here, put these elves on your side of the tree, I have three over here already." She handed Melinda two little plastic elves.

Melinda studied the tree before she decided where to hang them. "I don't know about that, I don't think she's going to fly home this time," she said. She picked up a blue ball and carefully hung in on a branch.

"Elaine said she was."

"I think she's coming in the white van," informed Melinda as she put a silver star on a low hanging branch.

"Don't be silly, the man that drives that van is in West Virginia," she said handing Melinda some tinsel. "Remember, not too much in one place."

Melinda shook her head. "No, she's with Matthew."

Janice stopped and looked at Melinda. "Did he kidnap her again?"

Melinda laughed. "No. This time she's happy. I'm just glad she's coming home, 'cause I made her a present for Christmas."

"You did. What is it?"

"It's a surprise, so you can't tell her," said the child seriously.

"I promise not to tell. What did you make?" asked Janice curiously.

"I made her a Christmas card and I even used glitter. And my teacher at school showed me how to make a friendship bracelet," informed Melinda.

"So that's why you wanted some of my embroidery thread and there was glitter all over your bedroom floor. I wondered about that," said Janice teasingly.

\*\*\*

Miriam looked out the window. It had started to snow and it was filling in all the places that had melted off a few days ago.

"It's so beautiful up here when it snows." She turned and looked at Rueben. He was building a fire in the fireplace. She still had trouble believing everything that had happened to her over the last eight months. She looked around her lovely little home and she sighed.

"Is something wrong?" asked Rueben looking up from his task.

"No. That was a sigh of contentment," she said. "A year ago I would have laughed at anyone who said I would be happily married and living in the Appalachian Mountains by Christmas. I would have said they were crazy."

He lit the fire and blew on it until the tiny flames grew bigger. He placed another log on the fire then stood up. "Come over here, wife," he said with a grin.

She walked across the room to him and he put his arms around her.

"I just thank the Lord that He led me to you before someone else married you."

She leaned her head onto his chest. "That wasn't going to happen anytime soon. I didn't even have a boyfriend."

"For which I am very grateful. I would have had to fight a duel for your hand," he said teasing. "I can't figure how you weren't already snatched up by some handsome man. Were you waiting for me?"

She smiled. He always seemed to say something that made her feel desired and desirable. She stood on tiptoe and gave him a kiss.

"If you've finished building the fire, I've got dinner ready for you." She walked across the room to the kitchen and started getting bowls out of the cupboard.

He put one more log on the fire. "That sounds great. I'm starved. I don't think I've ever chopped that much wood in one day before. It built up my appetite."

"Good, because I over did it making the stew. I think there's enough for six people," she said. "I got carried away with adding vegetables."

"Well, it certainly smells wonderful," he sniffed appreciatively.

As they ate she looked wistfully out the window at the falling snow.

Rueben noticed her melancholy expression. "Is there something wrong?" he asked. "You don't look as happy as you claim to be."

"No. I'm very happy here. The snow just reminds me of Christmas back home in New Jersey. I always loved the decorations and the music that they had all over town. If the truth be known, I'm happier here than I've been in a long time. It was always kind of lonely for me at Christmas after my parents died."

Rueben nodded. "I can see how you could miss that. I grew up without it, but Mrs. Hensley talked to me once about how she missed celebrating Christ's birth. Her husband gave her a special present and she puts it out every year."

She turned from the window and looked at him. "What kind of present?"

She watched as he got up and walked over to the front room closet. He pulled a small box from the top shelf and brought it back to the table. "One like this," he said handing the box to her.

She opened the handmade wooden box and nestled inside on a bed of cotton were wooden figures of Mary and Joseph, a small manger with real hay and a baby Jesus. She looked up at her husband in surprise.

"They're beautiful. Where did you get them?" she asked in awe as she noted the intricate details of the carved figures.

"John Hensley taught me how to carve them for you. He made a set for his wife years ago. It's not exactly a worldly celebration to honor Christ's birth. Reverend Forester has seen the set John made and he's never objected to it," he explained. "Do you really like it?"

She smiled up at him. "I love it. I can't believe you carved them. I shall always treasure them because you made them for me. Thank you so much."

"I put love into every piece," he said touching the figure of the tiny baby.

"I know just where I'll put them." She got up and cleared a place on the fireplace mantle to set up the figures. "Now it feels like Christmas."

***

"Dinner was wonderful, Mrs. Marcus," said Matthew.

"How many times do I have to ask you to call me Elaine?" she asked smiling. "It makes me feel really old to be called Mrs. Marcus. That's Brandon's mother, not me."

"Sorry. I'm not used to calling women by their first names," he apologized.

"And stop apologizing for everything. You are way too polite."

Elizabeth laughed at Elaine. "I never imagined you saying that to any of my friends," she said. "Back in West Virginia all the men I met are polite to the women. It was rather refreshing actually."

Maggie giggled. "He's too polite," she said nodding so hard her curls bounced.

Elaine smiled and began clearing the dirty dishes off the table. Matthew stood up and gathered his plate and glass. "I'll help you clean up," he offered.

"You will not!" said Elaine sternly. "You are company. Go sit in the living room with Elizabeth and the twins. Brandon can help me clean up."

Brandon rolled his eyes. "You're not helping me here, Matthew. I'm having to do more chores than normal just because you keep offering to do them." He took Matthew's plate and glass from him.

"I'm sorry. I don't mean to cause trouble," Matthew said embarrassed.

"How did you ever manage to kidnap my daughter?" asked Brandon. "I would have thought as soon as she asked to come back home you would have turned right around and driven her straight home."

Matthew blushed. "I'm so sorry about that. It was the reverend's idea. I would have never have done anything that on my own."

"Obviously," said Brandon. "And by the way. I have a question for you. How in the heck do you know which dirt road in the West Virginia mountains to take to get home? I must have driven down dozens of logging roads and never found the one that led to your town."

Matthew looked puzzled. "I look for the one with the telephone poles."

Brandon stared at him and Elizabeth laughed.

"They do have electricity and a few telephones up there," she informed him.

"The logging roads don't have poles," explained Matthew earnestly.

"Cripes," said Brandon. "Why didn't I think of that? We spent three days driving up and down the mountains for nothing."

"Mommy, Daddy said a bad word," tattled Martin. "He said cripes."

"Hush you little pip-squeak," said Brandon. "I think it's time for you to go to bed and me to help with the dishes. Now scoot."

"Yes, Daddy," said Martin.

# Chapter 15

Eve put an extra sweater and socks in Mark's backpack. "Are you sure you have to go?" she asked worriedly. "I'm so close to delivering these babies I worry when you're not here with me."

Mark stopped sharpening his ax and walked over to her. He caressed her tummy and gently pulled her into his arms. "It's only for two days and Mother is coming to stay with you. Stop worrying." He kissed her forehead then went and picked up the ax.

"I put extra sandwiches in the cooler for you. I know how hungry you get when you work hard," she said bravely putting on a smile for him.

He laughed. "I don't know why we even bring a cooler, it's cold enough out there to freeze our butts off."

"Hush, no talk like that in front of the babies," she warned.

There was a hasty knock at the door and Anna peaked in. "Are you ready, Mark? Your Dad's waiting in the truck for you. Hi, Evie."

She came inside and stomped the snow off her boots then put her overnight bag down by the sofa. "While the men are all off working, we're going to have fun cooking. Lydia and Miriam promised to come over this afternoon so Granny Hensley can show us how she makes her famous chicken pot pie."

Eve smiled. "I guess I won't have to worry about being lonely." She turned to Mark and accepted his kiss. "Be careful," she warned. "These babies need a father."

Mark tucked a blond tendril behind her ear then hurried outside. "I'll be extra careful for you and the babies," he called over his shoulder as he closed the door.

Anna looked at the worried expression on Eve's face.

"Try not to worry so," she said. "The men have been cutting trees and firewood for generations. They know what they're doing even if it looks dangerous. John's been taking our boys with him since they turned ten, he'll keep an eye on Mark."

Eve looked at her mother-in-law and tried to smile, but a tear trickled down her cheek. "I know all that. It's just that I have this overwhelming premonition that something terrible is going to happen to Mark. I feel it in my bones." She shivered and wrapped her arms around her chest.

Anna walked over and put her arms around Eve. "It's probably just all those pregnancy hormones rushing around in your body. I had it bad enough myself and you have it double. Come on. I'll put my clothes in the extra bedroom and help you finish that baby quilt we started quilting last week."

Eve nodded. She wiped her face on her sleeve and patted her stomach. "Daddy will be home in two days, you both be good until then."

"How far along are you now, Evie?" asked Anna as she came back from the bedroom carrying the baby quilt.

"Midwife Ansley says I'm about thirty-six weeks now, but she said twins often come early so I guess I could go into labor anytime. I feel as big as a house already, I don't know if my tummy will stretch any bigger."

"Well, let's hope they hold on a few more days. The longer you carry them the better off they'll be," said Anna. "Where is your sewing basket?"

"In my room." Eve went into her bedroom and brought out the sewing basket.

"I'll finish up the edging and you start on the other end with the quilting," suggested Anna. "Remember, small tight stitches help it hold together better through frequent washing."

Eve nodded and threaded her needle. "I'll have to wash it often?'

Anna smiled. "Well, unless you want it to smell like pee or puke."

Eve wrinkled up her nose. "Oh, yeah."

They spent the rest of the morning working on the quilt then stopped for lunch. Anna made them both egg salad sandwiches and they had just finished eating when Granny Hensley arrived with Reverend Forester. She thanked him for bringing her and headed straight for the kitchen to put down a bag of supplies.

Reverend Forester smiled at the women. "Mary wanted me to tell you she wouldn't be coming for the cooking lesson. Her arthritis is acting up and this cold weather isn't helping. Maybe next time." He put a box of supplies on the table then waved and left.

Anna helped Granny take off her coat.

"It's blustery out there today," Granny said. "Poor Mary's in pain today. Don't help my lumbago much neither."

As they were getting out the stew pot, Miriam and Lydia arrived. Eve's mother had decided to come learn Granny's secrets and she arrived soon after the others. Mrs. Leah Atkins was a small quiet woman. She didn't get away from home much as her rheumatoid arthritis made her self conscious of her crippled hands. Eve was her only daughter. She had four sons who helped out with chores, but she missed Eve's company since she'd gotten married and moved out.

"It'll be nice to have babies around again," she told Anna. "I wish my hands weren't so dang crippled up. I won't be much help to poor Evie when the babies come."

"Granny and I will be available for that," assured Anna. "You just come visit as much as you're able."

"My Evie's mighty lucky to have such a nice mother-in-law," Leah said gratefully. She cleared her throat and whispered. "Mine was a bitch."

Anna tried not to laugh, but she remembered old Mrs. Atkins and she had been a fierce woman with a bad temper. "I remember her."

Leah nodded. "I try to forget her."

"OK, ladies," called Granny. "I'm ready to be gettin' started."

Over the next two hours, Granny showed them all how to stew the hen and remove the meat from the bones. While the meat cooled she made her special flakey piecrust and a gravy. Anna chopped the vegetables for the pie.

The rest of them chatted while the pie baked in the oven, but Eve was unusually quiet. She couldn't seem to shake the feeling that something terrible was about to happen and she prayed that the men would be safe.

\*\*\*

The elderly lady shopper plucked at Jacob's sleeve and asked, "Young man, how do I know if this cantaloupe is ripe?"

Jacob put down the box he was carrying to stock the shelves and picked up a cantaloupe. "You see how there is a pinkish glow to this one underneath the white and green on the outside?"

She nodded.

"Now smell it," he held it under her nose. "Does it smell kind of musky?"

"Yes. Does that mean it's ripe?"

"Yes, Ma'am." He reached down and picked up the box, but she pulled on his sleeve again. He put down the box.

"What about this avocado?" she asked in shaky voice.

He picked up the avocado. "This one is nice and dark green almost blackish. When I gently squeeze it like this, it feels kind of soft."

Jacob spent a few more minutes answering her questions about the peaches and nectarines. After she left the produce section, he took the box of supplies and stocked the cereal aisle. When he went to the back storage room Mitch told him that the boss wanted to talk to him.

"I'll go see what he wants," said Jacob. He frowned and wondered if he had done something wrong. Jacob knocked on Bill Robinson's office door then stuck his head in.

"You wanted to talk to me, sir?"

Mr. Robinson waved him in while he finished a conversation on the telephone.

Jacob took a seat in front of the desk and waited.

Mr. Robinson smiled at him as he hung up the phone. "Jacob, I've noticed that you seem to know a lot about produce. I've watched you answering the customer's questions about the vegetables and fruit."

"I was raised on a farm and the rest of the things I learned about when I went shopping with my sister after my mother died. We kind of learned some of it by trial and error," he admitted. "I guess I know about most of the things we sell here."

"Would you be willing to be in charge of the produce section of the store for me? It would involve some early morning hours when you would have to go to my suppliers and pick out the vegetables and fruit to restock that department," explained Mr. Robinson. "I've been doing it myself for months since my produce manager retired, but I'm getting a little overwhelmed."

Jacob felt honored that his boss would trust him with a whole department. "I don't mind getting up early," he said. "I used to have to milk the cow at three AM."

Mr. Robinson smiled. "Good, good then. It would mean a pay raise, too. Could you start tomorrow morning so I don't have to do it? We won't need a lot of things for tomorrow because we'll be closed the day after that on Christmas."

"Sure thing, Mr. Robinson. Just tell me where to go and what we need."

They went to the produce section of the storeroom and Mr. Robinson showed him what was still in stock and they discussed what would need to be purchased. He told him where the supplier was located and gave a few suggestions on how to bid on the produce.

"The more money you save with them, the more we can save our customers," said Mr. Robinson. "Maybe I should go with you the first time."

"No, its alright, really," said Jacob. "I've dealt with suppliers before for my little community in West Virginia. We often bought things in bulk to save money."

"Very good then. Thanks, it takes a big load off my shoulders." Mr. Robinson slapped him on the back and headed back to his office. "Oh, I almost forgot. Could you tell Mitch I want to talk to him?"

Jacob returned to the storeroom to finish his stocking his shelves.

"What did the boss want?" asked Mitch. "You're not in trouble, are you?"

"I guess I got a promotion," said Jacob rubbing his chin. "I'm the new produce manager. I start tomorrow."

"Ugh," said Mitch. "I thought about that when Gary retired, but I hate getting up that early. I guess I'll be stuck back here by myself again until we find another flunky to help me out." He laughed. "Congratulations, I think."

"Oh, I almost forgot. He wants to talk to you now."

Mitch made a face. "I hope there's nothing wrong."

Mitch came back a few minutes later with a big grin plastered across his face. "Guess what? I'm the new assistant manager, can you believe it?"

Jacob slapped him on the back. "Congratulations, boss!"

Jacob was so excited about telling his father that he got a promotion at work that he didn't pay any attention to the knocking sound the engine was making as he was driving home that evening. Suddenly the car stopped completely. He coasted to the side of the snowy road and got out of the car. It was dark and he put on the emergency flashers and grabbed a flashlight to look under the hood. He couldn't tell what was wrong and he was standing there shivering trying to decide what to do when a car pulled in behind him.

"Car trouble is the pits in this weather," said a voice out of the dark.

Jacob looked up and saw a man approaching.

"It sure is, I'm freezing, and I can't tell what's wrong with it."

The man came over and looked under the hood. After a few minutes he said, "Why don't you let me give you a ride home? You can have it towed in the morning. It's too dark to tell anything tonight."

"Thanks. I think I'll do that." Jacob shut the hood and followed behind the man to his car. There was a woman in the front passenger seat and he climbed in the back.

"Where are you headed?" he asked.

"We're visiting friends for Christmas," said the woman. "We live in Utah, but made a lot of friends when we lived here in Idaho."

The man turned and glanced back at Jacob. "My name is David Bednar and this is my wife, Susan. Good thing we came along, there's not much traffic on this road tonight."

"I really appreciate the ride. My name's Jacob." He gave them directions and they dropped him off a few minutes later at his house.

"Thanks again," called Jacob as they left. "Have a nice visit."

Susan met Jacob as he was coming up the steps. "Hi," she said cheerily. "I came by to drop off some things for Esther. Who was that and where's your car?"

"It broke down a few miles back down the road. That was a really nice couple here to visit some friends. He said his name was David Bednar."

Susan's mouth dropped open. "That was David Bednar?"

"And his wife, Susan," said Jacob. "They used to live in Idaho."

Susan grabbed his arm. "Don't you remember him? He gave a talk in General Conference last October. He's one of the twelve Apostles!"

Now Jacob's mouth dropped open. "I remember now. Gosh!"

They both watched as the car drove out of view.

After they went inside, Jacob took Susan by the hand.

"I have some good news," he said shyly. "I got promoted to produce manager."

"Wow, congratulations," she said. "That's great."

"I still can't believe it," said Jacob. "It seems like nothing but good things have been happening since we moved here."

"Your family has had some great things happen. But don't think that just because you are living right that nothing bad will ever happen," she warned.

"You mean Mormons have bad luck, too?" he joked.

"You know what I mean," she said as she punched him in the arm. "Just because someone has trials in their life, doesn't mean they caused them or did something bad."

"I know. Trials can make you stronger. It was hard on my family when my mother died, but it made us depend on each other more and made my family stronger. And we know that one day we'll see her again," he said softly.

"Yes, you will," agreed Susan. "I guess I'll see you tomorrow."

"Right, we've been invited for Christmas dinner. See you then."

***

Christmas day started early at the Marcus household. The twins were up and going strong by five o'clock that morning.

"Mommy, Daddy, come see what Santa brought us!" they both shouted as they rushed into their parent's bedroom. Maggie tugged on Brandon's arm until he scooped her up and pulled her into the bed.

"It's too early to get up," he mumbled

"Daddy, you have to come," pleaded Martin as he tried to pull Maggie back out of the bed. "We got scooters!"

Elaine was laughing as they both tugged on Brandon's arm.

"Come on Daddy. Don't be a spoilsport," Elaine said, climbing out of bed. "You two go wait by the tree while we get our robes on," she instructed the twins.

The children bounced out of the room shouting, "We're going to get Elizabeth!"

The adults were sitting around the living room sipping coffee and watching the twins open their presents when Matthew found them.

"Hey," he said as he sat down by Elizabeth. "How long have you been up?"

"They woke us up about an hour ago. I can't believe you slept through all the squealing," she laughed. "You must have been really tired."

He nodded and yawned. "I'm still recovering from our road trip."

While the twins played with their new toys, Elizabeth helped Elaine make breakfast. They always had blueberry pancakes on Christmas morning.

It was later that morning, after everyone else had gone to visit Brandon's parents in Chula Vista that Elizabeth handed Matthew a present.

"I can't take this," he said shyly. "I didn't get you anything. We don't usually exchange gifts at Christmas."

"I know. But you have to take it. I bought it for you and it won't fit anyone else," she insisted. "I hope you like it."

He carefully undid the tape and removed the colored wrapping paper. "This is the first Christmas present I've ever had," he said smiling as he opened the box. He pulled out a dark green plaid flannel shirt. He held it up to his chest. "Wow, when did you buy this?"

"When I went to the store yesterday for some last minute things that Elaine needed. Do you like it? I thought it would match your eyes. And every guy in West Virginia can use a flannel shirt during the winter, right?" she asked hopefully.

"I love it. The ones I've been wearing are getting pretty worn out. Thanks." He wanted to lean over and give her a kiss, but felt too shy.

Elizabeth stood on tiptoe and kissed his cheek. When he blushed, she laughed at him. "I brought my own mistletoe," she explained holding up a twig of green leaves and white berries. "It's traditional to get a kiss if you're standing under mistletoe."

"Oh. I've never heard of that."

"Boy, I'm going to have to teach you all kinds of traditional things, aren't I?" she asked. "Tons of things."

He put the flannel shirt on over his t-shirt. "It fits perfectly. How did you know what size to get?" he asked. "My mother has always sewn most of my shirts, I don't even know what size I would buy."

"I looked around until I found a man who looked about your size and asked him what size he wore," she laughed. "What do you want to do today while everyone's gone to their grandparents house?"

"Could we take a walk outside?" he asked looking out the window. "I've never seen flowers blooming this time of year before. It doesn't even seem like winter down here in southern California. It's kind of weird."

"We can take a walk, or we could even go to the beach if you want."

"Really? Is it close by? I've never been to the beach before," he admitted.

"Didn't you see the beach when you and Mark were here last spring?" she asked.

He blushed again. "No. I'm ashamed to say we were too busy following you around. We never went to the beach."

She shook her head. "I'll call Maria and see if she would like to go, too. We usually do something together on Christmas while the younger kids play with their new toys. I'll bet the beach is deserted today," she said excitedly. "We could have it all to ourselves."

Elizabeth was right, there wasn't another soul on the beach when the three of them got there. It was too chilly to go into the water but they walked along the sand, picked up seashells and explored the tide pools.

"Elaine used to bring me here all the time after I started walking again," she told Matthew. "I had been in a wheelchair for two years and it was glorious to be able to walk around barefoot in the sand."

"It sounds like you've been through a lot. You must be one of the bravest people I've ever met," said Matthew admiringly.

Elizabeth shook her head. "I wasn't brave. I just did what I had to do."

Maria looked at Matthew. "Don't believe her. She was brave. You know she was almost completely paralyzed for a while. When I met her she was just beginning to walk again. She used to sit at the piano for hours re-teaching her fingers how to play. I couldn't believe it when we started high school and she began racing on the swim team with us," she said proudly looking at Elizabeth. "I think you're amazing."

Elizabeth smiled. "It was the only way I could be with my best friend. She was on the team so I started swimming, too. We did pretty good, didn't we?" She reached down into the water and carefully picked up a starfish.

Maria scowled. "I wish you were still here so you could help me with my homework from nursing school. It's the hardest thing I've ever done!"

"Now, don't believe her, Matthew," kidded Elizabeth. "She was a whiz at every subject she took in high school."

"Well, this is harder," protested Maria. "I hope I can make it through."

"I have no doubts at all," encouraged Elizabeth. She held out the starfish for Matthew to see. "Have you ever seen one of these before?"

"Only in pictures. It doesn't bite or anything does it?" he asked tentatively touching the rough surface of the creature.

"You handle poisonous snakes and are asking if this bites?" she laughed.

He ignored her and leaned over to pick up a hermit crab. "Look at this funny little thing," he said holding out his hand.

They walked a little further down the beach to where some large rocks had pockets of seawater around them. Maria climbed over a big rock following Elizabeth as she released the starfish back into the water.

Matthew watched the two of them. They reminded him of himself and Mark. His brother was also his best friend and they always encouraged each other when things seemed tough. He missed Mark now that he was married and living with Eve.

He climbed up beside Maria and said, "You know, Maria, I never did apologize for kidnapping you. I'm really sorry. My stupidity almost cost you your life."

"Maybe. But you were the one who took me to the hospital, so I forgive you," she said easily. "But I did learn one thing from that experience," she teased.

"What's that?" he asked concerned.

"Never get into a van with strange men, no matter how cute they are!"

Elizabeth laughed. "That's the truth."

They stayed at the beach for several hours until dinnertime then headed home.

***

Christmas at the Smalley house was always festive but this year it seemed even more so with the Brown family enjoying the celebration for the first time.

"That's the biggest turkey I've ever seen," said Esther watching as Maryanne basted the twenty-five pound bird and slid it back into the oven.

"I've never cooked one this big before, but with all these extra guests I had Robert get the biggest one he could find. It should be done in thirty minutes or so. Let's go see what they're doing in the living room." Maryanne wiped her hands and took off her apron.

The kitchen counters were lined with pies and plates of cookies she and Beth had made over the last few days. Susan had also made her special Christmas caramels and chocolate candies.

In the living room, Jacob was sitting on the floor playing Monopoly with Susan, Ephraim and Will. The two younger boys, Isaac and Ronnie, were playing checkers. Aaron and Robert were sitting on the sofa talking with the two missionary Elders who had been invited over for Christmas dinner.

Elder Whitsoe was from New Mexico and Elder Armstrong was from Georgia.

"What do you two think about all this snow?" asked Robert.

Elder Armstrong smiled, "I'm twenty years old and this is the first time I've ever had a white Christmas. I love it!"

Elder Whitsoe laughed. "He went out yesterday and made a snowman on the lawn in front of our apartment."

"Heck, Elder, don't make fun of me. You had a snowball fight with the Baker kids and I didn't make fun of you."

"True. It has been fun to see snow. We do have it up in the mountains near my home, but not usually before January and not in my own yard," admitted Elder Whitsoe.

Just then Beth came in the room carrying a letter. "Hey everyone, I have my brother's letter that came yesterday. He wanted me to read it to the family on Christmas day." She proceeded to read James' letter wishing them all a Merry Christmas and telling them all the latest news from his mission. When she finished she looked around the room until she spotted Esther.

"You know what?" she asked no one in particular. "James will be home from his mission in two weeks and I can't wait for him to meet Esther. I've been writing to him for months about how wonderful she is."

Esther looked up embarrassed. "You haven't really, have you?"

Maryanne laughed. "I have, too. You're just the type of girl he usually falls for."

"What type is that?" she asked questioningly.

"Sweet and innocent," said Robert. "Now everyone quit teasing her."

"I hear the kitchen timer," said Maryanne. "It's time to eat!"

After dinner the younger boys all sat around on the floor at Robert's feet and the adults found comfortable places to sit and listen to the story of Jesus' birth as told in the New Testament. It was a family tradition for Robert to read the story each year. Afterwards Beth played the piano and they all sang Christmas carols until it was time for Robert to take the missionaries back to their apartment.

"Can I ride with you?" asked Aaron. "I'd like to ask them a few questions when there aren't a dozen people around to interrupt."

"Sure, get your coat," said Robert.

Aaron sat in the passenger seat up front but turned around to look at the Elders.

"I've been reading The Book of Mormon," he admitted. "And I have a few questions. When the prophet Alma was talking about dying he said that we would all stand before God and be judged on our actions here in this life. So does that mean that Mormons don't believe that once saved always saved?"

Elder Whitsoe nodded. "Yes sir, we believe you need to do more than just confess that Jesus is the Christ. Jesus said if you love me, keep my commandments. So just saying that you believe in Jesus isn't enough to live with him in heaven when you die. Heck, even Satan believes that Jesus is real."

Aaron thought about that for a minute.

"That makes sense," he said. "And you believe that we will all be punished only for our own sins, not Adam's transgressions or anyone else's, right?"

"Right. How can a person be held responsible for sins someone else commits?"

"I believe that, too," agreed Aaron. "My church taught some of the same things as far as baptism by immersion and that there really is a hell. Alma talked a lot about people going to hell if they didn't live righteously. Some churches claim there is no hell and that everyone will go to heaven no matter how they live. That never made any sense to me."

"I think you've pretty much got it right so far," said Robert.

Aaron rode in silence for a few minutes. "I've also been reading about the priesthood you have in your church. That it is the same as in Christ's early church and you can heal the sick and perform ordinances in your temples like they did anciently. In the New Testament Paul was given the power to bind things on earth and in heaven. What does that mean exactly?" asked Aaron.

Elder Armstrong said, "That means that families can be forever bound together and be a family unit in heaven. Husbands and wives can be sealed together for time and all eternity in the temple, not just until death do you part."

"I thought that was what I was reading in one of the pamphlets but I wanted to be sure I had it right. I would like to take the missionary discussions and be baptized. I want to be sealed to my family," declared Aaron earnestly.

Robert turned to him and smiled. "Have you told your children about this yet?"

Aaron shook his head. "No."

"Well, that's sure a fantastic Christmas present then," said Robert.

"I know that Esther and Jacob have been waiting for me to come around before they got baptized. I guess they've waited long enough."

\*\*\*

Anna stomped the snow from her boots before she opened the front door. An unexpected blizzard had hit the mountain last night. She refused to let Eve out on the slippery ground and she had gone to the barn to milk the cow. When she opened the door the lovely smell of cinnamon wafted over her. She took off her coat and gloves, left her wet boots on the mat beside the door and put on her shoes.

Granny Hensley smiled at her when she went into the kitchen.

"You're up early, Granny," she said. "What's that wonderful smell?"

"I ain't been able to sleep past five o'clock for years. I decided to make a coffee cake for breakfast. You been out milking?"

Anna nodded. "Who will milk Sassy for you today?" she asked.

Granny laughed and her naked gums showed. "Mr. Aimsley will milk that silly goat for me. Him be a wonderful neighbor. He don't never let me go out to the barn when it gets nasty like this."

"Well, good for him." Anna's brow furrowed. "I wonder if the men got hit by this storm. Do you know where they were planning to go for wood?" she asked worriedly.

"Most like they went to the backside of the mountain. Last year they took trees from this side. This be a big storm though, they 'uns probably got snow, too." Granny leaned over and opened the oven door but the cake wasn't quite ready when she checked. "Needs a few more minutes, I reckon," she said.

Eve peeked around the door. "You're both up early. I'm sorry I slept so late, but these babies kicked for hours and then I had bad dreams. I'm still tired," she said yawning. She came in and sat down at the table. "I had a dream that Mark got hurt."

Anna walked over and gave her a hug.

"Pregnancy hormones at their worst," she commiserated. "I had bad dreams when I was pregnant, too. Mostly that something would be wrong with the baby. They never came true."

"Lessen you count that Mark was a little hell raiser!" laughed Granny as she patted Eve on the back. "This cake's 'bout done. Sugar and cinnamon can cure just about any black mood."

Eve smiled at her. "I love you Granny. You and Anna are two of the best things I gained when I married Mark."

It was eleven o'clock that morning when Eve's world fell apart. The women all heard a big commotion on the front porch and the door flew open. John and Rueben came in covered with snow and ice, a large bundle in their arms.

"A tree fell on Mark," said John wearily. "He's pretty busted up."

"Bring him into the bedroom," ordered Anna. "I'll get warm blankets. Granny, boil water for some hot tea, please. These men look frozen."

The two men carried the unconscious Mark into the bedroom and put him on the twin bed. When they peeled back the frozen blankets, Mark's legs were covered in blood.

Anna gasped and looked at John. He shook his head sadly.

Eve took one look at Mark and passed out on the floor.

***

It was only eight o'clock in California when the phone rang. Brandon was getting dressed. He had been off yesterday for Christmas but was heading back to work this morning.

Elaine was getting the twins breakfast. "Can you get that please, Brandon? We've had a little milk spill ... " she called to him.

Brandon smiled and picked up the phone. "Hello."

"Is this the Marcus home?" asked a woman's worried voice.

"Yes, it is."

"Is my son Matthew still there?"

"Yes, he is. Is this his mother, Anna?" asked Brandon.

"Yes. His brother has been in a terrible accident," her voice cracked as she spoke. "I need him to come home immediately. May I speak to him?" Anna was holding back the tears with all her might.

"Hang on, I'll go find him."

Brandon found Matthew and Elizabeth sitting on the front porch eating doughnuts and laughing at the antics of the squirrels that lived in the trees on their street.

"Matthew. Your mother is on the phone. Your brother has been in an accident."

Matthew jumped up and followed Brandon. Elizabeth hurried after them.

They could only hear one side of the conversation, but to Elizabeth it sounded serious. She held Brandon's hand while they listened.

"And both his legs were crushed?" groaned Matthew. "Isn't there anything that can be done for him?"

"No. John thinks his hips are broken, too." Anna started sobbing. "Matthew we need you. Please come home right away."

"I will. I'll drive as fast as I can, Mother," he said. "But it will take me at least four days to get that far."

"Be careful, Matthew. Don't have an accident on the way," she begged. "I can't bear to lose you both."

"I'll leave right now," he promised. "I love you." After hanging up, Matthew sat down on the sofa and put his head in his hands.

Elizabeth sat down beside him and put her hand on his arm. "What happened?"

He looked at her with fear and pain in his eyes. "The men back home had gone out on the mountain to cut dead trees for firewood. We do that every year," he explained. "They were hit by an unexpected blizzard the first night out. The next morning Mark was working a tree and the weight of the snow in the branches made it come down before it should have. He couldn't get out of the way in time. His legs were crushed." He started crying and Elizabeth felt a lump in her own throat.

"Won't they take him to a hospital?" asked Brandon.

Matthew shook his head. "We don't believe in that, remember?"

"But they might be able to do something to help him," argued Elizabeth.

Matthew sighed. "Mother doesn't think he'll make it. Both is legs were crushed beyond repair and probably his pelvis. He lost a lot of blood.

I'm sure I won't be able to get home before he dies." His face was stricken with grief. "I shouldn't have come here. I should have been out on the mountain with them."

"No! You couldn't have stopped that tree and you might have been hurt too," protested Elizabeth. "Don't feel guilty for coming here, please."

"I might have a way to get you home today. Come on. Get your things together. I have a friend with a private plane," said Brandon. "We'll worry about your van later."

"I'm going, too!" insisted Elizabeth.

Brandon nodded. "Hurry and get some things together then."

\*\*\*

Melinda stopped in the middle of playing with her new dolls and looked at her mother with wide eyes. "Mommy something very bad has happened," she said solemnly.

Janice picked her up. "Did something happen to Elizabeth?" she asked.

Melinda shook her head. "To Matthew's brother," said Melinda. "Elizabeth is going back to that place with the snakes because that other man got hurt."

Bill looked at Janice and shook his head. "How does she do that?"

Janice handed the child to Bill. "I'll call Elaine and find out what's happening."

Melinda started crying. "He got hurt bad, Daddy."

# Chapter 16

It had been a week since Mark's accident and he only regained consciousness for a few moments at a time. His pain was so excruciating that Granny had used up most of her herbal medicines to keep him even partially comfortable when he was awake. Eve hardly left his bedside and she was losing weight because of her fear. They all knew he was dying and there was nothing anyone could do about it.

Anna was beside herself with grief. "A mother is not supposed to see her child die before she does!" she exclaimed one morning to John.

"Where does it say that in the Bible?" he asked.

"If we took him to a hospital, maybe they could do something!" pleaded Anna.

John sadly shook his head. "Anna, even if they surgically removed his legs, there is too much damage to his hips and internal organs," he said sorrowfully. "I don't know how he's lasted this long."

She sat on the side of the bed and cried great wrenching sobs. John went over and sat beside her. When he put his arms around her, she leaned into him and cried harder.

"Why did this happen? We try to live good lives. We treat our neighbors well, we go to church, why does God let bad things happen?" she sobbed.

"Dying is the next step. To God it's not a bad thing to die, its just going home to Him," said John soothingly as he caressed her hair. "It breaks my heart to loose him too, but we can't change what is meant to be."

"I don't believe in predestination," she declared. "I don't think this horrible thing was destined to happen."

"It's your right to believe whatever you want but that doesn't change what's happening right now," he said gently.

She buried her face in his shoulder. He held her and let her cry until she had no more tears left.

Matthew and Elizabeth were staying at Mark's house with Eve and Granny. Matthew helped Granny take care of Mark and Elizabeth did all the household chores. She was very worried about Eve and the babies.

"Granny, I can't get her to eat hardly anything," protested Elizabeth when she returned to the kitchen with Eve's untouched breakfast plate.

Granny shook her head. "She be mourning for Mark already. I'm afeared for the babes, too. She can't do this much longer before they be getting sick," she said sadly. "I'll go check on her if you stir this pot fer me."

Elizabeth looked in the pot on the stove that had a clear liquid bubbling in it. "It smells funny. What is it?" she asked wrinkling her nose.

"I be making more arnica juice for his pains. It be almost ready. The heat's off, just stir it while it cools," instructed Granny as she left the kitchen.

Eve was holding Mark's hand and singing softly to him when he opened his eyes and looked over at her.

"You are so beautiful," he whispered through dry cracked lips.

Eve quickly stood up and kissed his cheek. "I always said you needed glasses," she sniffed. She held his head and gave him a sip of water then wiped his face with a cool cloth. The infection in his legs was causing his fever to increase and his forehead felt even hotter than it had a few hours ago. "Oh Mark, please don't leave me!" she sobbed. "I can't bear to live without you, you know that." She laid her head on his shoulder.

Mark looked lovingly at his wife. He raised his hand slowly and caressed her cheek. "I have to go Evie. I saw Grandpa Hensley last night and he said it was my time. Evie, please don't cry," he begged in a hoarse whisper.

Eve's sobs shook her whole body. "I can't bear this!" She flung herself across his chest. "Our babies need you!"

He patted her back. "I'm sorry to be such a disappointment to you, Evie. I would stay if I could," his voice faded as he fell into a drugged asleep.

Granny watched from the door. "Evie, let me sit here. You go rest for a little."

"No! I can't leave him!" Sobs wracked her body.

"The medicine will make him sleep. You need to sleep, too. You been in that chair all week," protested Granny. "He's not awake now."

Eve shook her head and clung to Mark's hand. "I'll sleep later."

It was Matthew who carried her to the bed in the master bedroom an hour later after she fell asleep with her head on Mark's pillow.

Elizabeth's heart ached for her. She watched Matthew as he tenderly covered Eve with a quilt and realized she couldn't bear to loose him either. Fear gripped her as she thought about leaving Matthew to go back to college.

Eve was back at Mark's bedside that afternoon when he quietly slipped away. She screamed a cry of anguish when his breathing stopped.

Matthew lifted her out of her chair and took her into her bedroom where she lay on the bed sobbing. "I can't live without him," she cried. "Matthew, how can I go on?"

"You have the babies to live for now," he said softly. "They need you." He left her weeping on the bed and his heart ached for her.

Granny sighed and covered Mark's face with the blanket. "Matthew, go fetch your parents. It be time we put this poor boy to rest," she said softly.

\*\*\*

Jacob and Susan were sitting in his car eating hamburgers and watching the snow fall softly around them. "I guess we should head back home before this gets too deep," he said reluctantly.

Susan finished the last french fry and smiled at him. "I had a wonderful time at the New Year's dance, didn't you?" she asked. "My feet still hurt from dancing."

"Well, your church dances are right quiet compared to the ones at the Pentecostal Holiness church socials," he said laughing. "But I did have fun."

"It's hard to believe that today is the first day of the New Year," she said thoughtfully. "Growing up, I imagined that by 2013 we would have cars that could fly."

"How silly," he teased.

She punched him in the shoulder. "Don't laugh at me!"

"Well, I imagined that the world would have gone up in flames by now because of all the sinning going on," he said seriously.

"I'm glad it hasn't burned yet. I wouldn't have met you then," she said coyly.

Jacob looked at her and cleared his throat. "I've been meaning to ask you something since Christmas when I got my promotion at work. I guess this is a good time," he said looking into her blue eyes.

She held her breath and watched him expectantly.

He pulled a little black velvet jewel box out of his pocket. He opened it and held it out towards her then took a deep breath. "Miss Susan Smalley, I was wondering if you would consider marrying me?"

"Mr. Brown, I would consider it an honor to be your wife," she said shyly. She held out her hand and he slipped the ring on her finger. The small diamond glittered in the light from the street lamp.

"It fits perfectly, how did you know my size?" she asked admiring the ring.

"I asked Beth what size you wore."

"You mean my sister has known about this for a week and didn't tell me?"

"I made her swear on a Book of Mormon not to tell," he laughed. He started the car and carefully pulled out of the parking lot. The snow was falling faster now and the roads were getting slick.

"Wait until my missionary brother comes home next week and I tell him this whole story. He always said that the motto 'Flirt to Convert' would work. I guess he was right," she smiled to herself as she stared at her engagement ring.

"It worked on me," admitted Jacob. "You were the cutest waitress I'd ever had the good fortune to meet."

"And you were the handsomest kidnapper I ever met," she said leaning over to kiss his cheek. "Happy New Year."

"Happy New Year to you," he replied grinning happily.

\*\*\*

The snow had melted and the temperature hung around forty degrees the day they buried Mark in the cold ground. All of the reverend's flock was there to say goodbye and it was a subdued group. Everyone knew that killer tree could have fallen on any one of the men cutting wood that day in the forest. The funeral was a quiet affair.

Eve was unable to control her sobbing throughout the sermon and it just about broke Elizabeth's heart to hear her. When they got home, Eve refused to eat and went straight to bed.

It was seven o'clock that night when her water broke and labor started.

Matthew fetched the midwife and took her to Eve's room. Both Anna and Granny were there to help. Eve was having a hard time of it in her depressed and weakened state. Granny was worried about her.

Elizabeth preferred sitting outside on the porch in the cold to being inside hearing Eve moaning in pain. It seemed such a horrible way to bring a child into the world.

"If childbirth is this awful," she told Matthew when he brought her a blanket. "I don't know how anyone would dare to have more than one baby."

Matthew tried to smile, but a piercing scream interrupted his snappy comeback. Instead he hung his head and sat down beside Elizabeth. "I don't think every woman has this hard of a time," he mumbled. "Evie's been through too much these last few weeks and she has no strength left for this. All we can do is pray it will be over soon."

The labor was blessedly quick compared to some.

The first child was born at eleven thirty-eight. Mark's son came into the world kicking and screaming, his wet red curls matted to his scalp.

Eve took one look and declared, "His name should be Samuel, after my grandpa. He had red hair just like that."

Granny took the screaming baby from the midwife's hands. "Why he don't weigh more than a five pound bag o'sugar," she said shaking her head. "He be a little mite."

Anna washed up her first grandson and wrapped him in one of the warm flannel blankets she had helped Eve make for the layette. When Anna handed him to her, Eve tried to hold him but she was too weak. Anna laid him beside her on the bed where Eve could see him. She reached over and touched his cheek.

"He's beautiful. I wish Mark could see him," she whispered.

The baby was only beside her a few minutes before her labor intensified as the second child tried to make its way into the world. Eve moaned and turned away from the baby and Anna handed him back to Granny.

"Push, Evie," instructed the midwife. "I know you're tired, but you've got to push hard. Come on now, you can do this." She held Eve's legs bent at the knees and wide open at the pelvis to allow the baby more room to descend. "Be ready when the next contraction comes."

Anna got up onto the bed behind Eve. She helped the girl sit up and braced her back for her while Eve struggled to push out her second child. As the contraction ended Eve collapsed backwards into Anna's arms. Anna wiped her sweaty forehead with a damp cloth.

"Rest for a minute, Evie. When the next one comes I'll sit you up again," said Anna. "Lean against me." Anna didn't know where the girl was going to get the strength to continue, but Eve surprised her when the next contraction came.

Eve pushed herself up and took two deep breaths. She closed her eyes and pushed with all her might. The baby's head was coming and the pain felt like it would tear her apart, but she didn't stop until the midwife said, "Ok pant for a minute, Evie. This one has a cord around its neck. Let me slip it over the head before you push again." After a few seconds she said, "It's OK. Now push!"

Eve took a deep breath and was relieved when she felt a gush of fluid and a release from the pain as the baby was born. Mark's daughter came into the world five minutes after midnight giving each child the right to a different birth day.

Eve collapsed back onto her bed while the midwife cut the cord. Anna moved out of the way so she could lay flat down in the bed.

The midwife handed Anna the wet squirming baby. She cleaned up her granddaughter marveling at the exquisite beauty of one so tiny. She had blond hair and bright blue eyes. The baby didn't cry like her brother, instead she inspected her new world with a look of wide-eyed wonder on her face.

Anna barely noticed when the placentas came. She was wrapping the baby in a flannel blanket when she heard the midwife gasp. Looking over at Eve she saw the results of a sudden gush of blood that washed over the end of the bed. She put the baby down in one of the cradles and rushed to Eve's side.

"What's wrong? What can I do to help?" she asked the midwife.

The midwife was frantically trying to massage the new mother's uterus encouraging it to clamp down inside on the open blood vessels that had fed the two placentas. "Her uterus is boggy, I can't get her to stop bleeding," panted the midwife.

Anna grabbed a stack of towels and proceeded to stuff them between Eve's legs to staunch the flow of bright red blood running off the bed onto the floor.

Eve was unconscious now and the midwife was furiously trying everything she knew how to do to stop the bleeding. Anna didn't think one person could loose that much blood and still be alive. She was right.

Eve never got to see Mark's daughter. She died the night the baby was born.

The warm break in the weather held for one more day while Eve was buried beside Mark in a small quiet ceremony.

When the temperature fell the snow started up again that evening.

***

The airport was crowded with family and friends the day Elder James Smalley returned from his mission. Besides his immediate family and all the Browns, members of the local congregation were there to greet him. James had left behind several young women from his high school who hoped he would notice how lovely they had grown while he was away for two years.

As soon as he saw his family, he gave his mother a big hug and kissed her on the cheek. "I never would have made it through my mission without those cookies you sent me every month," he told her. "Every companion I had said they were the best chocolate chip cookies they'd ever tasted."

Maryanne smiled. "You didn't tell anyone my secret recipe, did you?"

"No way," he laughed.

He had barely released his mother then he was attacked by Will and Ronnie.

"Oh my gosh, I can't believe these are my baby brothers!" he kidded.

"Hey, I wasn't a baby when you left," said Will punching him in the shoulder.

"Ow! Where did you learn to punch like that?" asked James rubbing his arm.

Will laughed. "From you!"

James picked up Ronnie and held him out at arm's length. "And look at you," he teased. "How old are you now?"

Ronnie tried to wiggle away without success. "I'm six years old and I'm not a baby. Look, I'm already losing my baby teeth." Ronnie smiled to show a gap where his two front teeth were missing.

"Well, look at that," said James setting his little brother back on his feet. He turned to greet his father and bumped into Esther. "Oh, I'm sorry."

"No, I'm sorry. I got in your way," she blushed.

James eyes widened slightly. "You must be Esther."

She nodded. "How did you know?"

"Susan said you had gorgeous black hair and a tuned up nose."

"What's with this sudden interest in my nose that I've been hearing," she huffed. "I have a totally normal nose!"

He laughed. "Hey, it's cute."

Esther blushed again. Before she could say anything in response, James was engulfed by Beth and Susan. She stepped back out of the way.

"I can't believe you're home," said Beth.

"It didn't seem like two years went by at all," said Susan.

James laughed. "Maybe not to you, but it seemed that way to me when I kept thinking about missing birthdays and Christmas with my family. But it was all worth it and I would do it again. I think it has been the most important thing I've ever done."

Robert nudged the girls out of the way and grabbed James in a bear hug. "Welcome home, son," he said.

After that James was swept away by his friends as they all walked to the baggage claim area talking and laughing.

Esther was walking with Jacob when Susan came up behind her and pushed between them. Taking Esther by the arm she held her back while the others continued down the hallway. "Well, what do you think of him?" whispered Susan.

"I don't know, I just met him," retorted Esther.

"But isn't he as cute as I told you?'

"Yes. But why did you tell him I have a turned up nose?" she demanded, turning to face Susan. "I can't believe you told him that!"

"You do have a pixyish nose. It's cute."

"Ugh!" she said storming off after Jacob.

"Well, you do. Why are you so touchy about your nose?" asked Susan hurrying after them. "And I told him you have gorgeous hair, doesn't that make a difference?"

Esther sighed but then she smiled. "Oh, never mind. It doesn't matter."

Susan slid her hand through Jacob's arm. "I just want my two favorite people, besides Jacob of course, to be as happy as I am."

Esther laughed. "Don't rush us. We might be totally unsuited to each other."

"Oh, I promise, you are perfectly suited to each other. Wait and see."

***

Melinda climbed up on the stool at the kitchen counter where her mother was preparing supper. "Mommy, Elizabeth has two babies."

Janice looked up from the pot of spaghetti sauce she was stirring. "What are you talking about, honey. Elizabeth isn't even married and she doesn't have any baby. That's silly."

Melinda looked exasperated. "Not one baby, Mommy. Two babies."

"How do you know ... oh, never mind. So how did Elizabeth get two babies?" asked Janice putting the lid back on the pot of simmering sauce.

"She went with Matthew to that snake place and the babies' mommy died. So she's helping to take care of them. Can we go see her babies?" pleaded Melinda.

"Well, Elizabeth is very far away right now. Maybe later." Janice checked the garlic bread and it was toasted. She took the tray out of the oven. "Go tell daddy that dinner is ready."

"I really, really want to see those babies, Mommy," insisted Melinda.

"I know. But we can't go see them right now."

Melinda climbed down from the stool. "OK, maybe later," she sighed. "I'll go get Daddy."

\*\*\*

It was taking both Anna and Elizabeth to provide care for the twins. Without their mother to provide breast milk for them, the babies had to be bottle fed, but they had not tolerated the milk supplied by Mark's cow.

After two days of them spitting up the milk, Granny solved their problem when she brought Sassy to stay in their barn. "Cow's milk is for bigger childrens," said Granny. "Little ones with no mama do better with goat's milk." And she was right.

That first night when they were born was hard on everyone. Mourning both Mark and Eve took a heavy toll. But the babies demanded so much attention they had brought everyone's focus on to them.

Anna had asked Eve's mother if she wanted to help, but with her crippled hands it took all Leah's energy to care for her own household.

"I just can't help, I'm so sorry. I miss my Evie so much it hurts," said Leah sadly.

Anna nodded. "I know. It's all right. We'll manage. I just didn't want you to feel left out. Come for a visit any time you can get away."

"Could we name Evie's daughter after her grandmother?" asked Leah. "Dinah was grandfather Samuel's wife."

"That's a nice idea," agreed Anna. "We'll name her Dinah."

As hard as it was with the around the clock feedings and all the laundry created by two cloth diapered babies, Elizabeth found herself totally at ease with their care. She fell in love with them both immediately.

"You really enjoy this, don't you, Elizabeth?" said Anna early one morning as they sat together feeding the babies.

Elizabeth smiled as she looked down at Dinah. "Yes, I do. Even at four in morning."

"She looks like she could be your child with that blond hair," commented Anna.

"I know," said Elizabeth wistfully. "I wish she was."

Anna nodded, remembering that Elizabeth would never have children of her own.

"I don't know what I would do without your help with them," said Anna. "I'm not young and full of energy anymore. The thought of raising these two is quite daunting. Matthew and I were wondering if you would ever consider staying here with us, permanently."

"Two weeks ago I would have said no. But now I'm not so sure that would be my answer," reflected Elizabeth. "You know I love Matthew, but I thought maybe I could bring him into my world." She put the baby up to her shoulder and patted her back.

"But after being here these last few weeks," continued Elizabeth. "I know that would never work. You are from a close knit community and he needs that. I would never ask him to give up everyone he loves to go away with me. And I feel such a bond with these two little orphans." She swallowed at the lump forming in her throat. "I don't think I could go away and leave them either."

"I understand that you might feel that way now, but what about your family?" asked Anna. "You would be leaving them all behind."

"Elaine and Brandon have their own young children. I'm already leaving their nest, so to speak, by going away to college. And I could always visit them." She sighed. "Sometimes life takes a strange turn, doesn't it? Who would have ever guessed when I was so happy to leave here last spring, that I would even be considering coming back to live here?"

Anna nodded. "I understand completely. I spent my first weeks here trying to run away, now I would never leave willingly."

Elizabeth finished feeding Dinah and gently placed her in her cradle. She looked up to see Matthew watching her from the bedroom doorway.

He smiled. "Are you finished? Can I talk to you?"

She followed him into the living room. "What time is it?" she asked.

"It's six o'clock. You haven't had much sleep. Do you want breakfast or are you going back to bed right now?"

She shrugged and yawned. "I should probably eat something first."

He nodded. "I milked Sassy and put the milk in the refrigerator. Come in the kitchen and I'll make us all some scrambled eggs and toast."

"You are so thoughtful. That sounds delicious." She sat at the kitchen table while he made breakfast. When he put a plate in front of her on the table then got down on one knee, it startled her. "What are you doing?" she asked sleepily.

"Elizabeth, will you marry me?" he asked placing a small gold ring beside her glass of orange juice. "If you need time to think about it, I'll understand."

She looked from the ring to his face. He needed to shave and his hair was tousled from being out in the wind but his eyes were full of his love for her. She felt a surge of passion as she looked at this man she had grown to love.

Instead of answering him, she picked up the ring and slid it on her finger. "I think it's a little big. I'll have to get it resized," she said smiling at him.

He jumped up and hugged her. "I was so afraid you would say no," he said grinning at her. "I've been afraid to ask you." He walked over to the stove and started filling his own plate with eggs.

"I do have one question though," she said looking serious.

He stopped putting food on his plate. "What's that?" he asked with some trepidation.

"If I marry you and go to church, will I have to pick up a snake?" She cringed at the thought and waited for his answer.

He laughed and shook his head. "Snake handling is purely volunteer."

She sighed in relief. "Thank goodness."

He brought his plate to the table and sat down beside her. "Eat your breakfast and then take a nap. I'll help mother with the twins' next feeding."

Looking up at him, her heart felt like it would burst with love. "No. I'll take a nap, but I want to feed them and let your mother rest. She's getting worn out. This has been a horrible week for her. Losing Mark and Evie has just about crushed her. I don't know how much longer she can hold in all the pain."

"I know. But the babies have helped," he reflected. "They've given her hope."

Elizabeth nodded. "That's true. I need to call my parents and my cell phone doesn't get a signal up here. Can you drive me to the reverend's house this afternoon?"

"Sure. The snow is letting up and Mr. Hamilton will have the roads plowed by then. What are you going to tell them?" he said between bites.

"Everything, I guess. I haven't talked to them since Mark's funeral. I'm sure they're wondering what's happening up here," she said.

After breakfast she slept for two hours but woke before the twins' next feeding. Anna was asleep beside her. She was exhausted and Elizabeth didn't wake her as she left the bedroom.

Matthew was already in the kitchen warming the babies' bottles. He smiled at her. "Samuel was getting restless. I figured I'd better have something ready when he woke up. He sure can holler."

"You're getting pretty good at this father thing," she said pleased.

"Thanks. I never expected to be one so soon, but I think I like it," he said with a grin handing her a bottle. "Here, this one's warm now."

When the phone rang that afternoon, it was Brandon who answered as Elaine was putting the children down for their nap.

"Hi, Brandon," said Elizabeth.

"Elizabeth, how are things? When are you coming back?'

"I'm not sure right now," she hedged.

"But you only have two weeks of semester break left before you have to be back at the university. We were hoping you would be able to spend a little more time at home," he said. "What's happening out there?"

"I need Elaine to get on the extension or put the phone on speaker so I can talk to you both at once," requested Elizabeth. "I have something important to tell you."

Elaine shut the twin's bedroom door and they put the phone on speaker. Her voice sounded far away and tinny as Elizabeth told them the story.

"Evie died last week when her twins were born. It was so awful. It still makes me cry to even talk about it," she said huskily.

"Oh, I'm so sorry. I know she was your friend," sympathized Elaine.

"I've been helping to take care of the babies. A boy and a girl. Elaine, they are adorable but I have a lot more respect now for how hard it must have been for you when Maggie and Martin were born. How did you ever get by on so little sleep?"

Elaine laughed. "It was awful. I felt sleep deprived for the whole first year."

"I wasn't much help either," reminded Brandon. "That was when I was working on a big murder investigation for months and was sometimes gone for days at a time."

"I remember," said Elizabeth. "It seems to me that I got up to help feed them a few times, but I should have done it a lot more often. I'm sorry I wasn't much help to you back then."

"You were busy with high school and the swim team and your piano recitals, I didn't want to interfere with all that," excused Elaine.

"Well, you must have been exhausted. Both Anna and I can hardly handle it even working together. And Matthew helps with all the other chores."

"I wasn't mourning the loss of a son and daughter-in-law like Anna," said Elaine. "It must be awfully hard on her."

"I know it is, but she's handling it. I think caring for the babies actually helps her."

"Well, who is going to help her when you leave?" asked Elaine.

Elizabeth took a big breath. "Actually, I'm not going to leave."

"What do you mean?" asked Brandon. "Are you staying there until you go back to school? We'll understand if you don't come back here with all that going on."

"No, I mean I'm staying here permanently. Matthew asked me to marry him and I said yes. We're going to raise the babies as our own."

"What about your scholarship? And the chance to play at Carnagie Hall? Haven't you dreamed about that for years?" asked Brandon.

"Somehow those things don't seem very important now."

"Don't be too quick to decide something that will determine the rest of your life," he warned. "This is a huge decision."

"Elizabeth, you're only eighteen," protested Elaine. "At least go back to school and think about this for a while."

"Elaine, I have thought about it. I've thought and thought," she said. "I can never have children of my own and this blessing has been given to me right now. It doesn't matter that I'm only eighteen, I want to do this. Seeing Mark die has made me realize how much I love Matthew. I can't bear to lose him. Please don't be angry," she begged.

Elaine looked at Brandon and nodded. "We know you've always been levelheaded. If this is what you want, then we won't stand in the way."

"Thank you. You don't know how much I wanted your approval," said Elizabeth.

"When are you getting married? Can we come?" asked Elaine.

"We haven't decided that yet. For now my life is taking care of these babies."

"Do you need me to go to Virginia and get your things from the university?" offered Brandon. "You can't just leave all your things there."

"Would you do that for me? I didn't want to ask," said Elizabeth relieved.

"I'll drive Matthew's van and pick up your things at the dorm on my way to West Virginia," he promised. "But there is one thing. If you're going to live up in the mountains, we need you to get a ground phone line in your house so we can call you more frequently. Can that be arranged?"

Elizabeth turned around and asked the reverend if it would be possible for them to get their own telephone service.

"I think that can be arranged, Elizabeth," he said. "I've never kept anyone else from getting a telephone. They just didn't feel the need."

"We can do that," she told Brandon. "There is one other thing I would really like for you to bring me from home though, besides all my clothes."

"What's that?" asked Elaine.

"I know it's asking a lot, but could you somehow manage to bring my piano?" she asked hopefully.

"Oh, Elizabeth, really? Your piano?" said Elaine in disbelief.

"I would love to have it in my new home."

Brandon broke out laughing. "Good grief, I'd have to rent a trailer but I'll try to bring it for you, Elizabeth."

# Chapter 17

Aaron looked lovingly at all of his children dressed in white sitting side by side on the church pew. His heart swelled with love at the thought that they could one day all be sealed together as a family with their mother and him. This was just the first step, being baptized into *The Church of Jesus Christ of Latter-day Saints*. He wished Leah was here with them but he felt her presence so strongly that he knew in his heart her spirit was pleased with them.

"I know this is a little late," he whispered leaning towards the children. "But no one wants to change their mind, do they?"

Esther rolled her eyes at him. "Dad, you were the last hold out. The rest of us have been ready for this since last fall."

Aaron looked at his two youngest boys. "Ephraim and Isaac, you aren't just doing this because I am, are you? I want you to get baptized because you want to do it," he said seriously.

Eleven-year old Isaac looked at him. "Dad, I know this church is the one I want to join. Really. I believe everything the missionaries taught us," he said earnestly.

Ephraim looked over at his father with a wicked grin. "Since when have I done anything just because you wanted me to?" he asked sarcastically.

Aaron sighed. "Good point."

At that moment the Bishop of the ward stood and the prelude music stopped.

"We'd like to welcome everyone out to the baptism of the Brown family," said Bishop Williamson. "It has been my personal pleasure to get to know and love each member of this fine family. Isaac informed me that even though our meetings are too quiet and subdued that they would like to become members of this ward," he chuckled remembering Isaac's description of a typical *Pentecostal Holiness Today* church service.

Esther nudged Isaac in the ribs. "What did you tell the Bishop in your interview?"

He looked at her innocently. "Just that we have electric guitars and snakes."

She bowed her head in embarrassment and sighed. "Great."

"Shhh," whispered Jacob.

They all listened quietly as Susan gave a short talk about the importance of being baptized by someone with proper priesthood authority. Then Robert Smalley explained about receiving the gift of the Holy Ghost who would always be there to comfort and guide them throughout their lives.

The congregation then went to the font room where Elder Armstrong baptized Aaron and his three sons. Last week, Esther had blushingly asked James if he would be the one to baptize her. He had welcomed the idea and today happily did so.

The whole service was over in less than an hour.

The Smalley's had invited them over for dinner afterwards.

As the Brown family all trudged through the snow up the sidewalk to the house, Ephraim took the opportunity to tease Esther.

"Esther has a boyfriend," he sang out lustily.

"Hush, you pest," she said blushing. "If you say anything in front of James I will personally snowball you to death!" To illustrate her point she grabbed a handful of snow and shoved it down the back of his neck.

"OK, OK. I get the message," he shouted as he pulled away from her grasp.

"I mean it," she said sternly. "I don't know if James even thinks of me that way. I'm sure that as a new return missionary he was just pleased that someone wanted him to do their baptism. Please don't embarrass me in front of him, Ephraim," she pleaded.

He stopped laughing and looked down at his sister. Suddenly he realized that he was now taller than she was by several inches. When had that happened?

"I promise I won't say anything in front of James. But I think he already likes you a lot. I've seen him watching you when you weren't looking," he said earnestly.

Esther perked up. "You have, really?"

Ephraim nodded. "And he gets that funny look in his eyes like Jacob gets when he looks at Susan. It's actually kind of icky sickening."

Esther grabbed him and gave him a hug. "I hope you're not making this up, because I really do like him, a lot."

Ephraim wiggled free of her grasp. "I'm telling the truth, honest. I just got baptized, I wouldn't lie to you now, would I?"

***

Matthew and Elizabeth sat in the car with the motor running to keep warm in the parking lot of a small gas station outside the town of Wharton. Even with the recent snowfall, all the roads had been plowed and the trip down the mountain had been uneventful.

"Brandon said they spent the night at Miss Millie's. He and Belle stayed there when they came looking for me last spring," reminded Elizabeth. "They should be along any minute now. He said her house wasn't too far from this gas station."

Just then Matthew's white van came into view pulling a U-haul trailer. Elizabeth got out and waved as it pulled into the parking lot. She walked over to it as Brandon rolled down his window.

"I'm glad I found you," he said. "I still have no idea which one of these dirt roads I'm supposed to take to get to Matthew's house."

Elaine climbed out of the van and gave Elizabeth a hug. "I can't believe how far it is from California to West Virginia. Traveling was slow with the trailer and all the snowy roads," she complained.

"I'm glad you made it safely. I'm so happy to see you both," said Elizabeth.

"It's beautiful in the mountains with all this snow," said Elaine.

Elizabeth looked through the windshield and noticed movement in the back of the van. "Who's that in the back seat? I thought you left the twins with grandma."

Just then there was a squeal from the backseat passenger and a small body came flying towards them. "It's me, Lizbeth!" announced Melinda as she jumped from the van. "I was taking a nap."

Elizabeth laughed at the child as she ran towards them, her curls flying.

"I didn't know you were coming, too," Elizabeth said in pleased surprise.

"She practically had an epileptic fit when she found out we were coming to see you and she couldn't come. I finally convinced Janice that we didn't mind bringing her," said Elaine. "She's been as good as gold the whole way."

Elizabeth leaned over and grabbed Melinda up and whirled her around in a circle then set her back on the ground. "I'm very glad you came." She tousled the child's hair.

"Lizbeth," said Melinda seriously. "You couldn't get married without me to be your flower girl. And I really, really wanted to see your babies."

"Do you want to ride with us in the car?" asked Matthew leaning down to Melinda's level. "I promise not to kidnap you."

Melinda looked up at him and nodded. "I told Mommy that you were a nice man and that it was OK for Elizabeth to marry you."

Matthew smiled. "Well, thank you for the nice recommendation." He patted her head and stood back up. "I appreciate all the help I can get."

Brandon winked at him. "I'll bet you do."

"We'll go slow and easy on the mountain roads," he told Brandon. "With you pulling a trailer we want to be extra careful. In fact, if you'd prefer, I could drive the van."

"No, after all the snow we've driven through so far, I think I can manage," said Brandon. "If I start to have problems, I'll lean on my horn."

Matthew nodded. "OK, then let's go."

After everyone was settled back in the vehicles, Brandon followed the car out of the parking lot. In a few minutes they reached the crossroads where he had found Elizabeth and Matthew together last spring. They turned left and drove a few miles and made a right turn up a steep hill then turned left onto another narrower road.

Brandon looked out the window and said to Elaine, "Look, there are the telephone poles going right up the hill just like he said. I can't believe I didn't think about that last year."

"Don't be too hard on yourself," she said. "We've only turned three times and I'm already lost. We must have passed at least four other dirt roads."

He looked over at her and winked. "You're too kind. I drove down dozens of those logging roads last year and never once thought about looking for telephone poles before I started driving on them."

"How were you to know they had power or phones up there?" she commiserated. "I bet there are probably some people living in these mountains without either one of those luxuries."

"You may be right," he admitted. "But I still feel dumb."

It took an hour of driving on narrow mountain roads with no guardrails before they saw the first house in Reverend Forester's little community. Elaine's hands were aching from holding white-knuckled to her armrests for the entire trip.

She had prayed the whole way that they would not slide off the icy road. She figured if they went over the side with the trailer, their bodies would lie there permanently as no one would be able to climb down to get them out of the wreckage.

When they pulled to a stop in front of the house, she finally breathed a sigh of relief and relaxed. While the women took Melinda inside, Matthew helped Brandon carry in the boxes of Elizabeth's belongings from the back of the van.

Anna and Granny Hensley were in the living room feeding the babies and Elizabeth proudly introduced the women.

"If it wasn't for Elizabeth, I don't know what I would have done," said Anna. "You have raised a wonderful daughter," she complimented Elaine.

"I can't take credit for that," admitted Elaine. "That's just Elizabeth."

After stacking the four boxes in the corner, Brandon was introduced. "You certainly live in an out of the way place," he said rubbing arms which ached from exerting all his energy to hold the van on the road.

Granny laughed. "We all moved here seventy years ago so's no one could give us grief over the snakes. It was right impossible to find us back then. We'uns didn't even have no electricity and no power poles to foller."

Brandon laughed. "Yes, Ma'am. I still had trouble finding you, even with the power poles. I'm pleased to finally meet you. Elizabeth has had wonderful things to say about you both," he said addressing the women.

Melinda had been quietly standing by Anna, enthralled by the babies. She looked up at Elizabeth and whispered, "They're so tiny, Lizbeth. They're littler than Maggie and Martin were. Can I hold one, please?"

"They were born a little early and their mama had been sick for a while. But they're already getting bigger, especially Samuel," said Elizabeth.

Anna stood up from her rocking chair with Dinah. "She's finished eating, do you want to hold her, Melinda?"

Melinda nodded. Elizabeth helped her climb in to the rocking chair and she put a pillow under her arm. Anna carefully placed Dinah in her lap. "There you go. Isn't she cute?"

Melinda nodded and touched the baby's tiny fingers. "Is she really going to be Elizabeth's baby?"

Anna nodded. "Both of them are going to be Elizabeth's babies."

"I'm glad. Elizabeth was always sad that she couldn't have babies. You know, because of that thing that made her brain sick. Now she has two," said a delighted Melinda. "Isn't that wonderful?" She leaned back and started rocking the baby.

Brandon cleared his throat. "Ah, Elizabeth. Where do you want the piano?"

"Over against that wall," she said pointing across the room. "I didn't want it too close to the fireplace and we cleared a space over there for it."

After getting John to help, the three men were able to bring in Elizabeth's upright piano. They maneuvered it up against the wall.

"It will probably have to be tuned again," warned Elaine. "I'm sorry to say it's been bounced around a bit on the trip."

"We has got a good man here that can fix it," said Granny. "Mr. Warner tunes all our musical gadgets for us."

"That's great," said Brandon. "I'd hate to think she couldn't get it tuned after all our hard work getting it here."

"I'm sure everyone is hungry," said Granny as she put Samuel into his cradle. "We all will go fix a little bite."

While she and Anna sliced banana bread and apples, Elizabeth showed Elaine around the house and told her how it had been made in only a week.

"You and your sons built this house and all the furniture?" Elaine asked John, impressed with the fine workmanship.

"Not by ourselves. All the men in the community got together and built several houses for all the new young couples," he said modestly. "This was for Mark and Evie. Since Matthew wasn't getting married last spring, we hadn't built one for him yet."

"What a generous thing for all of you to do," she said.

"It's our way up here. We're a close knit group. We work together and help each other when the need arises. It's like having a big family."

"I've had wonderful women friends to help me through the last few weeks," said Anna as she placed trays of food on the kitchen table. "With two funerals and two births, I could never have done everything by myself."

"And now on a happy note," interjected Granny. "We is going to have another wedding. All the women's been baking for a week now. And Ms. Mary made a right purty wedding cake."

"She did. Wait until you see it," said Elizabeth excitedly as they all helped themselves to the sandwiches and juice.

Later that evening after dinner, Anna, Granny, Matthew and John went home to sleep. Elizabeth stayed in the second bedroom which was now the nursery with the babies. Elaine and Brandon had the master bedroom while Melinda slept on the sofa.

It was in the middle of the night while Elizabeth was up feeding Samuel when Elaine woke up and came in to talk. She stood quietly in the doorway watching Elizabeth for a minute. "You've really taken to this mothering thing, haven't you?" she said smiling sleepily.

Elizabeth nodded. "I learned how from watching you with the twins."

"I think some of it comes naturally to you," said Elaine as she came in and sat down on the bed. "Everyone here is so nice and supportive, I guess I can stop worrying about you now."

Elizabeth put the baby to her shoulder and patted his back. She looked over at Elaine. "Yes, you can stop worrying. I'm happier now than I have ever been in my life."

"And tomorrow you'll get married. I never thought this day would come so soon. It's hard to believe that the years have gone by this fast since I first started taking care of you," sighed Elaine. "It's only been six years, but it seems much longer."

Samuel burped and Elizabeth smiled. "You'll never know how thankful I am that you came into my life when you did." She stood up and put Samuel into his cradle.

Elaine turned to leave. "I'll let you get some sleep."

"Brandon does know that I want him to give me away tomorrow, doesn't he?"

"Yes, I told him. He was pleased," said Elaine.

"Thank you for coming. See you in a few hours," said Elizabeth as she climbed wearily back into bed.

Elizabeth became Mrs. Matthew Hensley in a quiet ceremony in Reverend Forester's home. It was after the ceremony that the celebration became rowdy. The church was filled with as many people as it could hold, everyone glad they finally had something to celebrate after the sadness of the last few weeks.

Tambourines, electric guitars and drums played rockabilly music for hours as everyone devoured the homemade casseroles and desserts. Brandon took photos of the couple as they danced and cut the wedding cake. He knew Elaine would want to see pictures later, because right now she was seeing everything through blurry tears.

Granny Hensley carried her glass of punch over to a chair and sat down beside Anna in a slightly quieter corner of the room.

"Who'd a thought that this would happen?" she said with a smile. "Ain't it strange how some things work themselves out? Elizabeth was so unhappy when Matthew brought her here last spring, but somehow she felt a connection to him. A connection that brought all this to pass. My, my, who could have ever guessed?"

Anna smiled and nodded. "She understands what's important in life. It's not how much money you have or power or fame. The important things are love and family."

It was a subdued group that stood on the porch the next morning to say goodbye.

"I wish we could stay longer," said Brandon. "But I've been away a week now and have to get back to work."

Elaine hugged Elizabeth. She brushed a lock of her hair off her face and tucked it behind her ear. "Elizabeth, you promise to call us every week."

Elizabeth nodded. "I promise. And I'll send pictures of the babies so you can see how fast they grow. I remember how much Maggie and Martin changed every month."

Melinda stood solemnly beside Elaine listening to the grown ups. She looked up and smiled at Elizabeth. "I can still feel you even though you live far away now, Lizbeth."

"You can? I can't feel you very well. I'm sorry," admitted Elizabeth. "I didn't even know you were coming to visit me."

"That's OK. That just means that I can surprise you sometimes," said the child.

"I hope I can come visit next summer. Matthew told me he would teach me how to fish."

Elizabeth looked at Matthew and smiled. "I'm sure we can arrange that."

"Well, we better get going. Matthew has to get us to the airport by eleven," said Brandon. "Congratulations, you two." Brandon felt his own eyes water as Elizabeth gave him a goodbye hug.

"Take care of yourself," she whispered. "You're the one who has to dodge bullets. And tell Belle to watch over you for me."

"Hey, I'm pretty fast on my feet," protested Brandon.

"Maybe so, but bullets are faster," she reminded him.

# Epilogue

It was a few weeks later that Reverend Forester stopped by the house to drop off a package for Matthew. "It was in that post office box that I use down in Wharton," he said handing a large manila envelope to Matthew. The label was addressed to Matthew in care of the reverend.

"I wondered if anyone could send us mail," said Elizabeth.

Reverend Forester nodded. "If they use this post office box number I'll make sure it gets to you. No mail gets delivered this far up the mountain," he explained.

"Thanks, Reverend," said Matthew as he inspected the package.

"Good day." The reverend left them to deliver a few more pieces of mail to members of his flock.

"What is it?" asked Elizabeth looking over Matthew's shoulder.

"It says it's from Jacob Brown out in Idaho." Inside the big padded envelope he found a letter, several small booklets and a blue paperback book. He opened the letter and read it out loud to Elizabeth.

> "Dear Matthew and family,
> We were all devastated to hear from Reverend Forester about the deaths of Mark and Evie. Our hearts break knowing how you must all be in pain over losing them.
>
> We do want to assure you that we know you will one day see them both again and that there is a way for you all to be together as a family forever.
>
> As you know our family has been baptized into The Church of Jesus Christ of Latter-day Saints. They follow many of the same ideals that the Pentecostal Holiness church follows. However, they believe that their members should be in the world but not of the world. They shun sin of all types but they live out in the world to be good examples and to try and bring others into Christ's fold.
>
> I have enclosed some reading materials that I know you will find interesting. Please pray about the information and if you find it to be the truth, as we did, then share it with Reverend Forester. You might also tell him the following story about Joseph Smith.
>
> When men from the early days of the Church were traveling in what was called Zion's Camp, Joseph Smith taught that they were to

*conserve natural resources and avoid killing. One time when he was preparing to pitch his tent he discovered three rattlesnakes. While others wanted to kill the snakes, the Prophet said, "Let them alone—don't hurt them! How will the serpent ever lose his venom, while the servants of God possess the same disposition, and continue to make war upon it? Men must become harmless, before the brute creation." The snakes were then carried across the creek and released. Joseph told the men to refrain from killing any animal unless it was necessary to avoid starvation.*

*I read about that story in the <u>Church History in the Fullness of Times</u> student manual which is published by the Church for the Educational System in Salt Lake City, Utah. It's from the chapter on the journey of Zion's Camp on page 144. I'd be happy to send you a copy of that book, too, if you're interested.*

*My family's prayers are with you all through this hard time. We were happy to hear that you and Elizabeth got married and have adopted Mark and Evie's babies. Bless you both.*

*Below is our new address, please write soon and let us know how you are doing.*

*Best wishes and love, Esther and Jacob"*

Enclosed with the letter they found several pamphlets including: Man's Search for Happiness, The Restoration of the Gospel, and The Proclamation to the World. And with them a copy of *The Book Of Mormon, Another Testament of Jesus Christ.*

Matthew looked up from the letter. "It's going to be a long winter, it was nice of them to send us reading material to pass the time, wasn't it, Elizabeth?"

THE END

Made in the USA
Charleston, SC
07 January 2013